OREGON DISCOVERY

TRAILS OF HEART BOOK 4

RACHEL WESSON

LONDONGATE PUBLISHING

This story is dedicated with love to my dear friend, Nancy Cowan, who never fails to inspire me.

CHARACTER LIST

Hughes Homestead

    Rick Hughes

    Jo Hughes nee Thompson - his wife

    Nancy & Lena Hughes - their six year old twins

    Adopted three trail orphans

    Sarah Hughes - 18 - Rick's niece

    Carrie Hughes - 14 - Rick's niece

    Almanzo Price - 18

    Bridget Murphy - housekeeper

Jones Homestead

    Scott Jones (former Boss of Wagon Train)

    Becky Jones nee Thompson - his wife

    Jake and Ruth - six year old twins

    Nathan and Annie - three year old twins

Clarke Homestead

David Clarke
Eva Clarke nee Thompson - his wife
Patrick known as Pat - 7 1/2 years
Samuel known as Sam - 4 1/2 years

Thompson Homestead
Paddy Thompson
Della Thompson, his wife

CHAPTER 1

OREGON 1860

*T*he sun was already hot despite it being early morning. Matilda Masterson, or Tilly as her friends called her, eased her feet into the sparkling cool water. It was decadent and delicious at the same time. She giggled as the small fish nibbled at her toes, imagining her deceased mother's reaction to her eighteen-year-old daughter wading with her skirts tucked up around her knees, her bonnet, shoes, and stockings on the bank of the small river.

She looked over at her friend Fiona. She didn't share Tilly's reservations having been used to being barefoot until she joined the Masterson household at the age of fourteen. She grinned back at her mistress. "Feels heavenly doesn't it?"

"Yes Fiona, I feel human again for the first time in ages. This was such a good idea." Tilly bent down dipping her hanky in the water to wash her neck and face. She really wanted to strip down but they didn't have time for that. They were late starting today due to having to fix a wagon axle which broke yesterday. The other women were doing some laundry further up the river near the campsite but Tilly had wanted it to just be the two of them. She had taken two horses, one for herself and one for Fiona, so they could ride back a little bit to the small sheltered creek. They were still within shouting distance of the camp, not far enough to cause alarm yet enough distance for her to spend time with Fiona in peace.

"Tilly, you can come help me do the laundry anytime you like," Fiona replied grinning at her friend. "Just don't tell Master Richard I was the one who suggested it."

Tilly scowled. "Don't ruin our morning by talking about him. Did you see him last night? He and father had some disagreement and he strutted off to his wagon. He looked like a cockerel only twice as nasty."

Fiona grinned at the description. "Why were they arguing?"

"I have no idea. Father rarely talks to me anymore. Not that he ever told me anything he considered important. He believes women should look decorative. Our sole aim in life is to please our menfolk and produce an heir. Anything else is against God's wishes." Tilly's face screwed up as she repeated what her father had drummed into her for as long as she could remember.

"I can't see why God would want you to marry someone nearly three times your age," Fiona replied heatedly.

Tilly splashed her friend, "He's old but he's not over 50."

"You sure about that? He acts older than your father and he's ancient."

"Fiona Murphy is that any way to speak to your employer?" Tilly asked in a voice reminiscent of her mother.

"Forgive me, Miss, it's my Irish temper. Always gets the better of me," Fiona replied in a thick Irish accent making them both laugh. Tilly didn't see Fiona as a servant but as an equal, a fact she had to hide from her father and her fiancé. Fiona Murphy was the only friend she'd ever known and she was so grateful the Irish girl had agreed to come on this godforsaken trip.

Tilly had no idea why they had to leave San Francisco and head to Oregon. Her father didn't see fit to tell her. He expected total obedience and if he didn't get it, she paid a heavy price as she had learned in the past. When she had refused to marry Richard, her parents had locked her in the attic. They told her she would get food and water when she came to her senses. If it hadn't been for Fiona sneaking up water as often as she could, Tilly didn't think she would have lived through that week. In the end, she hadn't agreed to the engagement, but her mother's sudden death meant her father had to produce her in public. Ironically, by dying her mother had done something to help Tilly for the first time in the young girl's life.

It wouldn't be done for a Masterson to miss her Mother's funeral. Her father had introduced Richard as her fiancé to all the mourners. Tilly was just as determined as ever not to marry the hideous man but she had yet to figure out a way out of her predicament. Running away, although attractive, wasn't a practical option as Fiona so rightly pointed out. It was far too dangerous for two young women with no money. They had to think of another plan.

"Fiona, what do you think Portland will be like?"

"I have no idea, Tilly. Same as all the other places we've lived, I guess. One rule for the rich and another for the poor."

"Fiona Murphy, how are you so cynical at such a young age?" Tilly was just about to splash her friend again when they heard what sounded like gunshots. Then a scream. Fiona pulled Tilly to the ground, half in and half out of the stream

"What was that?" Tilly's voice quivered.

"Shush Tilly."

Lying beside Fiona, she could feel her friend's heart beating fast. Tilly raised her head to see if she could see anything but Fiona wasn't taking any chances. She pulled her back down.

"We can't be seen if we keep our heads down. The men will fight them off and then we can go back to the wagons," Fiona said, her confident words not matching her trembling voice.

Tilly was shivering, the combination of fear and wet clothes wasn't a good one. More gunshots and then the sound of horse hooves. She pushed Fiona to one side and risked taking a look over the ridge of the stream. She saw her father racing towards their spot. Before she could do or say anything, a shot rang out and he fell from his horse. The animal continued running but didn't come anywhere near their hiding spot.

From this distance, Tilly couldn't see if her father had survived or not but she saw a few riders circling the wagons, aiming their guns at the adults. Her heart beat so fast as she saw the people they had traveled with gunned down mercilessly. She couldn't see any faces but the men shooting appeared to be Indians.

As she saw one racing after a child, she bowed her head. Fiona pulled her back down out of sight, the two of them cuddled together, both holding their hands over their ears. Each praying they would not be discovered. The noise of the attack grew louder. It seemed like another group of men on horseback had joined in. A couple more shots and then everything fell silent.

Tilly and Fiona lay still, too scared to risk looking up again.

"Do you think they will come looking for us?" Fiona asked.

"Father and Richard will find us when it's safe. For now, we best stay here quietly." Tilly whispered back to her friend. She wasn't going to tell Fiona she'd seen her father shot. That news could come later.

She was trying to be brave for both of them given she was a year older than Fiona. She was also Fiona's employer and her mother had lectured her for years of the impor-tance of being a good mistress. Although her mother had taken the view servants needed to be kept in their place and not given expectations beyond their station in life, Tilly preferred to think her mother would have expected her to protect Fiona.

The sun rose higher in the sky. Where they were afforded them little protection. Tilly regretted taking off her bonnet. The sun's rays combined with thirst were making her feel lightheaded. Fiona had closed her eyes but whether she was sleeping or had passed out, Tilly wasn't sure. She moved slightly closer to her friend, intending to check on her when she sensed something behind her. She turned to look. The last thing she saw was buckskin before she passed out.

CHAPTER 2

HUGHES HOMESTEAD, PORTLAND OREGON.

"*R*ick Hughes, please listen to me and go to the doctor, I'm worried about you," Jo said, kissing her husband on the cheek. Rick didn't get a chance to answer as someone knocked on the front door.

"Sarah, can you get the door please," Jo asked her adopted daughter.

"Yes Ma," Sarah said smiling nervously. She knew Edwin was calling to see her Pa. She wished now she had a chance to warn Rick and Jo about the purpose of Edwin's visit but maybe it was best coming as a surprise. Rick and Jo disliked Edwin's parents intensely and believed Edwin shared his parents' bigoted opinions. The Morgans didn't agree with equality and had made it known they thought all Blacks should be kept as slaves. Mr. Morgan regularly disagreed with the contents of Uncle David's writing column and he believed Uncle Scott was at the least part Indian. While it was true Scott Jones had lived with Paco's tribe prior to becoming a wagon train leader, he was fully white. The tribe had rescued Scott as a child and raised him in their ways. Unlike the Morgans, Paco and his tribe were welcome and called regularly to see Rick, Jo, their twins, Nancy and Lena as well as Carrie and herself. Almanzo's best friend was Paco's son, Walking Tall.

Sarah opened the door, kissed Edwin on the cheek and led him in to her pa's small study. She wanted to say something to encourage him but couldn't think of anything appropriate.

Edwin Morgan played with his hat, his flushed cheeks marking his embarrassment. "Mr. Hughes, could I see you in private please?"

Sarah watched Rick closely as he smiled at Edwin, obviously attempting to put him at ease, although his smile didn't reach his eyes. Rick might not like Edwin or any of the rest of the Morgan family but he wouldn't be rude.

"You best let Jo stay, she's the real boss in this house," Rick replied.

Sarah caught the tender look her Pa sent Jo. Please say yes, Pa, she muttered to herself as Jo spoke, "Almanzo, Sarah please leave us in private.

Sarah threw an encouraging look to Edwin but he was staring at the ground so hard, he missed it. Reluctantly she followed Almanzo out of the room.

"What's that all about, Sassy?"

"Stop calling me Sassy. I'm not a child anymore," Sarah said heatedly avoiding Almanzo's question. She hadn't even told Carrie her sister, that Edwin was going to propose. She hated the nickname Paco had given her. The Indian had said she needed to be more respectful to her elders. She disagreed.

"No, I guess you're not. Michael Nolan called you a spinster the other day." Almanzo said.

"Is that why you punched him?" Sarah asked, the drama taking place between her parents and Edwin momentarily forgotten.

"Heck no. I punched him because he was cheating at cards."

"Almanzo Price, if Pa hears you were playing cards again, he is going to tan your hide."

"Rick isn't going to hear, though is he? No-one is going to tell him. It's not like we are gambling. Not really. It's only a bit of fun." Almanzo shrugged.

"Wait till Mrs. Porter or Mrs. Nolan hears about your bit of fun. Then there'll be trouble," Sarah said knowingly. She had been on the wrong side of Mrs. Porter's vicious tongue on more than one occasion.

"Mrs. Nolan wouldn't say anything bad about her son. She thinks he walks on water. Anyway, if you live your life according to those old ladies, you will never do anything. They spend their lives confessing imagined sins to the priest. I think it's so they can listen in on other people's confessions."

"Almanzo Price. That's a dreadful thing to say. You better not let Rick or Jo hear you talk like that."

"They won't. I have to go to town. See you later and try

not to upset Rick and Jo too much," Almanzo said but Sarah wasn't listening.

Sarah fought hard against the urge to listen at the door. Edwin's father and Rick had got into a huge argument last year over Oregon joining the Union. Mr. Morgan, a vocal supporter of slavery had argued against Oregon joining the Union last year. Rick had called him a bigot amongst other things but only after Mr. Morgan had started abusing the extended Thompson family. It was funny how Jo and her sisters were still known as the Thompson girls even though they had adopted their husband's surnames. Maybe it was because grandma Della was such a forceful character. Sarah was glad Della wasn't here visiting or she would be listening to a lecture on the evils of the Morgan family.

Edwin wasn't like his father. At least she didn't think he was. They didn't spend much time talking about politics or stuff like that. She couldn't think of anything else but Edwin when he was near her. He was so handsome now he had developed muscles from mining every day. His hair was longer. She loved the feel of it on her fingers as she massaged his scalp.

His kisses made her blood sing. It was getting harder not to take things further.

They had agreed not to talk about the Indian situation. Edwin got annoyed with Sarah's loyalty to Paco and his tribe. He was jealous about her friendship with Walking Tall even though she'd reassured him, Walking Tall was a friend who happened to be happily married. Almanzo and

Walking Tall spent a lot of time together over the years so she knew the Indian almost as well as her adoptive brother.

She didn't want to think about Edwin's dislike of her friends. When she was with Edwin and he was kissing her and telling her how beautiful she was, none of that mattered. He had been back in town two months now and they had spent every second they could alone. They hadn't done anything too bad but she knew Jo wouldn't be pleased if she knew how far Sarah had let things go.

The door to Pa's study opened. Edwin marched past, his face like thunder. Picking up her skirts, Sarah ran after him as he stormed out the front door.

"Edwin, wait. What did he say?"

"No." Edwin's terse comment was thrown over his shoulder as he marched off.

"Wait, I can't move as fast as you. What do you mean no? Didn't he say anything else?"

Edwin gave a half-hearted shrug before turning to face her. "He said what I told you he'd say. I'm too young and you're too old. I mean, not old but older than me. Dang it anyway Sarah, I told you we were wasting our time. I'm going back to the mines and I am not coming back until I have money for the ranch."

Edwin marched over to his horse, mounted and rode off without another word. Sarah didn't know whether to run after him or confront her Pa. She decided on the later. Now while she was brave or foolish enough to take on both her parents. Holding her shoulders back, she took a deep breath before walking back into the house, closing the door behind her. She entered the study. Jo glanced at her, a warning look on her face. But Sarah didn't acknowledge it.

"Sarah, this can wait. Your pa is tired," Jo insisted.

"Sorry Ma, but it can't wait. Not when Edwin is threatening to leave Portland. I won't lose him." Sarah swallowed hard hoping to quell her nerves. Over the years she had on the odd occasion defied her Pa but never over something this big.

"Pa, I'm old enough to know my own mind. I love Edwin and want to marry him. I would prefer you give your blessing. But I intend to marry him regardless. If he leaves Portland, I'm going with him."

"Sarah Mary Hughes, don't speak to your pa like that," Jo's voice shook with anger but Sarah was too annoyed to listen.

Sarah glared at her Ma. "I'm sorry." She knew the apology didn't sound genuine. How could it? She wasn't sorry. She loved Edwin. She didn't care what he did for a living or the fact he was a year younger than she was.

"Pa, please. You've known Edwin ever since we first moved here. He's a hard worker and a good man."

"He's also a year younger than you, Sarah. A woman needs an older man. Especially when the woman in question has a temper and a wild streak." Pa gave her a stern look. "You need to marry someone mature and with enough sense not to consider mining for gold or silver. "

"Pa, that's not fair. You know he only went to the mines

to try to get some money to buy some land. He did well too."

Sarah watched her Pa closely. He had a reputation as a tough man but he was also fair. Her Ma had always said the best way to deal with her Pa was to appeal to his sense of justice. She sweetened her tone.

"Pa, please give us a chance. Edwin swears we will come back to Portland in the next three to five years. Once he has sufficient money to buy out the old Saunders place and start a ranch of his own. "

"Sarah, I told you before. When you marry, I'll give you some of my lands," Rick said, sounding tired.

Sarah felt guilty at the tiredness in his voice but it didn't last. She had to make him see, her future lay with Edwin.

"Edwin has his pride, Pa. He doesn't want your land, he wants to start his own ranch."

"You can't blame the boy for wanting to provide for his own family, Rick."

Sarah shot her Ma a look of gratitude although calling Edwin a boy had rankled. He wasn't a boy. Not after spending the last two years in the mines high up in the mountains. When she thought of the risks he was taking daily, her blood rushed to her head making her dizzy.

Her Pa stayed silent. Sarah was about to interrupt him when a look from her Ma warned her not to. Patience not being her strongest asset, she tapped her foot nervously as she waited for her Pa to say something. Anything. The silence lingered.

Sarah risked a tentative smile. "Please, Pa. Say yes. I love

Edwin and he loves me. If I don't marry him, I'll become a spinster for real. Michael Nolan will be proved right."

"What's that idiot Nolan got to do with anything? He hasn't the brains he was born with. If his pa was around, he'd take that boy over his knee and give him a good thrashing," Rick said crossly.

"Rick, calm down. You can't afford to get riled up especially over the likes of the Nolan boy," Jo reprimanded her husband softly. "Sarah, go get your father a glass of cold water. Tell Bridget I will be with her in a few minutes."

Sarah hesitated.

"Do as I said, Sarah." At the note of steel in her Ma's voice, Sarah moved quickly out of the room. Tempted as she was to listen at the door, she was too well brought up to be so rude. Instead, she went to the kitchen where Bridget was busy making pies.

"Did your pa agree?"

Sarah wasn't shocked Bridget knew everything. It had been like that since the small stocky Irish woman had come to work for them.

"Not yet. Do you think he will, Bridget? Sarah asked, the smell of the pies reminding her she hadn't eaten yet today.

"I can't say, Miss Sarah. Edwin Morgan is a little young for you." She paused in her baking to push some hair off her face leaving a trail of white flour on her cheek. "Don't you be giving me one of your dirty looks now little missy. The age difference is a fact. It's not going to change because you want it to. But it doesn't matter what I think. I'm not your pa."

"He thinks the same as you do. Edwin is too young for me. Who would have thought a year made such a difference? " Sarah asked although she knew it wasn't really the age difference upsetting everyone. It was Edwin's family or at least their reputation. But Edwin wasn't like his parents and when they were married, he would accept her friends and family as his own. Including Paco, Walking Tall and the rest of the Indians. He loved her, she knew he did.

"Women mature faster than men. That's just a fact," Bridget blew her hair out of her eyes. "Many fathers prefer their daughters to marry older men who are mature and stable to provide a good home."

"My Edwin is mature and he's working hard saving for us to have a home." Sarah took a bite out of an apple. "Did you marry someone older, Bridget?"

"No, my husband was the same age as me. We were sixteen when we met. Tom was handsome and fun, unlike the man my daddy had picked out for me. Daddy was more concerned with making a good marriage for me than my happiness."

"A good marriage?" Sarah questioned.

"By marrying me off to his nearest old neighbor who had no children, he could increase his land holding." Bridget laughed, her belly moving. "I'd love to see that man's face when he heard I took off with Tom. That old man, he used to come visit me and I tell you, Miss Sarah, I never smelt such bad breath. He was disgusting. Always chewing and spitting tobacco. "

Sarah laughed but stopped at the look on the house-keeper's face. "What's wrong?"

"Just thinking Miss Sarah. I never saw my daddy after I ran off. He was right about Tom being a bad one but I wouldn't listen. If Daddy hadn't been so keen on getting me hitched to an old landowner, I may not have married Tom so quickly." Bridget leaned over and took Sarah's hand. "Miss Sarah, you remember your pa loves you. He's not like my Daddy. He has his reasons for the decisions he makes but they are always made with your best interest at heart. Even if you don't always see that. Mr. Hughes is the kindest gentleman I ever met. Your mama is a real lady too."

Sarah fell silent. The housekeeper's story had upset her but it was more than that. Pa and Ma weren't her real parents but her Uncle Rick and his wife Jo. They had taken care of her and Carrie after their real ma and brothers died on the wagon trail. They had adopted both girls and would have adopted Almanzo too but he refused.

"You take that look off your face, Miss Sarah. You know Mr. Rick and Miss Johanna loves the bones of you. That pair couldn't love you more than your real parents."

Sarah flushed at how easily Bridget read her thoughts.

"I know you think you love Edwin and he believes he loves you. But you are both young Miss Sarah and you are very different. You don't have to rush into anything. Don't do anything to cause a rift from your parent's, you may never be able to repair it."

Sarah didn't want to listen to Bridget so she tried changing the subject. "I'm sorry you didn't have a happy marriage, Bridget."

"What you sorry for? It wasn't your fault, my husband was a bad one. Maybe if he hadn't been so young, he wouldn't have taken to the drink so quickly. " Bridget grew so misty eyed, Sarah was afraid she would cry. "If I had my time over again, I may have listened to my Daddy about Tom. It would have saved a lot of heartache."

Pa! She'd forgotten his glass of water. "Bridget. I forgot Pa wanted a glass of water. " Sarah dropped a kiss on the housekeeper's cheek before taking a glass of water back to her Pa's study.

Calm down first, she told herself. Try to listen to what they say. She stood at the door for a couple of seconds before knocking and entering on her pa's command. The look of love he sent her nearly reduced her to tears.

"Pa, I'm sorry. I got talking to Bridget. and I forgot about your water."

"Sarah, your ma and I have been talking. I will agree..."

"Oh Pa, thank you." Sarah rushed to her father's side.

"That's my impetuous girl. You never listen. Let me finish the sentence. I will agree to Edwin courting you for the next year," Rick said, in a tired but firm tone.

"But Pa..."

"Sarah Mary Hughes, listen to your elders," Rick snapped losing patience. "If you do not agree to my terms, there won't be any wedding. If you and Edwin are serious, a year isn't going to make any difference."

"What if he finds someone else? Michael Nolan said the girls in the towns near the mines are really pretty."

"Oh darling, is that what has you upset?" Jo moved to her adopted daughter's side putting her arm around her shoulders. "In Edwin's eyes, nobody could be prettier than you. But, if he did go off with someone else, then you will have had a lucky escape."

"The girls in those towns aren't anything like you, Sarah Hughes. They, well... let's just say they work for their living." Rick's discomfort would have amused Sarah if she wasn't so angry. Her pa really did believe she was totally innocent and didn't understand what a soiled dove was. But she wasn't about to educate him now. The longer he thought of her as innocent the better.

Maybe if she came and told him Edwin and herself had already slept together he would say yes. She bit her lip. Edwin wanted her, she knew that. But she didn't want to upset Rick and Jo by anticipating her marriage vows. Despite them not agreeing with her, she loved them. Deep down. She tried another tactic.

"You were younger than me when you decided to marry Uncle Rick." Sarah knew her use of the term uncle had hit the mark. Jo's eyes widened with hurt. She felt bad for a couple of seconds but they had to see she was serious about Edwin.

"Yes I was but I hope I was more mature than you are acting right now. This discussion is closed."

Jo's curt dismissal hurt but Sarah knew she deserved it. Rick and Jo had adopted her and Carrie when they were orphaned on the trail. Uncle Rick had promised their ma, his sister, he'd look after them. He'd kept that promise and more. Jo had become an instant mother younger than Sarah was now. Neither Carrie or herself were ever treated differently or loved less than Rick and Jo's natural children, the twins.

She'd behaved badly and for what? It hadn't made them change their mind about her and Edwin. She picked up her skirts and ran from the room letting tears run down her face.

She'd show them. She'd run away and marry Edwin. They couldn't stop her. Almanzo would try his best, he'd do anything to keep Rick and Jo happy even if it meant humiliating her. She would have to go when he wasn't around.

CHAPTER 3

HUGHES HOMESTEAD

*a*lmanzo pushed the door open, barely aware he was holding his breath. Was Rick in bed? Jo and Bridget were talking in the kitchen. The smell of cooking coming from the kitchen was mouth-watering. Tempted as he was to eat, he decided to sneak up to his room. He didn't want Jo to see the state of him.

"Almanzo Price, what time do you call this? Where have you..." Jo paused, clearly shaken by his injuries. "What happened to you?"

"Nothin'," he said not looking at her.

"Doesn't look like nothing. What did Rick tell you about fighting? You're 18 now not 10."

"I know how old I am. I didn't have any choice. They ..." Too late he realized he'd said too much.

"Who?"

"Doesn't matter. I'm going to wash up."

Hand on her hips, Jo blocked his way. "You start talking. I want to know who they are?"

Almanzo glanced at her. Her cheeks were flushed and her eyes glittered with temper. Most people assumed Becky Jones, Jo's twin, was the one to fly off the handle faster. Usually, she was but when Jo felt anyone had threatened her family, she was quicker to rile than an injured bear.

"I'm waiting."

"Jo, it was just a lark. They didn't mean any harm."

"I can see that." Jo's sarcasm sliced through him. He hated disappointing this woman who had provided him with a home since she'd rescued him back on the trail. He'd have died if it wasn't for her. And Rick. They'd given him shelter, food and above all a family. Despite having twins of their own, they never let him or their nieces feel like outsiders. But he was. Nothing was ever going to change that. His own parents had left him behind to die. They didn't believe he was worth anything. They were right.

He stayed silent. He didn't want to put her in danger. She had enough to worry about. She kept staring waiting for him to explain

"Let me handle it, please. As you said I'm a grown man now."

She gave him a hard stare but then threw her hands up in the air. "I don't know how to get through that thick head of yours. Rick will be up later. He'll want an explanation."

Almanzo gave Jo's arm a gentle squeeze as he walked by

her to get some water. He had to clean up a bit before he went to see his friend.

* * *

ALMANZO CLIMBED out the window and down the roof before dropping to the ground at the lowest point. He had to speak to Walking Tall and didn't want to alarm Jo any further. He waited a couple of minutes to make sure nobody had heard him leave then he ran in the direction of the meeting point. He'd sent signals he needed to see Walking Tall. Hopefully, the Indian had picked them up and his friend would be waiting.

He got to the spot on the edge of Rick's ranch where they always met. It was right next to the river which separated Rick's land from Scott's. Walking Tall dispensed with all greetings as soon as he saw his face.

"Harvey and his group?"

"Yes. You need to get to Paco. There is big trouble brewing," Almanzo took a second to control his anger. "Harvey said a group of Indians ambushed a wagon train. They killed all the men, most of the women and some children. But they took two of the younger women hostage. The Indians fled leaving some survivors."

"Why the Indians left?" Walking Tall asked in English.

"I don't know, something to do with soldiers coming," Almanzo said.

"What tribe?"

"You know they don't know or care about stuff like

that," Almanzo answered impatiently. "They think you are all the same."

Walking Tall scowled as Almanzo talked. Almanzo knew it hurt the Shoshone to be blamed for the actions of others. They tried to live in peace. "Did you hear anything?" Almanzo asked.

"I not hear but that does not mean it has not happened. I go talk to my father. He will know what we should do."

"Be careful Walking Tall, they know you work at Scott's ranch. They were saying some horrible things."

"They wish to put me on a horse with a rope around my neck," Walking Tall responded.

Almanzo stared at his friend. He had never told him what Harvey had threatened to do.

"Harvey has a big mouth and makes lots of noise," Walking Tall said grimly. "He is not as dangerous as those who keep mouth closed. They are the ones to watch."

Almanzo watched as his friend disappeared. He knew he should go home but he needed to talk to someone. Rick wasn't well and Jo would only worry. He decided to go visit Scott. He may be able to calm the situation in town with the whites.

As he rode over, he wondered whether the story was true. Indians had taken captives before but not around here. He didn't want to think about how scared the girls would be if it was true. He could still remember the fear and adrenalin when Becky was kidnapped. He hadn't known at the time his father was part of that. His real pa had been a horrible man. He had tried for years to understand how one man was so full of hate but he couldn't. Some nights he stayed awake wondering what he'd done to make his pa leave him behind. Why had his ma left him? Jo would sooner walk over hot coals than leave any of her children alone and in danger. That went just as much for him and the girls as her own natural children. Becky and Eva were the same. If anyone touched a hair on the head of their children, they would kill them. What was it about him that made his parents abandon him with barely a second glance? Sure, his ma had argued with his pa about leaving him behind but she had still left with his pa.

He raced along until he came close to the ranch when he slowed deliberately. He didn't want to cause panic by his sudden arrival. Luckily Scott was in the stables.

"Al, anything wrong? Is it Rick?"

"No it's not Rick but there is trouble."

Scott put down the bridle he was mending. "What sort of trouble?"

Almanzo explained what had happened in town. As he talked, Scott's expression grew grimmer, his hands fisted by his side.

"Walking Tall will have reached Paco already. They are camped out on the south side of the ranch. I best go talk to him."

"Shouldn't you go to town first and try to silence Harvey and his friends?" Almanzo said, his tone hesitant. He liked Scott but was in awe of him.

"No, it's best I talk to Paco. Have you told David?" Scott asked.

"Not yet, I came here first."

"I would offer you some coffee but I'd rather Becky not see you. She isn't feeling too well. If she sees the state of your face, she will be angry."

"Jo wasn't pleased either. I can ride to David and tell him if you want to go straight to Paco."

"Great, we will meet you at David's. Thanks, Almanzo."

"No, we will meet you at the camp. If Harvey and his group go looking for trouble, that's where they will be."

Scott nodded and shook his hand before he went to the house. Almanzo guessed he would tell Becky he had to go out but not tell her why. He grabbed a drink of water from the well and then got back on his horse and headed for David's ranch. One benefit of the family owning adjoining properties was they could reach each other quickly in the event of an emergency. Although each ranch was large, they had arranged the houses so they were close enough. If they had situated the house at the far end of each ranch it would have taken days to get to them all.

"Evening Almanzo." Eva got up from the porch seat, laying her mending to one side. Smiling she came to greet him, "Are you here on ... Good Lord, what happened to your face?" Eva looked as horrified as Jo had earlier.

"Harvey and his friends. Is David here?"

"He's reading the boys their bedtime story. Why did Harvey attack you or will I wait for David?"

Almanzo didn't want to scare the young boys and a couple of minutes wouldn't hurt. " I'll wait until he is finished. I'd rather tell you together," Almanzo kind of hoped Eva would leave him to talk to David alone but he couldn't suggest that.

"Come in and I will get you some coffee. Have you eaten?"

Almanzo's stomach grumbled.

"Guess not," Eva said smiling. "How are my sister and her family?"

"Jo and her family are fine or at least they were when I left. Scott said Becky wasn't feeling too good today.'

"Poor Becky, it's hard being pregnant when you have young'uns under foot. I shall go over tomorrow and see what I can do."

Almanzo didn't comment. Having babies was women's stuff. He had just finished his dinner when Scott came down from the boys' bedroom.

"I thought I heard voices. Did you walk into a pole?" Although David was joking his eyes were full of concern.

"We have trouble in town. Harvey and his friends."

"What is that lot up to now?" David asked, his distaste evident

"They said the Indians attacked a wagon train and two girls were kidnapped. The men were all killed before the soldiers came to their aid."

"Where? Which tribe?"

"I don't know. You know they don't care about those details. They were like a pack of dogs baying for blood. Harvey was saying stuff about Walking Tall so I punched him."

David gave him a look which spoke volumes but at least he didn't criticize him openly in front of Eva.

"I couldn't stand by and let them talk that way." Almanzo had to excuse his actions.

"You should have walked away. George Harvey is a bigoted, self-centered son of a …."

"David Clarke, little pitchers have big ears," Eva warned her husband gesturing upstairs.

"Sorry darling," David apologized. "Did you warn Scott?'

"Yes, he sent me to speak to you. I spoke to Walking Tall first, he didn't know of any attack so he has gone to see Paco. Scott went there too."

"Where are Paco and his tribe camped? On Scott's land?"

"Yes down near the river. But I don't think being on Scott's land will help them this time," Almanzo couldn't bear to put the truth into words. "Harvey was talking about lynching them."

David took his gun down from above the door and checked it. Then he turned to Eva. "Get the children up. I want to take you to your pa's and then we will go on to Scott's. I will send Jessie for the sheriff. He is a fair man. He won't stand for this.

"Won't the sheriff be out looking for the missing girls?" Almanzo asked.

"True, I hadn't thought of that." David looked at Almanzo before turning his attention back to Eva.

"David, I am not getting the children up again. Go to

Scott. Jessie was Scott's right hand man for years. There is nothing he can't handle. I can fire a gun. We have the root cellar if all else fails."

Almanzo knew there was a deep cellar under the house. It was something Scott insisted was built into every house. It was used to store foodstuffs for the winter months but also for protection if necessary. It would buy the family time in the event of an attack. Almanzo knew nobody had expected it to be used as protection against other whites but these were the times they lived in. The gold and silver mines had attracted all types, some of them less pleasant than the worst of those they had met on the wagon train.

Almanzo borrowed one of David's horses while one of Scott's ranch hands looked after his. He listened as David briefly explained the situation to the men. He knew Eva and the children were in good hands. The hands who worked for David Clarke idolized his wife and family. They were mostly single guys and Eva did her best to provide them with some of the home comforts they missed. They could perhaps have done without the weekly bath she insisted on but they were grateful for her cooking, her laundry skills and the fact she watched over them as a substitute mother. His thoughts wandered to the two young girls in captivity. How were they doing? Their families must be in despair. He could only imagine how bad it would be if Sarah and Carrie had been kidnapped. Rick and Jo would be frantic.

CHAPTER 4

INDIAN CAMP

*T*illy opened her eyes but swiftly closed them again at the pain. She moved slightly on the bear skin bed, liking the feel of the fur against her skin despite her stomach not being keen on where her bed covers had originated. Tentatively she rubbed her fingers over her face.

"It is best not to touch. This should help."

Tilly forgot about the discomfort as her eyes flew open at the sound of the woman's voice. Her English wasn't fluent but not because it was a second language. It was more like it had been a long time since she had spoken it. She looked at the Indian closely. Her skin was tanned to a nut brown but she had blue eyes. Her hair although dark looked like it had been colored.

"Who are you?" Tilly asked, drawing back from the woman.

"My name is Broken Wing. Don't look alarmed. I am here to help you not hurt you."

Tilly immediately looked for Fiona. Her friend was out cold. She moved to check her but the Indian put out her hand to stop her

"She is sleeping. I gave her something to help. She has been burnt too but is worse than you. Her skin is paler. See?"

Tilly looked closer at Fiona. Her skin was indeed red raw with little blisters from where it had been exposed to the sun. Despite the Indian's word, she checked her but to her relief, Fiona was sleeping.

"I will get you some more water and something to eat," Broken Wing said quietly.

"Why are we here? Why did your people kill the others?" Tilly demanded taking a step back from the Indian.

"None of my people killed anyone. They rescued you two. They were unable to save anyone else." Tilly thought the woman looked sad but why would she care about white strangers?

Tilly wanted to know more but the woman had already left. She moved quickly despite her bad limp. How had she been injured? Was it some sort of punishment inflicted by members of the tribe? She tried not to think about the newspaper articles she had read on how Indians treated female hostages.

Instead, she looked around the dwelling. It seemed to be made of branches woven together with a hole at the top.

She wondered what it was for. She squinted up at the sky but her face hurt too much. The woman didn't take long. She handed Tilly a drink.

Tilly sniffed it wondering if it was safe.

"It is only water. You do not need another draught," the Indian said in response to Tilly's actions.

"You already drugged me?" Tilly said, disbelief written all over her face.

"It was necessary to keep you quiet. The men were worried you would scream and give us away." The Indian woman's matter of fact tone pushed Tilly to respond truthfully.

"I would have," Tilly conceded. "In fact, I ..."

"You won't do anything to jeopardize your friend. You have kind eyes. You care deeply for this girl yet I do not think you are sisters." Broken Wing interrupted in her calm voice.

"She is my friend," Tilly replied shortly. "So if I scream, you will murder me?"

"Not me."

Those words sent a shiver of fear down Tilly's spine. She looked toward the exit.

Broken Wing's eyes followed her gaze. "There is a guard on duty. He will not come in. You are safe."

"How can that be true when we are surrounded by savages?"

The woman shut her eyes quickly as if hurt before responding quietly. "The color of a man's skin does not make him a savage. This is a lesson you should learn."

Before Tilly could answer, the woman was gone.

Tilly moved closer to Fiona, her brave front having disappeared now they were alone. She wished her friend was awake although she envied her peace. She closed her eyes as she lay down beside Fiona. Maybe this was all just a nightmare. Shutting her eyes, she prayed for sleep and hoped she would wake up in their wagon. Better still back in their home in San Francisco. It had been bad there but it was better than this nightmare.

* * *

SHE WOKE SOMETIME LATER. Fiona was still asleep. Thirsty she looked for the water Broken Wing had brought in earlier but it was all gone. Could she be brave and go looking for some? She glanced at Fiona before deciding she had played the part of a prisoner for long enough. She was going to demand they be returned to their own people.

She moved slowly, enjoying the feel of the earth on the soles of her feet. She looked around but seeing the coast was clear, she walked through the exit. There was nobody guarding them which she thought was a bit odd. She looked from left to right. The women and children all seemed caught up in various chores. A few men were sitting around a fire deep in conversation. She couldn't understand a word of what they were saying. She moved in the direction of the river, her thirst overruling her fear of stepping on something she shouldn't. Not for the first time, she regretted leaving her shoes and stockings at the river. Not that she was thinking of anything reasonable when she had first seen the Indians.

She had just got to the edge when an Indian stepped out in front of her. He glared at her as she screamed. He reached out a hand. She retaliated by slapping him forcefully across the face, hurting him before he touched her. He moved his head back, his eyes narrowing in anger. Raising his fist he moved to strike her but another Indian man grabbed his arm from behind. They wrestled for a couple of minutes before the Indian Tilly had struck gave in. He moved away, one hand on his cheek all the time glowering at her. She looked toward the Indian who had saved her. He was grinning at her. He said something but she couldn't understand him. He gestured at the water and then made a sign of drinking. She nodded. He reached down and making a cup using his hands offered her a drink. She pushed down her objections figuring she would insult him terribly if she didn't at least take a sip. Her stomach roiled at the sight of his less than clean hands but she forced her lips to the water. It was the right thing to do, as his smile grew bigger.

"Pretty hair. Face not bad for a squaw. You come share my blanket now?"

She stepped back but whether in shock he spoke English or his words, she couldn't be certain. She shook her head, her brain not working properly. He moved to stroke her face but she jerked out of his reach.

"Come with me. I protect you." He insisted moving closer. The smell of his breath combined with whatever he used to make his skin glisten, made her stomach heave. She pushed him away just in time to prevent her vomit covering him. He kicked the ground in disgust.

"You shouldn't have done that. You embarrassed him in front of the whole village." Broken Wing's words seeped into Tilly's brain as she tried to quell her stomach.

"I didn't do it on purpose. But he made me drink from his hands and the smell…" Tilly's nose wrinkled as her stomach heaved once more. But there was nothing left inside. She dry heaved for a couple of minutes before Broken Wing seemed to take pity on her. Taking a jug, she gathered some clean water which she gave to Tilly to drink. Then she handed her a cloth miming she should wash her face and mouth.

"Thank you," Tilly said quietly.

"Red Feather is a kind man. He would be a good husband," Broken Wing said, her eyes teasing.

Tilly wasn't in the mood for jokes. She had to get out of here and back to civilization. "I am not staying here never mind marrying an Indian. What do you take me for?"

"Someone who acts hastily without thinking," said Broken Wing, her disapproval evident. She looked at Tilly sternly making the younger woman feel more uncomfortable. "You should consider your circumstances. Men surround you yet you walk around like a woman of easy virtue. Indian maidens would never behave this way."

"I was thirsty and went to get a drink. I didn't anticipate a marriage proposal." Tilly knew she had spoken sharply but the other woman's condemnation had hurt.

"I told you to stay in the lodge. You are safe here provided you do what you are told," Broken Wing responded just as sharply.

Fed up with being found wanting, Tilly decided to take a stand.

"I demand you take me to your Chief. He must release us at once."

Broken Wing eyed her sadly. "My Chief cannot do that."

"Oh, he will. Let me speak to him." Tilly moderated her tone. "Please."

Broken Wing looked at her sadly. "Your family must be worried about you and your young friend."

Tilly didn't comment. She wasn't about to admit nobody cared whether herself or Fiona returned or not. She wrapped her arms around her body, watching Broken Wing closely as they moved back into the lodge. The Indian gently woke Fiona. This strange woman, half Indian, half something else had shown more care for Fiona and, if she was truthful, herself, than any other adult Tilly had known. She sniffed not wanting to show weakness by crying. It was pointless feeling sorry for herself. She had to get them both out of the camp and back to real life.

As they left the lodge heading toward the Chief, Tilly looked closely at the Indians. The women wore dresses made from some sort of animal covering. They stared at herself and Fiona, their gazes curious rather than unfriendly. They didn't make any attempt to speak. They appeared to be doing most of the work, not just preparing food but collecting firewood and two were fixing their lodge. She noted they moved in twos and threes, didn't wander alone as Broken Wing had said. Maybe her walk to get a drink had been a bad idea after all.

Then her gaze wandered over to the men. They all wore buckskin pants but their chests were bare save from some beaded necklaces. None had paint on their faces, yet they didn't look like the Indians she had seen in the forts. Those had a look of despair about them but these ones, despite looking thinner, sat up proudly. They had a defiant air about them, not threatening but leaving Tilly in no doubt they would fight to the last to protect what they considered theirs.

Fiona edged closer to Tilly, taking her hand as they walked in line behind Broken Wing. The Indian woman spoke rapidly to an older man with an air of authority about him and then pushed Tilly and Fiona forward. "Speak slowly and with respect," she warned the girls.

Fiona nodded mutely but Tilly ignored the warning. Instead, she walked right up to the Chief.

"I demand you take us to the nearest white town. Now." Tilly used the tone her mother had adopted when speaking to servants.

The Chief's eyes widened but before he could say anything, one of his braves stepped forward. He made to pull Tilly back but she rounded on him and slapped him hard. He was going to return the slap but the Chief spoke sharply. Then he turned his attention to Tilly.

"You must stop using violence in my camp. I do not like it."

Shocked he spoke English, Tilly retaliated by speaking sharply. "I don't like to be manhandled. If your men don't put their hands on me I won't hit them." Tilly believed she was being perfectly reasonable even if Fiona groaned behind her.

"Tilly, you need to be nicer. Having an attitude with the Chief isn't going to help," Fiona whispered but her words fell on deaf ears.

"Are you intent on fighting your way out of my camp?"

The Chief's question surprised Tilly.

"Yes, if I have to." She answered thinking she was stating the obvious.

The Chief signaled and two Braves stepped forward. One grabbed Tilly's arms and forced them in front of her while another tied them tight.

"What are you doing? Release me at once." Tilly protested, aiming a kick at the two Braves.

An Indian standing to one side said something and everyone laughed. Tilly glared at him before turning her attention back to the Chief.

"What did he say?"

"He says you are like fire. Nice to look at, hot to touch. He wouldn't mind you in his bed," the Chief replied giving her a disdainful look.

Tilly's mouth opened and closed. She didn't know what to say.

"Tilly, shut up. Everything you say makes things worse," Fiona whispered. "Apologize."

"I will not apologize. I haven't done anything wrong," Tilly protested hotly.

"You should listen to your friend. She is smart. You have a lot to learn." The Chief turned to Broken Wing and spoke quickly. She nodded in response, a sad expression in her eyes. Then she moved to the girls.

"Come, follow me."

Fiona moved to follow but Tilly wouldn't. "Wait, where are you going?" When Broken Wing didn't answer, Tilly turned back to the Chief. "I insist you set us free."

The Chief glared at her while Broken Wing hurried back to her side, taking Tilly's arm in hers and pulling her away forcibly.

"I asked you to be respectful. All you succeeded in doing was make the Chief very angry. Come now before he punishes you."

"What do you call this?" Tilly said waving her hands around.

"A safety precaution." Broken Wing replied sharply before leading Fiona away. Tilly stared after them for a second, then looked again toward the Chief. He ignored her although she knew he saw her glance at him. Uttering a word she would have never admitted to knowing a few days previously, she followed Fiona and Broken Wing. How on earth were they going to get away from the Indians now?

CHAPTER 5

*A*lmanzo rode alongside David in silence. He saw the older man look around him as he was doing the same. There were no dust clouds, no sign of Harvey or his men coming. But that didn't mean he wasn't lying in wait somewhere. Almanzo wasn't sure if Harvey was dumb enough to set foot on David or Scott's land. David would report everything back to the paper he wrote for. The paper was unusual in that it didn't take the usual anti-black, anti-Indian approach most papers did. In fact, the editor had been accused of being an abolitionist. Almanzo wasn't sure if he was or not but he knew David believed in equal rights for everyone. He could remember his pa grumbling about David Clarke and his love for blacks only his pa had used a much more horrible word. Almanzo tried to shut down the part of his mind, he didn't want to think about his pa now or ever. He had thought he hated him when he left him behind to die. But it was nothing to how he felt when Rick and Jo had finally told him the truth about his pa's role in kidnapping Becky. He'd been 15 and despite his age had to run out of the house to be violently sick. He couldn't believe, after everything Scott, Rick and Jo not to mention the rest of the party had done for him, his pa had put them in danger. His pa hadn't even checked on whether his own kid had survived. He hadn't cared enough. Neither had his ma.

"Open eyes my friend," Walking Tall stated as Almanzo almost ran over him. He'd been so caught up in his thoughts, he hadn't noticed they were almost at the camp. He colored. He should have been more alert. The Indians always posted sentries, especially now they knew they were being threatened.

"He Who Runs is with my father. He sent me to bring you to him. Hello David," Walking Tall greeted David with a big smile.

"You look well, Walking Tall. How are your wife and child?"

Walking Tall looked so proud. "My wife is with child again and our son will be two years this summer. He is very smart and wise already. Paco says he like him."

Almanzo smiled. Typical of Paco to take the credit. He couldn't imagine being married with children yet Walking Tall was only a year or so older than him. If he was going to marry anyone, it would have been Sarah. His heart twisted as he pushed her from his mind. His adopted sister was in love with Edwin Jarret and had been for years.

They walked over to the camp where the men were gathered around the fire. Almanzo didn't see any of the women which meant the conversation was serious. He greeted Paco and the other Indian braves he knew and took a seat beside Scott.

"Did they hear about the missing women?" he whispered.

Scott nodded but didn't say anything. He gestured to Almanzo to stay quiet. David sat on his other side but didn't say a word, his gaze focused on Paco. Almanzo was shocked at the change in Paco, he looked so much older than the last time he saw him. It had been about six months. Not long enough for Paco to have aged. He looked smaller and more troubled than ever.

"My scouts tell me what you say is true. A wagon was attacked and two young women were taken hostage. Their men were killed," Paco stated.

"Have they been harmed?"

"Not yet," Paco replied to David's question. Almanzo didn't like the emphasis on yet.

"What can we do?" Scott asked.

"It is difficult. In the past, our tribes were enemies. We have been friends for a while but it is not a deep friendship. We must proceed with caution."

"So we can't do anything?" Almanzo asked forgetting he was supposed to stay quiet. It was very rude for a younger man to address the Chief without waiting to be asked for his opinion. He felt the stares of everyone as all but Paco

41

turned to look in his direction. "I am sorry, I forgot my place."

"You are impetuous my friend. A little like He Who Runs when he was younger. These women, they are friends of yours?"

"No, Paco, but ..." Almanzo faltered.

"But..." Paco prompted.

"The men in town aim to bring all Indians to justice. They hate you and the tribe almost as much as they hate David Clarke."

"We are honored to be among good company," Paco said smiling at David. The two men shared a deep bond of friendship, each recognizing a kindred spirit.

"Forget about the men in town. The sheriff will handle them. Bradley Rodgers may not be vocal enough for my liking but he is not a coward and doesn't hold with vigilantes," David said calmly. "But we would like to try to get these women back. We must help. They deserve to be back with their families. What's left of them."

Silence lingered for a while before Walking Tall spoke up.

"Let me go, Father. I will take Al and a couple of the other men. We can go hunting and pretend to stumble over the camp."

"I will bring furs and some food with me, make it look like we are coming back from Canada. Maybe we can trade." Almanzo added, his blood feverish with the wish to be included.

"Rick will have my head if you go off looking for these women," David protested, looking at Almanzo

"Rick doesn't have to know. He would help if he wasn't ill. You know that," Almanzo argued back. Paco stayed silent letting the whites fight it out between themselves as he always did.

"I am going. I am not a child," Almanzo insisted. "Thanks to Walking Tall, I can ride and fight as well as any Indian."

"Not quite any Indian my friend. I can still beat you," Walking Tall said, an amused expression on his face. The smile slid off quickly as his father said something. Almanzo didn't understand the words, but the body language was easy to read. Paco was telling his son to take the matter more seriously. Almanzo knew Walking Tall was hurt but he didn't reply to his father. That would be disrespectful. Walking Tall always made light of the most dangerous situations. It was his way. Usually, Paco indulged him but not this time. That only showed how worried Paco was, not just about his tribe but also about the captives.

"We should go now. The longer we wait, the more dangerous it is for these women," Walking Tall said.

"If the white men show up, the Indians will kill the women first."

Paco's comment made them all think.

"Scott and I will head into town and see if we can stop Harvey and his friends," David stated. "Walking Tall, please keep Almanzo out of trouble. I do not wish to face my wife or her sister should anything happen to him."

Almanzo was about to protest but didn't. He knew the men cared about him. They considered him part of the Thompson extended family. Only he wasn't family was he? He was just another orphan from the trail.

CHAPTER 6

*I*t took two days and two nights to reach the camp where the women were being kept hostage. Almanzo had colored his face and skin to blend in with the other warriors. It wouldn't fool anyone close but from a distance, he didn't look like a white man.

"You can pass for my half-brother," Walking Tall said smiling.

"I smell like your brother," Almanzo retorted his nose wrinkling at the stink of bear grease his friend had insisted he rub into his skin.

They watched the camp but couldn't see any sign of the women. Walking Tall and the other braves argued about how best to approach the camp. In the end, it was decided Walking Tall would go in alone. Almanzo didn't agree but there was no arguing with Walking Tall once his mind was made up. He was definitely Paco's son.

Almanzo sat on his hands as he waited for Walking Tall

to return. He couldn't move about as the others said he made too much noise. He didn't think he did, he thought it was because Running Bear was with them. The Indian brave hated whites as much as Harvey hated Indians. Almanzo wasn't sure why the brave was in Paco's group. He had been told Running Bear's father had been a good friend of Paco. Almanzo couldn't understand the Indian he knew being friendly with a man who hated anyone ,least of all whites. But then he of all people should. his pa was just like Running Bear, full of hatred for an entire race. As Mr. Price had said often enough, the only good Indian was a dead Indian.

It seemed like forever, but it was only an hour or so later, Walking Tall returned, scowling.

"They have the women but refuse to let them go."

"What do they want?" Almanzo asked. "Don't they know the soldiers will attack?"

"They want a promise their lands will not be taken and they will be free," Walking Tall responded, his frustration obvious from his facial expression.

"Nobody is going to promise them that," Almanzo stated the obvious but before he could expand, Running Bear interrupted him.

"Why shouldn't they ask for what is rightfully theirs? Your white friends came and stole from us."

"Running Bear, enough," Walking Tall spoke sharply. "Al is a friend of mine. Do not show disrespect."

"I was going to say, I don't agree with them losing their lands," Almanzo clarified slowly. "But people will die if they don't let those women go free. Do you want that on your conscience Running Bear?"

"In war, men die," Running Bear spat back, his hostility clear for everyone to see.

"It's not just the men. Women, children, old people, babies, the white men who come won't care. They will kill anyone they find, not just those who attacked the train." Almanzo spoke sharply but Running Bear kept silent. He knew Almanzo was right.

"That was a big puzzle," Walking Tall stated. "The Indians say they not attack train but found women later. They say white men did it."

Almanzo turned toward Walking Tall. "But that's not what Harvey said?"

"You believe this Harvey because he is white?" Running Bear taunted, his face a sneering mask.

"No, he is a lying dog but the women would be able to tell their rescuers what happened," Almanzo spoke his thoughts aloud.

"Dead people do not speak," Running Bear spoke louder.

Almanzo and Walking Tall's gaze caught. "It's a trap. We must get those girls back to town so they can tell Sheriff Rogers what happened to them. Quickly before it is too late." Almanzo didn't wait for anyone's permission but headed to his horse.

"Wait, I am coming with you. I need to translate."

Almanzo flashed his friend a grin. He had forgotten most Indians didn't speak English as well as Walking Tall and while he knew a few Indian words, he was more likely to get into trouble than to rescue the girls.

* * *

THEY APPROACHED THE CAMP CAREFULLY. The Indians were waiting for them. Almanzo greeted the Chief, surprising him by speaking a few words. Although they weren't the Chief's language, he knew enough of the tribal languages to understand. Judging by his pleased expression, Almanzo had done the right thing. The Chief explained his position again to Walking Tall and the other Indians. Almanzo couldn't understand as they were speaking so fast so he took the opportunity to study their surroundings. The other men surrounding the Chief didn't look as friendly but they weren't hostile either. If anything, they looked fed up and more than a little frustrated. Almanzo sensed they were angry at being blamed for something they hadn't done. So, it was true the Indians hadn't attacked. He found it easier to believe these strangers than he did Harvey whom he had known for the last eight years.

As Almanzo looked around, he spotted an Indian woman staring at him. She looked away when he stared back at her but then she looked at him again. He couldn't see her face properly as she was too far away but something about her was familiar. She had a young child with her, a girl about six years old. The child was curious about the meeting, tugging at the woman's hand trying to get free but the woman held onto her tightly.

He wanted to meet her but that was the quickest route to being killed. These Indians didn't want white men near their women. Unlike some other tribes, they didn't sell or trade their women to the whites.

Almanzo glanced again in the direction of the woman but she was gone as was the child. He waited until there was silence between the Indians before asking Walking Tall if they could speak to the white women. Walking Tall confirmed the Chief had ordered the women brought to him.

It took several minutes for the women to arrive and when they did, Almanzo could see why. One of the girls was fighting and kicking every step of the way. She reminded him of Becky. The other girl was more docile although her eyes were looking at everything, taking note of things. They widened when they landed on Almanzo.

Almanzo stood as the girls came closer. They were dressed in their own clothes but on their feet, they appeared to be wearing moccasins. A hint they had been taken in a hurry?

He addressed them in English forgetting he was dressed as an Indian. The pale redhead listened although she tried to give the impression she wasn't. The other one stopped fighting long enough to spit in his direction before sending a kick aimed at the nearest Indian's lower leg.

"Calm down, please. You are not helping," Almanzo instructed quietly.

"I don't intend assisting in my own degradation." The

woman retorted. She spoke very well, her accent clipped. She wasn't local to the area.

"My name is Almanzo Price. The Indians with me are my friends. We came to rescue you."

"You? You look as much like a savage as the men around us. In fact, you look like those who attacked our train and murdered our ..." Her voice caught on the last word. She dashed her hand against her face, he saw then they were bound in front of her.

"Walking Tall, can you ask them to release the bonds?"

"I did. They said no as she is like fire. Nice to look at but dangerous to touch," Walking Tall responded, his eyes lit up with admiration for the girl.

Almanzo looked at the woman who was glaring at Walking Tall.

"He is a fine brave man who came to help you. Don't look at him like that," Almanzo's tone was insistent causing her to glare at him.

"He's a savage."

"He is your only hope of life. The savages are the white men who attacked your train, killed your people and aim to destroy this village on the pretext it was the Indians who were the aggressors." He paused long enough to get her attention. "You will not live to tell the truth unless you let us help you."

Tilly paled at his words but only for a second or two. Then she thrust her head back. "Why should I believe you?"

"Why not? I don't see anyone else trying to rescue you.

"I don't need your help. Fiona and I were doing just fine."

"Listen, lady, you need to simmer down. You and your friend Fiona are in grave danger."

"I..."

"Use your ears woman. God gave you two for a reason," Almanzo hadn't realized he'd spoken so sharply until the Indians started laughing. He glared at them which made them laugh more. "Just what is so funny?"

"Fire Daughter has burnt you too. She has been the same since they rescued her. They had to bind her hands as she kept trying to kick or slap them." Walking Tall spoke in English. "They do not like mistreating people but she refused to see they were trying to help." Walking Tall gave the woman a long stare before going back to sit with the Chief.

Almanzo looked at the woman and saw she had the grace to look ashamed. Yet she didn't apologize. She shut her eyes and when she opened them again the shame was gone, replaced by defiance.

"I wish to go to the nearest city. I need to speak to the Sheriff. You must escort me now," Tilly said in the haughtiest tone imaginable. Almanzo should have been annoyed at being addressed as a servant but instead, he was full of admiration for the woman. She must be terrified but she wasn't going to let anyone see her fear. Unfortunately for her, her attitude was only going to endanger her more.

"Yes my lady, anything you say. Just let me try and

prevent wholesale slaughter first." Almanzo bowed to her as he saw his sarcasm hit home.

"Slaughter?"

"The men who attacked your train want to kill all these people. Apart from binding your wrists, have they mistreated you in any way?"

She shook her head.

"Have they given you food and drink?" Almanzo asked, his tone kinder.

She nodded the shame back on her face.

"Perhaps you could think about that for a couple of minutes. If they wanted to rape and kill you, would they feed you first?" Almanzo asked softly.

Her horror at his words showed in her eyes. He was just about to apologize when her next words stopped him.

"You sir are no gentleman to speak of such a thing in a lady's presence."

"In case you haven't noticed, darlin', you are in the middle of an Indian camp, not at a Boston tea party," he drawled as her eyes opened wider. "Your life and the lives of every person in this camp is at stake right now. Perhaps you could stop thinking of yourself for one minute and look around you."

Almanzo returned to where Walking Tall was sitting and sat down beside him.

"She has made an impression," his friend whispered but Almanzo was far too angry to respond. He had been rude, something Rick and Jo had taught him not to be.

"I am trying to get the Chief to move his tribe closer to

ours. Then we may be able to help protect each other," Walking Tall confided.

"He does not want to?" Almanzo asked.

"No, he says there is no danger as he provided shelter to the women just as he did to other women in the past."

Almanzo's head shot up. "Other women? You mean there are more white women living here with these Indians?"

"Yes, my friend and you should change your expression as your disapproval crosses the language barrier. These men provided shelter for those who were missing or ill. You should not judge them badly," Walking Tall said quietly.

Shame caused Almanzo's stomach to roil. He had just judged an entire tribe harshly based on his own racist views. Despite telling himself he had left behind the beliefs his father had instilled in him all those years ago, he had immediately believed the women were being held captive.

"I am very sorry. I should have used my head," Almanzo apologized.

Walking Tall nodded slowly, the pain in his eyes causing, even more, shame to course through Almanzo's body. In acting without thinking he had caused his best friend pain. He felt lower than the underbelly of a rattlesnake.

"Can you ask the Chief if I could meet these women please?" Almanzo asked.

Walking Tall scrutinized him for a couple of seconds before rattling off something to the Chief. The old man smiled, before gesturing for one of his braves to show Almanzo around.

"You wish to meet with other white women?"

"Yes please, thank you. Thank you Chief," Almanzo remembered his manners. He put his hand on Walking Tall's shoulder and squeezed by way of an apology before he followed the brave toward the back of the village.

"Wait. Can we come with you?" the dark-haired girl said.

Almanzo looked to Walking Tall who again rattled off something to the Chief. Then Walking Tall took out his knife and seconds later, the girl's hands were free. Almanzo glared at her until she said thank you.

"Please keep quiet. Do not cause more trouble," Almanzo said under his breath. Then he held out his hand to the redheaded girl. "Fiona, I will not hurt you. Take my hand and I will help you." He spoke so gently, the tone the same as he used with a nervous colt. The girl stared him in the eyes and then moved to take his hand. Her grip was stronger than he expected. He held her hand as he moved after the brave leaving Fire Daughter to follow. He hadn't asked her name.

As they walked toward a group of women, he noticed the older woman from earlier move quickly in the direction of shelter, well as quickly as someone could with such a bad limp. Something made him call out.

"Wait, please. Don't leave."

The woman stopped moving but didn't turn around. She had understood English. He turned to Fiona and asked her to wait where she was. "Look after Fire Daughter and keep her out of trouble." Fiona gave him a half smile as he pointed at her fiery friend.

Then Almanzo moved slowly toward the woman.

"Please don't be afraid. We come in peace," he said quietly, his heart beating so loud he was sure she could hear it.

Still, the woman didn't turn around. He moved closer.

"You understand me. Are you one of the white women the Chief mentioned?"

She shook her head violently but he was close enough to see her skin, while tanned, was not the nut berry brown of the people around her. Her hair, although braided, was fair despite having been made to look darker. Who was she and what was she so afraid of?

"Please speak to me. I will not make you come with us. If you wish to stay here you can," he said softly.

She turned, a solitary tear rolling down her face. Her eyes were glued to the ground but it didn't matter. His head slowly understood what his heart was trying to tell him.

"Ma? It is you, isn't it?"

CHAPTER 7

HUGHES HOMESTEAD.

*C*arrie raced through the kitchen.

"Who's chasing you girl?" Bridget called.

"No-one but I'm late for dinner. Again." Carrie called back but kept moving. She'd forgotten the time and she hated being late for anything. Especially now with an atmosphere in the house. She didn't know what was wrong with Rick, but it was like walking on eggshells around the adults. They were usually patient and kind but Jo had become rather snappy the last few days. She didn't want to get on the wrong side of her ma.

Pushing open the door, she found her sister Sarah lying in bed. "What happened to you? Your cheeks are all red and your eyes are puffy. Did you have a row with Edwin?" Carrie asked with concern.

"Mind your own business."

"No need to bite my head off," Carrie retorted, stripping off her pants and putting on a dress. "You better hurry

56

up. Dinner will be on the table in ten minutes. You know we can't be late."

"I'm not hungry."

Sarah always had a good appetite. Worried it was something serious, Carrie sat down beside Sarah. "What's wrong Sassy?"

"Quit calling me that. I hate it."

"I thought you liked it. Paco was right when he started calling you that. You do talk back to the adults a lot," Carrie's impatience overrode her concern.

"I am an adult now," Sarah said pushing her sister's hand away. " For goodness sake, why does everyone insist on treating me like a child?"

"Maybe 'cause you act like one. Nancy acts older than you do at times," Carrie said firmly.

Sarah sat up on the bed, wiping the tears away with her hands. "Nancy acts older than everyone. Paco calls her the old soul for a reason," Sarah confirmed.

Carrie smiled thinking of their little sister. Well, their cousin if she wanted to be correct. Rick was her mother's brother but she couldn't remember her real pa. Her ma's memory had faded over the years. Rick and Jo were the only real parents she ever had. She loved them and considered their twins Nancy and Lena, her younger siblings.

"Are you worried about Al?" Carrie asked.

"No. Why?"

Carrie looked open mouthed at her sister. She knew Sarah had a selfish streak but even she must be worried about the missing girls and their adoptive brother out looking for them. "He's been gone ages. I know Ma and Pa are worried about him and the girls."

"They are better off dead."

Carrie's head snapped up. "What did you say? How could you?"

"Grow up Carrie. Who is going to want two girls who have been living with Indians for almost a week? If they aren't dead, I bet they wish they were." A stinging slap rang out. Sarah screamed in pain. "What did you do that for, you little brat?"

"How could you say something like that. You don't know anything about the Indians. They could be like Paco and the rest of *our* friends. Remember how the tribe helped to save Becky from the kidnappers and helped us to settle in Oregon."

Sarah reddened a little at Carrie's emphasis on our. She turned away not wanting to acknowledge her sister was right. "Edwin says it is not decent. What if they come back with an Indian in their belly?" Sarah said, her cruel words shocking Carrie to the core.

"I hate Edwin Morgan and you should too. He is a despicable excuse for a man. I am going to tell Pa and Ma what he's been saying. That will be the end of you walking out with him."

Sarah paled before dropping to her bed. "Please Carrie, don't say a word. I'm sorry. I am just really worried about Pa and Almanzo and the others. Of course I hope the girls come back safe and sound."

Carrie eyed her sister. She couldn't say anything to Rick

and Jo, not for her sister's sake but for Rick's. He had enough to worry about.

Carrie concentrated on putting on her stockings. Why couldn't her sister have fallen in love with Almanzo. He was so much nicer than Edwin Morgan. Now was not the time to tell Sarah she thought Almanzo was in love with her. He had been for years but nobody seemed to see it. Sarah had never mentioned anything. Carrie knew she wasn't wrong though as Stephen had the same suspicions. She smiled thinking of Stephen. He'd kissed her for the first time earlier. She hadn't been surprised as she'd been in love with him forever. Well at least since they had met on the wagon train. She bit her lip as her body tingled remembering the touch of his lips against hers, the feel of his fingers as he held her face so tenderly. He had been so gentle.

"What are you thinking about?" Sarah asked, her voice sounding stronger.

Carrie flushed as her sister's voice intruded on such personal thoughts.

"Carrie Hughes, what have you been up to?"

"Nothing. I was just thinking about the material I saw in Newlands. It would be perfect for a new dress for the 4th July party."

Sarah threw her eyes up to heaven. "I can believe a lot of things but since when did you care what you wore?"

Carrie didn't answer. There was no point when Sarah was in one of her moods. Carrie quickly finished her hair and went downstairs. Let Sarah sulk. She had better things to do.

Carrie pushed open the kitchen door. Bridget was standing at the stove, her face as red as a tomato.

"Have you stopped running now Miss Carrie?" Bridget teased her.

"Yes thank you, Bridget. You look very hot. Do you want me to take over?"

"Bless you, child. I think I need to go stand in the doorway for a little while. I keep getting all hot and bothered."

Carrie's heart tightened. "Are you ill?"

"Not ill, child, just nature's way of telling me my child bearin' days are over. Seems to me women get the raw deal on this earth."

Carrie stirred the gravy, embarrassed at what Bridget was saying. Although she should be used to their Irish maid. She'd been a straight talker from the first day she'd started working for the family.

"Bridget, why do you keep calling me a child? I am almost 15. That's old."

"Miss Carrie you only just turned 14. Why young'uns want to be older is beyond me," Bridget shook her head. " You will look back one day and wonder where all the years went."

"But I am a woman now. Not a child." Carrie hoped the housekeeper would think her cheeks had pinked up due to the heat of the stove.

"You are growin' into a fine young woman Miss Carrie.

I will try to remember not to call you a child again but you'll have to forgive me if I forget. My old mind isn't what it used to be. I'd forget my own head if it wasn't stuck on my neck."

"Bridget, you are not old. Not really. Grandma Della is older than you, isn't she?" Carrie asked.

Bridget laughed loudly. "Don't go sayin' that in front of Miss Della. She'd not be too happy."

"Grandma Della wouldn't mind. Grandpa keeps telling her she is getting on."

"Your grandpa is teasin' her. Sure, he adores the bones of that woman. Easy tellin' that was a love match."

Carrie didn't want to think of Jo's parents being in love so changed the subject.

"Bridget, would you have time to help me make a new dress for the 4th of July dance?"

"*Help* you, Miss Carrie?" Bridget's eyes glowed as she teased her.

Carrie flushed as her guilty gaze met Bridget's. "I do try to sew nicely but you always say my seams are crooked."

"You sew like you were blind, chil... sorry, love," Bridget corrected herself quickly. "I tell you what. You take on some of my other chores and I will make your dress."

Carrie beamed.

"Is there a special someone who will be at this dance Miss Carrie?" Bridget's smiling eyes sparkled with curiosity.

Carrie's heart beat so fast it hurt. She wanted to confide in Bridget but if she said anything, Stephen could be in trouble. She shook her head trying to make herself believe she wasn't lying if she didn't speak.

"Hmm, your face tells a different story. I reckon I can guess who the young man is too. He's a good lad, strong and steady. Knows what he wants."

"He is lovely, isn't he?" Carrie clamped her hands over her mouth as Bridget smiled knowingly at her. "You tricked me."

"No, love, I didn't but you can't hide your feelings. You wear your heart on your sleeve, Miss Carrie. Always did right from the day I met you. You and Stephen Thompson make a fine couple but you know your pa thinks you are too young to be courtin'."

"Pa is so old-fashioned and strict," Carrie said stirring the meal furiously. She hated being critical of anyone but it was true, her folks lived in the last century. "Gretel Fredrickson is getting married next month and she is only 15."

"Your pa only wants you to be happy. Miss Sarah wouldn't listen to me and I guess you won't either. But Master Rick only ever does things to keep his family safe and well provided for."

"Is that what is wrong with Sarah? Did she have a row with Pa?"

"Yes, Miss Carrie. Your sister wants to marry Edwin Morgan and your pa thinks she is too young."

"She will always be too young to marry that boy. How could she like him? The Morgans hate everyone but particularly the Indians." Carrie grimaced remembering the awful row she had witnessed between her uncle David Clarke and Edwin's father. David had written about the horrible conditions the Indians were expected to endure on the reservations. Mr. Jarret had called David a whole range of names, only some of which Carrie understood.

"Yes, your pa is very upset. So it is best, for now, you don't say anythin' about you courtin'. He has enough on his plate."

Carrie stirred the gravy faster, her face screwed up in concentration. She hated thinking about illness. People who got ill died. Ma and Benjy hadn't got any better when they got sick. Sarah had but only because Jo nursed her so well. Why couldn't Jo fix Pa? She jumped as Bridget put her arm around her shoulders. She hadn't heard the woman walk over to her.

"Don't fret love. People get sick and get better all the time."

"My real ma didn't. And my brothers. What if…" Carrie couldn't put her thoughts into words.

"Stop thinkin' like that," Bridget said soothingly. "Master Rick is strong. He will get better."

Carrie hoped Bridget was right but she couldn't help think her voice wasn't as confident as her words.

"It's all the trouble with the school board. I hate those people. First, they insisted we had two schools, one for the rich and another for the poor. Now they want to…."

"Good afternoon Miss Johanna, were you coming to check on dinner?" Bridget's voice, louder than usual, cut across what Carrie had been saying. She looked up and caught Jo looking at her, her expression thoughtful. Carrie saw the deep black circles under her ma's eyes and felt worse. How could she have been so happy earlier with Stephen when there was an illness in the house?

"Bridget, since when have I had to check on dinner?" Jo teased her housekeeper. "Carrie, darling. How nice to see you helping Bridget."

"Thanks, Ma. Bridget is going to help…" at Bridget's cough, Carrie corrected herself, "Bridget is going to make a new dress for me and I am going to do some of her chores in return."

"I see. It took you a long time to admit defeat, Bridget. I thought you were determined to make my daughter sew like a professional."

"She sews like something Miss Johanna but not like any seamstress I ever met," Bridget responded rolling her eyes as she laughed.

Jo and Carrie laughed before Jo added, "I guess the world would be a boring place if we each had the same talents. I wish I could crochet like you Carrie, you have a real gift for making pretty things."

"Thanks, Ma, you were the one who taught me how. I can make you a new collar for your dress and for Bridget."

"I ain't goin' to the party," Bridget said firmly.

"But you have to Bridget. There are lots of miners coming and they don't have anyone to dance with. You might find yourself a new husband," Carrie said. She wanted everyone to be just as happy as she was.

"One of them was enough for me, thank you, Miss

Carrie. I never want to see a man's boots under my bed again. Not if I live to be a hundred years old." Bridget started banging some pots. It was time to leave her domain. Rick and Johanna may own the house but Bridget oversaw the kitchen.

Carrie and Jo decided to sit on the porch for a few minutes enjoying the last of the sunshine.

"Ma, is Pa going to go see the doctor?"

"I don't know Carrie. He says he will but he wants to wait until the school governors visit is over first."

"I wish he would just start a new school. Like he did when we first came here. Then he could run it just as he wanted. He wouldn't have to take orders from anyone."

Jo linked her arm through Carrie's. "Since when did you get so grown up? It seems like I closed my eyes and you have gone from being a little girl to a proper young woman. I feel old."

"Ma, you're not old. You're not even thirty yet," Carrie protested. She snuggled closer to her ma taking advantage of being alone with her. That was a rare occurrence given the busy household. "Why does Bridget get so annoyed when anyone talks about her getting married again? I was only joking."

"I know love but Bridget didn't have a good marriage. Her husband wasn't like the men you know. He hated everyone including himself. He was very unkind to Bridget."

Carrie didn't know anything about Bridget's husband other than he had died on his way to Oregon leaving

Bridget to fend for herself. Like most people she couldn't afford to go home so she stayed. She had written to her Daddy but he hadn't responded. The Reverend had heard about Bridget, spoken to Rick and Bridget moved in shortly after.

"Is that why she lives with us? Because we aren't rich enough to have a maid, are we?" Carrie asked.

"Bridget is so much more than our maid. She's a member of our family," Jo corrected Carrie softly.

"I wish she would just call me Carrie. Makes me feel funny, her calling me Miss."

"I would prefer if she called me Jo or Johanna too, but Bridget has her ways, and we aren't going to change them. We treat her the same as we would any other family member and that is all that matters. Now tell me about your plans for the dance?" Jo tilted her head to the side.

Carrie took a deep breath. How could she explain to her ma that she was in love with Stephen? He was Jo's younger brother. The silence lingered. Jo grinned at Carrie before caressing her cheek. "Does my little brother figure in your plans?"

Carrie went rigid with shock. "What?"

"Carrie Hughes," Jo said giving her a hug. "You have been trailing around after Stephen since that day at Soda Springs when he drank too much and had a belly ache. It's hardly surprising you want to look pretty at your first dance as a grown up."

Carrie glowed with pleasure at being called an adult.

"Will Pa mind?'

"Rick might find it a little difficult to let you grow up Carrie but he is not going to stand in the way of your happiness. He is protective of both you and Sarah – possibly even more than Nancy and Lena."

"I don't understand why. The twins are little, they need him more." Carrie knew Rick was protective but children needed more attention than adults.

"We all need Rick in different ways. He feels responsible for you girls as your ma gave you into his care. You and Stephen need to be patient and sensible. Please don't do anything to upset your pa."

Carrie saw the tears Jo was trying so hard to keep from falling. She gave her an impulsive hug.

"We won't, Ma. I promise."

Jo didn't say anything but hugged Carrie very tightly for a couple of seconds before she let go and left the room. Carrie guessed she was going to wash her face. Jo didn't like anyone to see her upset, least of all her husband.

Carrie stared at her, a cold ball of fear in the pit of her stomach. She wished Grandma Della was due to call as she could always help make Jo feel better. But could Della help this time? Was Rick more seriously ill than she had first imagined?

CHAPTER 8

*D*ella Thompson pulled up outside her daughter Becky's home. She loved the large homestead almost as much as her own smaller place. Scott had built a large home, not least because he regularly had visitors who stayed for weeks at a time. Scott insisted that the way to living peacefully with the Indians was to have people on both sides of the argument get to know each other better. So he invited prominent people from politicians to newspapermen to stay. He then told them his story and introduced members of Paco's tribe. His Indian family camped down near the river when they came down from the mountains, they didn't like living in a house.

Della smiled thinking of Paco's first sight of the homestead. The Indian who wasn't scared of anything refused to step inside. He kept telling Della and anyone else around, the roof would fall in on top of him. Scott, Rick, David, Paddy and some of the Indian Braves had carried Paco against his will and dumped him in the sitting room. It hadn't changed Paco's viewpoint and the Indian still resisted going inside. Paco had aged in the eight years they had been living in Oregon. Della could understand why, given how badly the Indians had been treated. Why was there so much hate in the world?

She raised her hand in greeting to one of the ranch hands. She didn't know his name, Scott tended to employ casual labor as and when he needed it. He preferred Indians to work with the horses. Della couldn't see her grandchildren. They mustn't have heard the wagon, otherwise, they would come running to see who was visiting. Becky was nowhere to be seen. Maybe she was resting although as soon as Della had the thought, she dismissed it. Ever since she was born, Becky had been moving. She never stayed in one place for long. Even when sitting down, her hands had to be working on something. Paddy used to say it was as if there was a fuse lit inside her which never went out. Della smiled at the reference. Becky had made a better life for herself than anyone could imagine. Back in Virgil, her daughter had imagined a life married to a rich man where she could be a lady of leisure or spend her days on horseback. As Della looked around at the evidence of her daughter's hard work from the kitchen garden to the whitewashed picket fence, she could see how far from a lady of leisure her daughter had become. Despite their initial opposition and concerns, Scott Jones had turned out to be the perfect husband.

Well almost. Della wished Scott didn't want such a big

family. Becky was pregnant again and she was worried about her. Two sets of twins in seven years were enough for any woman. She loved her grandchildren but she was scared for their future. She sighed deeply spotting the flag Scott had erected outside his barn. Oregon had joined the Union last year with the dubious honor of being the first state to join with an existing racial clause. Now with the talk of war in every newspaper, she was afraid. She'd thought she would never be as frightened as she had been on the Oregon trail eight years ago but this was a new fear.

They had been through a lot since they first arrived, with the Indian wars and the financial crash of 57. But despite all the upheavals and bad news, her girls and their husbands had not only survived but prospered. All three girls were mothers of healthy children, had beautiful homes and good marriages. The only cloud on the horizon was Rick's illness. At least that had been the only issue. Maybe they had been too lucky? Was there a price to be paid for all their good fortune?

Now the newspapers were full of plans for war. Her son Stephen and the adopted grandson Almanzo were almost 18, they would be the first ones to go and fight should war break out.

Della gave herself a mental shake. What was the point in inviting trouble? As her mother-in-law used to say, there was plenty enough bad things going to happen without inviting them to your door.

Now was the time to concentrate on the things she could do. Becky needed her help whether she admitted it or not. She parked the wagon and got out wondering where everyone was. Usually, someone came to greet visitors but the porch was empty. She tied the horse to the rail before opening the front door, calling out a greeting. Silence answered. She walked quickly into the kitchen where Ruth, her six-year-old granddaughter was working at her letters.

"Didn't you hear me, child?"

Ruth didn't answer, nibbling at her lip as she traced the A on her slate. Della spoke to her again. This time Ruth looked up, squealed and ran to give Della a hug. Then she ran outside saying she was going to find her ma. Della stoked up the cooker and put the water on to boil. She was gasping for a cup of tea. While the water was boiling, Della moved toward the kitchen sink, spotting Becky a little way outside. She was looking at something in the distance.

BECKY LOOKED up as the kitchen door opened and her ma came out. She gave her a big hug despite wondering why she was here. She hadn't said she was coming to visit.

"Is Pa all right?"

"Yes, fine. Why?" Della asked but her eyes didn't meet her daughter's face.

"Just wondered if there was anything wrong. It's not like you to turn up unannounced," Becky said scrutinizing her ma. She looked tired but it was probably the heat. It was hard to sleep when it got so warm.

"I came to see my family. I didn't realize I needed an invitation," Della snapped.

"Ma! Don't get all worked up. I am thrilled to see you. Now how about a cup of tea."

"Why don't you take a seat on the swing and I will bring it out to you?"

Becky looked at her ma closely. Her mother never suggested anyone sit down when there was so much work to be done. She had to weed and water the garden and the sun would be too high if she left it much longer.

"Becky, sit a while. The garden and other chores can wait."

Becky sat more out of shock than anything. It was nice to get a little break. Constant nausea overtaking her body was making life more than a little uncomfortable. She sat back in the shade. If her ma wanted to fuss a little bit, who was she to stop her?

Della didn't take long to make the tea and brought it outside with a plate of cookies.

"No thanks Ma, my belly isn't feeling too good."

"Try them. They will help with the morning sickness. Mrs. Newland gave me the recipe and she should know."

In addition to running the store with her husband, Mrs. Newland had appointed herself as the midwife to the surrounding area. In most cases, the women preferred another woman to help birth the baby. They only called in Doc White if there were complications. Becky smiled.

"What are you smiling at?"

"Do you remember we told you about the Indian who

tried on Mrs. Newlands unmentionables. She whacked him across the face."

Della smiled. "She is some woman. Who would have guessed she'd become a force to be reckoned with. Rumor has it, she had a row with Mrs. Morgan last week."

"I dislike that woman intensely. What did Mrs. Newland do?'

"She served an Indian woman who had been waiting in line. Mrs. Jarret thought she should be served first seeing as she is white."

"Good for Mrs. Newland. Although if anyone had said to me when we first got acquainted with her, she would turn into a friend, I would have laughed. Do you remember how she used to moan?" Becky asked rolling her eyes to heaven.

"I remember. But I think it was because she was fearful of the future. Now she has friends and family around her, she has less to worry about."

"I don't know about that, Ma. If she continues upsetting Mrs. Jarret and her cronies, she may find life gets more than uncomfortable.'

"I hope she does keep doing exactly what she is doing," Della said firmly. "I wish Mrs. Morgan would disappear and take her family with her. Did you know Edwin asked to marry Sarah? Rick said no, of course, but Jo is worried about it. She said Sarah wasn't too happy."

Becky bit her lip suddenly feeling emotional. Tears weren't far from her eyes which was so unusual for her, she found it really disconcerting.

"Becky, what's wrong? Is it the baby?"

"No Ma. I just get all teary all the time. It's so annoying," Becky answered.

"It's called pregnancy darling. What upset you? Sarah?"

"Oh Ma, how did she turn out the way she did? She was a quiet sweet girl on the trail and she has turned into a .... Well I can't put it into words."

"She is a selfish little madam. I think Rick and Jo were too soft on her. I know it was difficult learning the truth about her da but there are those who have it worse. Almanzo for example."

"He has turned out to be a fine young man, hasn't he. It's a pity Sarah didn't fall in love with him." Becky bit her lip as she considered her niece.

"Love works in mysterious ways. I just hope Sarah doesn't get carried away. Rick and Jo have enough on their minds.

"What do you think is wrong with Rick, Ma? He doesn't look well and he seems to get tired so easily. I know Jo is worried sick."

"He keeps avoiding Doc White. I think Jo will put her foot down soon and either Rick will go into town or Doc White will call to the homestead."

"Do you think it's really serious, Ma?"

Taking one look at her ma's face, she didn't need her ma to answer. It was written all over her. The tears came again but she brushed them away angrily.

"Becky sweetheart, I think you should go back to bed.

You look worn out. Why not let me help for a while?" Della said softly.

"I will be grand, ma. You know me. Can't keep still for five minutes," Becky said forcing a smile on her face. "Thank you for the tea."

"Well at least sit there and enjoy it in peace. I will make a start on dinner. Ruth can help me."

Becky didn't remind her ma that her daughter was only six. Her ma had firm beliefs in children learning to help from a young age. Becky didn't have the energy to fight with her ma or anyone else at the moment.

She sat back in the swing and closed her eyes telling herself she would get up in a few minutes. Sometime later she woke to the sound of her son's shrieks of laughter.

Becky pushed her hair out of her eyes as she tried to focus on her son, Jake. Ruth's twin was pushing the horse too fast as usual. She wanted to haul him off and hug him close but he would hate her for it. Although only six years old, he was fiercely independent. When she complained about it, Scott reminded her there were children barely older than Jake working full time in the big cities like New York.

"Ruth Jones, if I have told you once, I told you a thousand times if a job is worth doing, it's worth doing properly." Della's voice carried on the wind. Becky gave one last look in Jake's direction before going inside to rescue his twin from her ma.

"Ma, she's only six. Leave her be." Becky pulled a sniveling Ruth into her arms and gave her a cuddle.

"She's old enough to start learning. You have enough on your hands with four children and another on the way. You still look tired, Becky."

"Ma! I am fine. I am not ill, just pregnant," Becky said trying but failing to hide her irritation.

At Becky's tone, Della looked upset. Della bent down toward Ruth and gave her granddaughters arm a squeeze. "I am sorry love, I didn't mean to shout at you. I am in a bit of a heap this morning."

"What's heap?" Ruth asked, her curiosity getting the better of her.

"Your gran is a little bit worried about your ma. She thinks I should rest more," Becky said quickly trying to offset a string of questions from her daughter.

"No you shouldn't do that ma, you are getting fat. Soon you will look like Mrs. Porter."

Becky had to hide her smile from her daughter and judging by her ma's quick turn, she did too.

"Ruth, it's not nice to make comments about people," Becky corrected her little girl.

Ruth sniffed, turning her nose up. "I don't like Mrs. Porter. She's mean and says horrible things about Paco. He's my friend. She isn't. And she is fat," Ruth said with conviction.

Della burst out laughing even though Becky sent her a fierce look.

"Ruth, sweetheart, I know you love Paco, but we can't say nasty things about people we don't like. It isn't nice," Della explained only to be interrupted by Ruth.

"Ma calls Mr. Jarret a jumped up... What was the name you used ma?"

Becky decided it was time to ignore Ruth or there was no knowing where the conversation would end up. Her ma was tidying the kitchen. It drove her nuts her ma always started working in the kitchen no matter how clean it was. She felt like a child again, being found wanting.

"Ma, sit down and have another cup of tea before you drive me crazy."

Della Thompson opened her mouth but then closed it again. She glanced at Ruth. Becky took the hint.

"Ruth can you take Annie and go check on the hen house. Your brother was supposed to clean it out but..."

"I'll do it, Ma," Ruth said, putting her slate and chalk on the shelf.

"No. I want Jake to do it but I need you to take care of Annie. Don't let her play with the hens. They may peck her."

Becky waited until the girls were gone before sitting down. Despite her brave words, her legs were aching. It hadn't been so long since she was pregnant, but she'd forgotten how tiring it was. She looked up in time to see her ma brush away a tear. Her ma never cried. Her stomach dropped as she took her ma's hand. "Ma, what's wrong?"

"There's nothing wrong. Can't I just come see my daughter?"

"Ma, tell me why you are so upset. Please," Becky said softly.

Della stayed quiet for so long, Becky was sure she was going to tell her someone was dying or had died. Horrible thoughts crowded through her mind. She was just about to say something when her ma spoke.

"It's your pa, he's convinced there is going to be a war."

"With the Indians?" Becky asked a bit impatiently. "It's been going on for years, why would it start worrying him now?"

"Not with the Indians but between the North and South. I think he is making too much of it but you know he reads every newspaper he can get his hands on. He says it's not a question of if but when."

"He is being ridiculous," Becky said hotly. Her temper was shorter than usual, being pregnant in the heat didn't help. She was relieved nobody was dying but her pa's pessimistic attitude annoyed her. He was always thinking the worse. "Nobody wants a civil war in America."

"I don't know if that's true, Becky but your pa isn't usually wrong about things. You know what he said about the treaties and the Reservations. All of that is coming true as we know."

Becky stroked her ma's hand absentmindedly. She didn't want to think about the horrible things that had happened since they moved to Oregon. The upsurge in Indian attacks and the number of Indians killed by troops supported by local militia was too painful to contemplate. Scott, David, Rick and others like them had done all they could to help Paco and his tribe but it hadn't been enough. Although Paco and his immediate family were safe, the same couldn't be said for other members of the tribe. Some had joined the fight on the side of the Indians but more had been innocent victims of retaliation attacks. The hostility toward Indians was growing to the point most settlers wanted them forced onto reservations preferably miles away from Portland and the Willamette Valley. If the North and South went to war, what would happen with the Indians? The soldiers would be called to fight, wouldn't they? A bolt of nausea hit Becky. Who else would be called up to fight? "Ma, what about Scott and the other men. They wouldn't have to go fight in the war, would they?"

"I don't know, Becky. Your pa seems to think younger men would be called up first."

"Stephen? Oh no Ma, he wouldn't. They couldn't." Becky almost begged her ma to tell her she was wrong. " Oh my goodness, Almanzo too."

"I shouldn't have said anything. Maybe your pa is wrong this time."

"What's Paddy wrong about?" Scott had come in while his mother in law was talking. He bent and kissed her on the cheek before greeting Becky as always with a butterfly kiss on her mouth.

"Pa thinks there might be a war. Ma is worried about Stephen, Almanzo and the rest of the boys. You don't think there will be a war, do you?" Becky looked up at her husband but he didn't meet her gaze.

"I don't believe so. Look how quickly President Buchanan stepped in to prevent war with Britain."

Becky looked at Scott closely. He was deliberately

avoiding her gaze making her suspect he was telling them something to make them feel better. She didn't get a chance to pursue it as her ma interrupted.

"I still can't believe we came so close to war with another country over a pig eating potatoes. Men! If they had to have babies, they wouldn't be so quick to want to kill them."

"Calm down, Della. Nobody is going to kill anyone. Becky, why don't you make your ma another cup of tea. I am going to check on Jake." Scott retreated out the door. He never stayed around if there was a hint of an argument between the Thompson women.

* * *

"Scott was clever asking Paco and Walking Tall to look after his animals while he was working as a trail guide."

"We are lucky ma. I was reading an old newspaper and the stories of people still suffering in the big cities from the panic in '57 are scary. I am so glad we moved out here," Becky said.

"Do you remember asking me if I regretted moving? That time when the ox died and we were stuck in the horrible dust," Della's lip twitched at the memory.

"Can I ever forget it? I thought there was no hope for me and Scott and now look at us. Four children and counting." Becky rubbed her stomach. She hoped it wasn't another set of twins but she would never admit that out loud.

"Have you seen Eva, Ma?"

"Eva is grand. She is worried David is taking on too much with his writing and the work on the ranch but she is happy."

"I wonder how many people back in Virgil would believe David Clarke is a writer on the newspaper." Becky wondered aloud. Her brother in law had suffered due to his father's reputation as a drunk. The people of Virgil would be amazed at what David Clarke had achieved in such a short period of time. She could see him in the senate. "He has a way of reporting the news, it makes it clear what he is saying."

"He does but sometimes his views aren't too popular. He has abolitionist tendencies," Della stumbled over the unfamiliar word. "Many don't like that."

"Ma! You brought us up to believe everyone was equal," Becky said shocked at the implication David was wrong.

"Yes, Becky and I believe that," Della quickly corrected her daughter. "But his articles on John Brown and the action at Harpers Ferry weren't popular. There are many who believe Mr. Brown was wrong to do what he did."

"David didn't agree with his actions but with his sentiments. John Brown, for all his faults, believed in freedom for everyone," Becky clarified.

"But David should think of his family. His children must live in Portland. There is a lot of bad feeling towards Indians and Blacks especially with many losing husbands and fathers in the Indian wars."

"Well, it was their fault for joining the militia," Becky snapped.

"Becky Jones, don't let anyone hear you saying that. You would be lynched."

"I am only talking to you Ma. The local militia appears more eager to kill Indians than the army. They don't care who they kill either. I know the Renegades committed dreadful acts but Indians like Paco don't need to suffer too. If I killed a man, nobody would come and kill you and pa, never mind Jo and the children in revenge. It's one rule for them and another for the whites. That is what annoys David so much."

"Scott feels it too yet he doesn't go around broadcasting his views." Della commented before saying, "Don't look at me like that Becky. I agree with David but sometimes it is best to keep your opinions to yourself.'

"If everyone did that ma, nothing would ever change." Becky didn't want to fight with her ma so she quickly changed the subject. "Is Pa coming back to collect you or will Scott drop you home after dinner?"

"I drove myself over, I can drive myself home," Della said, her tone suggesting she was still angry.

"I know you can ma but I prefer it if you didn't drive around alone. You know there is still a chance of attack. Scott will ride back with you. Now, why don't you help me with dinner?" Becky cajoled knowing her ma liked to feel useful.

"Let me do dinner and you go put your feet up for a bit. Your ankles look a bit swollen. Go on, go rest."

"But the younger children?" Becky's protest was half hearted. The continuous nausea was making her tired. And grumpy although she wasn't about to admit that.

"Becky, I am not dead yet. I can make dinner and mind children. I've had plenty of practice!"

"Yes, ma." Becky would have run if she could. Her ma was rarely in bad form but today she was in a shocking mood. Was it because Gran had died? They knew she'd been sick but still, everyone had been surprised she didn't pull through. As David pointed out, they'd expected Gran to live forever.

Becky sat on the edge of the bed looking at her ankles. They were huge. Thick ankles and being sick all the time. Pregnancy wasn't that much fun. She lay back on the bed closing her eyes before opening them again. She didn't want to sleep. Every time she tried, she imagined it was Scott who was ill not Rick. At night, she lay in bed beside him watching him breathe. She couldn't imagine how Jo was dealing with Rick's illness. She pulled the pillow closer as she gave into the tears that had been threatening all morning. She prayed things would get better for her sister but she had a horrible feeling the worst was yet to come.

CHAPTER 9

*C*arrie ran on hearing Jo's scream. She met Bridget in the hallway as they raced to Jo's bedroom.

"Rick, wake up. Please, wake up."

"What's wrong Ma?" Carrie asked as Bridget moved toward the prone figure on the bed.

"Sarah's gone, she's run off with Edwin. She left a note, Rick read it and he won't wake up." Jo shook her husband but there was no response. Bridget moved her gently away before putting her head on his chest.

"His heart's beating. It's just a funny turn Miss Johanna," Bridget said calmly taking charge. "Miss Carrie, get changed and ride for your uncle Scott. Go carefully mind. We don't want you hurt too."

Carrie didn't wait to be asked twice but ran to get her pants on. She met Nancy and Lena on the way, Lena gripping Nancy's hand, the other in her mouth.

"Pa isn't feeling well, girls. He gave ma a fright but you can go in to her now. Bridget is with them."

"Where are you going?"

"I am going to get Uncle Scott, Nancy. Now you girls be good."

Carrie couldn't wait to reassure them, she had to get going. She ran outside thankful Walking Tall had shown her how to ride bareback too. She didn't have time to start saddling up. At the last minute, she stuck a gun in her pants. Scott had insisted they all learn to shoot. She wasn't any good but it might deter someone.

BECKY WAS WOKEN by the sound of her niece screaming for Scott. Forgetting she was pregnant, she jumped out of bed thanking God she hadn't got undressed. Her ma was holding Carrie by the arm trying to make sense of what she was saying. Scott came running with a couple of the casual workers.

"Carrie love, calm down. You aren't making any sense."

"Jo sent me. You got to come. Sarah's run away."

"Sarah? Why?" Becky's questions were interrupted by her ma.

"She's gone with Edwin Morgan hasn't she?" Della asked.

Carrie flushed. She nodded her head as if by admitting Sarah's guilt she would be implicated too.

"When Carrie? How long ago? Are you sure she is with Edwin?"

At the glare from his mother in law and wife, Scott continued. "She is better off with him than riding around on her own."

"Marginally!" Della said under her breath.

"I don't know Uncle Scott. I went to call her as she was late for breakfast and she wasn't in her room. We had a row yesterday before dinner and I didn't speak to her after that. I don't know if she left last night or this morning."

"How is Rick?" Della asked quietly.

"Grandma Della you need to come. Pa passed out. Ma got him back into bed but she needs you. Uncle Scott, Almanzo hasn't come back yet."

"Why did Sarah run?" Scott asked.

Carrie told them of Edwin's proposal, Sarah's row with their parents and then Sarah leaving. "She left a note. It said they would be married by the time we read it so not to bother looking for her."

Scott's face twisted at this comment. He exchanged a look with Becky. Della caught it too.

"Scott, it seems pointless to go chasing after her now. What is done is done. It might be better to let them get married, her reputation is in the gutter now anyway." Della stood up. "Come on Carrie, let's get you home and see how your folks are. Scott, Rick may agree to go into town with you?"

Della's meaningful look at Scott didn't go unnoticed. Becky gripped the edge of the table, her white knuckles almost popping through her skin. Her ma was even more worried about Rick than she was.

"Jo wants him to see Doc White but he won't. Do you think you could make him go Uncle Scott?" Carrie asked, her big eyes staring up at Scott. "He listens to you."

Becky had to turn away. Carrie looked so young and lost begging Scott to take Rick to the doctor. If she got a hold of Sarah Hughes, she would shake her. Her brother in law was ill enough without having to worry about all this. She should go to her sister too. But as soon as she stood up she sat back down. She would go, but later when the nausea had cleared a bit. If only Almanzo were here. Jo could lean on her adoptive son but instead, she was worried about him being in danger too

"I will take him into town. Jo will want to come with me. Della can stay with Jo's family. Becky will look after the twins. Carrie, can you ride on to David? Or do you want me to send one of the men?"

Carrie was torn. She wanted to get home to see for herself Rick was okay but she knew that the men were all busy, especially as Almanzo, Walking Tall and some others still hadn't returned.

"I will go. Can I take a horse? Poor Biscuit needs a rest."

Scott raised his eyebrows at the horse's name but he didn't comment. He spoke quickly to the brave nearest him. The man flashed a smile before running toward the corral.

"Carrie, first come inside and have a cold drink. Where is your bonnet?"

"Becky, I don't care about my complexion, not now," Carrie snapped, immediately regretting having done so.

"I was thinking about you getting sunstroke darling."

Carrie's eyes fell. How stupid could she be? She felt Becky's arms around her.

"Sweetie, you are brave and wonderful. I didn't mean to snap. I just don't want you getting sick too."

"Yes Aunty Becky."

"Thank God our Jo had you today. You are the best daughter any mother could have."

Carrie beamed with pride but then flushed at Becky's next words. "After you get David, will you ride on to Ma's house and tell Pa and Stephen?"

"Yes Becky, I wish Almanzo was home."

"Me too, sweetheart. But maybe he is on his way."

Carrie hoped her aunt was right. She knew the missing women needed help but her family was falling apart. She needed Almanzo home. They all did.

CHAPTER 10

Almanzo stared at his ma. She wouldn't look at him. The rest of the camp faded into the background as if it was just the two of them out here in the open. He took a step toward her, holding out his hand as if by touching her, he would wake up from a dream.

"Ma?"

The woman shook her head violently still looking at the ground.

"Lucy Price," Almanzo whispered. "Your name is Lucy Price."

The woman lifted her eyes to his... "Lucy Price is dead. It is best you forget her."

The woman looked into his eyes for a couple of seconds before turning and walking away. He couldn't move. The clock swung back and he was the ten-year-old orphan left to die as his ma and pa drove their wagon away. He froze, staring at her. She'd been alive all this time, yet even now she didn't want to know him. Had she ever wondered about the son she left to die alone?

He felt rather than heard the woman the Indians called Fire Daughter move to his side. She lay a hand on his arm but still, he couldn't respond. She repeated her question.

"Who is that woman? It looked like you recognized her."

"My mother. She went missing, presumed dead on the trail when we moved to Oregon eight years ago," he said, his tone highlighting his disbelief. He looked at the girl's face expecting to see censure and disgust but instead her eyes were full of pity. He didn't want anyone feeling sorry for him.

"Excuse me. I must get back to the Chief. Can you bring Fiona?"

She nodded, not that he gave her much of a choice as he stormed off in the direction of the gathering of men.

"What is wrong?" Walking Tall asked him as he approached but he ignored him. Instead, he walked straight up to the Chief. He looked so fierce the Chief's eyes widened and two younger Braves leaped up ready to come to their leader's defense.

"My mother is one of your prisoners," Almanzo's tone was harsh.

"I do not have prisoners. Every person is free to leave when they wish. All the women choose to stay rather than be returned. Apart from these two."

"Liar."

"Almanzo Price," Walking Tall's sharp tone got through

the haze in his head. He looked at the Chief who was staring back at him. His eyes were clear, his expression one of kindness rather than deceit.

"Sometimes the truth is hard to hear. Which woman?" The Chief asked.

The brave who had accompanied Almanzo spoke in his own tongue in answer to the Chief.

"Broken Wing. She was very sad and half dead when she came to us. It took a long time to heal her wounds." The Chief spoke slowly as if trying to pick the right words.

"She had the fever, just like me." Almanzo prompted.

"No, it was not the fever," the Chief said sadly. He looked into Almanzo's eyes. "She had been beaten very badly. Many broken bones. Her leg never healed. Lots of bruises. Her spirit was broken too."

Almanzo gazed at the Chief. He knew he spoke the truth. He could see it in his eyes.

"When? Did she tell you she had a child? A son? Did she ever try to find him? Why did my mother choose to stay with you? Why not go back to where she belonged?" He threw out the questions so rapidly the Chief didn't have a hope of responding. Walking Tall came to his rescue. He translated quickly. The Chief looked at Almanzo when he replied but he used his own language leaving Walking Tall to translate.

"She was ill for a long time. She didn't speak for months. We thought she would never speak again. She feared everyone even the women. One of us finally spoke to her. He had some white man's language. She said she

91

had married a bad man who killed her son first and then tried to kill her. If he knew she lived, he was going to find her and kill her. She wanted to die."

"Yet she didn't," Almanzo said bitterly.

"She almost did. It took much medicine to make her better. Brown Owl was kind. He showed her not all men were the same. He made her smile first then laugh. They had a child. A young girl."

"I have a sister?" Almanzo asked, not sure how the news made him feel.

"Yes. She has lived seven summers."

"And this Brown Owl? He is the reason she never left. Where is he?"

"He died." The Chief's voice faltered as a shadow of pain crossed his face. "Afterward, we offered to take Broken Wing to join Wagon Train but she says no. She stays here with daughter. Said, white people, not accept the girl."

Almanzo couldn't argue with that. He had seen how the locals treated half-breeds. His ma obviously loved her child as she didn't leave her behind. Unlike him.

"Many men offer to be new husband. Broken Wing says no. She prefers to live alone." Walking Tall translated, his eyes full of concern. Almanzo ignored him, he couldn't show any weakness now or he may just fall apart.

"I want to talk with her," Almanzo said firmly.

The Chief raised his eyebrows at Almanzo's tone. Walking Tall coughed, a hint to Almanzo he should be more respectful.

"I apologize for my tone. It was a surprise to find my mother alive. She left me for dead eight years ago."

The Chief considered him for a couple of minutes, the other Indians sitting in silence. Almanzo knew most of them didn't understand enough English to follow the conversation.

"Broken Wing is not like that. She is very caring. Towards everyone, not just her own girl," The Chief spoke confidently. He obviously believed every word of what he said.

"Well, she must have hit her head pretty badly. My parents both hated Indians. Pa used to say the only good Indian is a dead one. She agreed with everything he said," Almanzo spat the words out, the anger he had blocked out as a ten-year-old resurfacing.

"You are angry, young man. This I understand but you must cool your rage. You will not meet with Broken Wing until your anger is gone. The woman is a member of my tribe and I respect her. She does not act like you say, not now. Maybe in the past. But she may have been forced. You were a child. You are an adult now. When you can see things like an adult and not a child, you may speak to Broken Wing."

"But…" Almanzo didn't get to say anything else as Walking Tall gripped his arm.

"Thank you, Chief. We will camp outside the village and come back in the morning," Walking Tall said in his own language. "My friend, Almanzo, is a good man. He is hurt and angry but his temper will be gone tomorrow."

"You are welcome to camp in the village just not near Broken Wing's home. I will not forget my manners so long as your friend doesn't forget his."

"He won't," Walking Tall sounded so confident, Almanzo wouldn't be surprised if his friend had him bound hand and foot to make sure he didn't go near the woman. His ma? Living with Indians? Having another child. Not wanting to leave. It didn't make sense. But then what type of woman abandoned her ill child and left him alone to die?

CHAPTER 11

*R*ick was sitting up in bed by the time Scott arrived, followed shortly after by the women-folk. Della came into the bedroom and immediately ordered Rick out of bed.

"You have to go into town and see Doc White. No more messin' around. You have responsibilities, Rick Hughes." Della's nagging didn't upset Rick but brought a smile to his face.

"Easy knowing you aren't worried about me, Della, if the first thing you do is start nagging me."

Jo caught the look of terror in her ma's eyes but Della played her part well. "Day I start worrying over a strong man like you is the day you put me in the grave. Now, are you going to get up yourself or do I have to help you?"

Della took a step toward the bed making Rick comply with her demand. "I can do it myself but not in front of an audience. Why don't you go get some coffee? I am sure you have other things to talk about?"

"Like what? My granddaughter eloping or my grandson going missing looking for kidnapped white women? I can't think of anything to say on either topic." Della made for the door. "This family will be the talking point of Portland. Again." Della closed the door leaving Jo alone with her husband. Jo suspected her ma was trying to put the focus somewhere other than on Rick.

"Poor Della, she is so upset over the children. If I got my hands on Sarah now…" Rick said but they both knew he wouldn't do anything worse than hug her close. They were both devastated as they feared Edwin Morgan would not live up to Sarah's expectations. Still, there was nothing they could do about Sarah now. They had other priorities.

"Rick, forget about the children for now. You need to concentrate on your health. You gave me a real scare this morning." Jo clasped her hands in front of her waist, they kept shaking otherwise. "Will you please go and see Doc White? You know he wants to do some tests."

"I know darling but what about the school? The governors are only dying to get rid of me. They want to push their own plans into place. A white only school for those well off enough to attend. That isn't what we wanted." Rick was devastated by the authorities plans for schooling. His dream of providing an education to every child was receding faster than a field of crops under a locust attack. He could see Jo no longer cared about anything else but her immediate family. Although disappointed, he could understand she could only worry about so much.

"I don't care about the school Rick. I know I should but I just want you to get better. Our girls need you, our family needs you. Most of all I need you." Jo's restraint broke as the tears ran down her face. He pulled himself up out of the bed and took her in his arms, nestling her head into his shoulder.

"Darling, don't cry. I will go see Doc White. Today with Scott. I promise." Rick's guilt overwhelmed him. Jo was a strong woman but he was her husband. His role was to protect her not cause her more problems. She was right. Their family came first before anything else even his dreams for the school.

Jo hiccuped as she tried to stop the tears but they kept coming. "Wear your good suit. And your new shirt," she eventually managed to say. "I will go see to Ma and the rest," she muttered softly as she turned and fled the room.

Rick sat back on the bed, what little strength he had, had disappeared. If truth is known, the incident this morning had scared him too. He'd had funny turns before, far more regularly than he had let on to Jo but that was the worst one. He hoped Doc White would know what was wrong, and more importantly had a remedy for it. But inside he knew it wasn't good. Paco had hinted at terrible times ahead and given Sarah was gone, Almanzo hadn't returned yet and now this, maybe the Indian had seen something. He sat listening to the noise of his family in the house.

He had been so lucky meeting Jo. She had helped him rescue his nieces and Almanzo, given him two beautiful daughters, assisted him with building their home but most of all she'd given him unconditional love. All he wanted was to grow old with her in their home surrounded by family. Was that dream too much to ask for?

A knock on the door brought him out of his thoughts. He pulled on a pair of pants quickly before asking his visitor to come in.

"You not dressed yet? Della is threatening to come in and help…" Scott said lingering in the doorway.

Rick smiled at his brother in law. Scott had proved to be a real friend as well as a brother in every sense of the word. They may not always agree on everything but they did on the important stuff. He knew he didn't have to ask but it didn't stop him.

"Scott, you and David will take care of Jo and the children won't you?"

"Don't be stupid Rick. You will be here to do that," Scott said.

Despite Scott's false bravado, he didn't meet Rick's gaze.

"We both know that isn't true. I have to pretend to Jo but please let me be honest with someone."

Scott let out a ragged breath. "How long have you known? Is that why you wouldn't see Doc White?"

Rick stared Scott in the eyes. "I don't know anything. Not for certain but I don't need a doctor to tell me my heart is giving out. I don't know why but I have a feeling. It just won't go away."

"A feeling? Now you sound like one of the women," Scott's attempt at a joke fell flat. "Sorry. I shouldn't have said that. Paco's concerned about you."

"Yes, we had a long talk. You know he believes a man knows when his time has come."

Scott knew all too well. Too many times, the man he considered a real brother rather than his brother in law, had been correct about health related issues. Paco, like many Indians, believed your spirit knew when the time was coming to move into the spirit world. He didn't think confirming that knowledge would prove helpful to anyone.

"Jeez Rick, you can't think like that. What would Jo do if she knew you felt this way?"

"My wife knows. Deep down but she just won't admit it. She is a fighter like all the Thompson women."

As if she heard her name, Della Thompson shouted she was coming in if he didn't make an appearance in a couple of seconds. Scott helped him up from the bed.

"Come on, let's ride into town and see what Doc White has to say. Could be you just have a bad case of indigestion," Scott said as he helped Rick into his jacket.

"Don't let Bridget hear you saying stuff like that or she will hide hot peppers in your next dish."

Scott pulled Rick into a hug for the briefest of seconds. "The answer is yes. You just concentrate on getting better."

Then he was gone before Rick could say anything back. He took his hat from the back of the door, his eyes

RACHEL WESSON

lingering for a couple of seconds on the photo of Jo and himself taken for their wedding day. If he had known then how little time they would have together would he have made different choices? Would he live long enough to see Almanzo come home safely? Maybe Sarah too?

CHAPTER 12

The Chief suggested the two white women continue to sleep with the Indian girls. Almanzo could see the Indian was trying to protect their reputation. The older man knew a little of the white culture, he guessed from speaking with the white women who choose to live with the tribe.

"Fire Daughter, Fiona, the Chief wants you to continue sleeping with the Indian maidens. It is safer for you," Almanzo explained.

"Call me by my real name. Please. I hate the one you use."

Almanzo stared at her for a few seconds until she realized he didn't know her name. He thought her flushed cheeks made her even more beautiful. Although she wasn't classically pretty, her eyes were slightly too far apart and she had a strong roman nose, she was beautiful in his eyes.

"My name is Matilda but my friends call me Tilly."

"Nice to meet you, Tilly, although we could have chosen better circumstances." He teased her just as he would Sarah and Carrie. Her cheeks flushed even more but the look she gave him suggested she enjoyed it. "Please go to bed. We can talk more in the morning."

"But what about your mother? Aren't you going to speak to her?" Tilly asked.

Almanzo replied, trying to hide his impatience. "I am not allowed. The Chief believes I need to calm down."

"She was very kind to us. She cooked us a delicious meal. I had never had pronghorn before. She had new shoes made for us as we both left our own at the river bed. She told us we had no need to be afraid, that her brothers and sisters wouldn't hurt us," Tilly said earnestly. She looked at him as if willing him to believe good things about his mother. "I thought she was rather fair skinned to be an Indian but I never thought she was white."

"I don't think she sees herself as white anymore," Almanzo said despite knowing he sounded like a spoilt child. He couldn't help reacting badly.

"I...I don't know what to say only please listen to her. She seems like a very good person," Tilly said quietly.

Almanzo couldn't reply. What sort of mother left her child alone to die? Fiona looked at him, her face full of understanding. What would she know about his predicament? Just as that thought crossed his mind, he gave himself a shake. These women had enough problems to deal with. He forced himself to be gracious and his voice actually sounded a little cheerful.

"Goodnight Tilly. Look after yourself as well as Fiona."

* * *

He left the ladies and walked slowly back to where his friends had set up camp. Running Bear was looking at him, a gloating expression on his face. Almanzo refused to acknowledge him.

Walking Tall glared at him. "You must sleep now. Before you take a turn at guard duty. Harvey and his friends may still attack. We need you to be vigilant." Walking Tall was obviously still furious with the way Almanzo had spoken to the Chief. He ordered him around like he would any other brave.

"I can't close my eyes. What if you found out the mother who abandoned you to die, was alive and well and living with a white man," Almanzo spat at his friend.

"I would be glad she was still living. We would have much to talk about," Walking Tall replied honestly.

Almanzo glared at Walking Tall.

"I know you are hurt, angry, feeling betrayed but none of those feelings will help you. Do you not think your mother feels the same?" Walking Tall asked.

"She left me behind." To his horror, his voice shook with emotion. He had to screw his eyes shut to stop tears falling. Darn it anyway, he wasn't a ten-year-old boy anymore.

"Perhaps she had no choice. You have not heard her side of things. All you know is what you remember as a ten-year-old boy. You are different now. Much changed. Perhaps she is too. Give her chance to explain. Then you can make mind up," Walking Tall said softly before turning over to go to sleep.

Almanzo stared at his friend's back. It was easy for Walking Tall to preach forgiveness, his ma hadn't abandoned him. No, his friend's ma had died in a massacre and Walking Tall would give anything for the chance to speak to her again. One last time.

Almanzo punched the earth under his bedroll in frustration. He didn't want to hear the voice of reason in his head. He wanted to stay mad. Being angry meant he didn't dwell on the memories he had of when he had been much younger. His ma had stepped in front of his pa's fist more than once protecting him. She'd made him cakes and bought him candy on the rare occasion they had gone into town. She had protected him, loved him even. But then why did she leave him to die?

* * *

AFTER A SLEEPLESS NIGHT, Almanzo finally fell asleep as dawn was breaking. Walking Tall never called him for his turn at guard duty, he guessed his friend knew he would be too distracted to be of any use. He didn't get to rest for long as he was soon woken up by the sounds of the camp around him waking up. The children were playing, the women talking as they worked. He sat listening to the noise, not understanding most of what was said but he was still struck by how happy everyone seemed. There was no underlying atmosphere of fear or tension. He wondered if their Chief had made a conscious decision not to tell his people of the danger or whether the Chief wasn't taking the threat seriously.

He stretched and went in search of Walking Tall. His stomach rumbled but he wasn't hungry. It was nerves. Today he would get the answer to a question that had plagued him for years. Did he want to know? Or was what he imagined preferable?

That decision was taken out of his hands. As soon as he left the lodge, he saw her waiting for him. His ma. She was sitting very still, her eyes closed. He wasn't sure if she was praying. He couldn't remember her ever praying when he was little. Pa had frowned on going to church saying it was a load of busy bodies poking their noses in everyone else's business. The first couple of times he had gone with Rick, Jo, and the girls, he had felt the same but now he enjoyed it. He found listening to Reverend Polk peaceful. It helped the Reverend was a young man with a new wife. He had left his home back East somewhere to bring the Word of God to the inhabitants of Portland and surrounding area. Some of the older folk thought he was a bit young and lacking in wisdom gained with years. Grandpa Thompson didn't agree. He said there were men older than Reverend Polk who had half the knowledge the reverend did. Anyway, what was he doing thinking about the Reverend now when his ma was sitting just yards away?

CHAPTER 13

*A*lmanzo walked toward his ma but when she didn't acknowledge his approach, he sat down on the ground and waited for her to finish. He took the time to study her. She looked older, well obviously, she would, given the length of time since he had last seen her. But what struck him most, was she looked well fed and well cared for. There wasn't a bruise or mark on any of the skin showing. Given she was dressed as an Indian woman, he could see her arms and legs clearly. One leg had been badly broken and hadn't healed correctly but it was a very old wound. He waited, trying not to lose patience.

"You have learned to wait," she said her voice trembling slightly.

He guessed she was nervous. "I learned to do a lot of things." Although he tried not to be angry, his reply sounded snappy. She blinked hard making him regret his harsh words.

"Sorry, Ma. I just… Well, I never guessed I would see you again. How are you? Are you happy?" Almanzo asked realizing it was important to him how she felt.

She gazed up at him for a few minutes before she moved closer to him. Taking one of his hands, she held it up to her face. "I can't believe you are my son. All grown up. You have become a handsome strong boy. I heard how you spoke to the girls last night. You are kind hearted too. Not at all like…"

"My pa. I hope not. I hate him and I hate…" Almanzo stopped himself just in time but she caught his meaning.

"Me. I understand your feelings. I hated myself too. For a very long time. Brown Owl, he was my husband, convinced me it was time to leave the hate behind."

"He told you to forget about me too?" Almanzo felt the tears prick at his eyes but he refused to let them fall. He was not going to cry in front of this woman.

"Never." She denied fiercely. "I never forgot you but I thought you were dead." She stared at him, the truth written all over her face but he still couldn't let himself believe her. He picked at some yellowing grass struggling to grow in the sandy earth beside him.

"You mean you wished I was," he steeled himself as she flinched at his words. "How could you leave your only child behind to die? With strangers?"

"I didn't have any choice," she protested weakly.

"You left with Pa, I don't remember you begging him to let you stay with me," he said, his cruel tone making her flinch. He hated being cruel but he couldn't stop himself.

He wanted to hurt her as badly as he had been hurt as a ten-year-old child.

"He told me he would kill you himself if I tried to stay with you. I hoped you would have a chance. You might be found. By someone who would help." She spoke quickly as if afraid he would stop listening.

Her short answers fell silent as he looked at her in disbelief. "Who did you think would help me? The sick people who were all dead or dying around me? If you had stayed maybe some of them could have survived too."

"If I stayed you would have died that day. I had no choice. Mr. Price would have killed you."

"You mean my pa."

"No, I mean Mr. Price. He was never your pa. Your real pa died when I was pregnant. I had to marry Price. I had no choice. My parents kicked me out for getting pregnant. Price offered me a way out." She clasped and unclasped her hands, her gaze not leaving his face. She was telling him the truth. All these years, he had believed that monster had been his pa when he was no relation at all.

"Why didn't you tell me before?" Almanzo asked, trying his best to keep his voice calm and free from emotion.

"Tell you? You were ten years old. Anyway, it was better if you kept calling him Pa. He liked that."

"But he never liked me. Kept telling me I was a disappointment. Every time he beat me," he said, trying hard to stop his voice from shaking.

"I know son and I swear if I had thought he would treat you like that, I would have never married him. But I was so young and so scared. I thought they would take you away from me and I couldn't lose you. I was prepared to do whatever I could to keep us together," she stared at him, her eyes pleading for understanding and forgiveness.

But he wasn't ready to forgive and forget. "You failed miserably on that front." His harsh words seemed to burn into her soul. She bowed her head but he didn't feel better. Hurting her, hurt him even more.

"Why did he hate me so much?" he whispered.

"I never had another baby. He used to blame me but seeing you showed the fault was not mine. Or at least there was proof I could have children whereas he…" she stopped for a second as if remembering the past hurt. "It meant he wanted to have you as his son, so other people would see him with a son. But he hated you for not being his. He was a twisted man, with anger running right through to his soul."

"How did you get away from him?" Almanzo asked.

"After he left you behind, I ran twice. I was trying to get back to you but both times he caught me and punished me. The second time, he beat me so bad, I think he thought he had killed me. He got the wagon and left me behind. I lay there wishing I was dead. My life was over anyway. I had lost you."

His ma was crying at this point yet he still couldn't open his arms and hold her close. He wanted to, God knows he did but he couldn't bring himself to make that move. Instead, he watched her as she cried and when her tears stopped falling, he was still watching.

"I was hurt bad. Really bad. Then the Indians came and I was terrified. Price had filled both our heads with so much hatred for these people. I thought they would scalp me there and then. Instead, they took me to their camp. Their medicine man worked on healing my wounds. In time the wounds faded but the scars inside were still there." She fell silent.

"Then you met Brown Owl."

His ma nodded but the look of love followed quickly by loss on her face almost bowled him over. She had loved the Indian, just like the Chief said.

They sat in silence for a few minutes. He trying to absorb everything she had said, she trying to recover from opening her mind to the years of abuse she had sustained at the hands of his so-called father.

He realized they both needed a little time. He was about to suggest he go and come back later when his ma asked him if he would like some breakfast. She seemed keen to share food with him so he agreed. She led him to her fire. He thought the child he had seen yesterday would be there but it was just the two of them. They ate in silence and then while drinking something which he didn't recognize, she continued to speak.

"Brown Owl was so gentle. He spoke a little English so could teach me some of his language. He taught me other things too, like how to dry meat and prepare food. He was so kind and generous. I told him about you and he told me your sprit would forgive me. It took some time but I grew to trust him. He never hurt me. In time, we had a child. Her name is Mia."

"My sister," he stated, not in disbelief but in awe. He had always wanted a sibling. A real one. He loved his adoptive family, but this was different.

"Yes, Almanzo. Mia is the reason I didn't leave the tribe after Brown Owl died. I couldn't bring her back to my parents. They were angry enough at my getting pregnant with Sam's baby. They would be horrified at the thought of an Indian granddaughter."

Almanzo didn't comment. He knew there weren't many places in the USA where a half breed child would be made welcome. Instead, he focused on his real father.

"Sam? My real father's name was Sam?"

"Yes. He was a kind man. Very like Brown Owl. He was Price's first victim."

Almanzo sputtered and coughed as his drink got caught in his throat. "You married my father's killer?"

CHAPTER 14

HUGHES HOMESTEAD

*J*o walked back and forward, her eyes staring across the horizon willing her son, Almanzo, home. Was he hurt? She couldn't bear it if anything happened to him too.

Rick was in town with Doc White. The kindly doctor had insisted Jo go home, saying she needed some rest. She guessed he was trying to protect her a little from the news the tests may reveal.

She heard the door open behind her.

"Come in and have some breakfast, Miss Johanna. You need something to eat."

"No thank you, Bridget. I couldn't."

"Now Miss Johanna I ain't asking you. I'm tellin' ye to get your backside on the chair and eat. I have enough to be doin' with worrin' over Miss Sarah and Mr. Almanzo and now Mr. Rick. I don't need no more troubles."

Jo smiled weakly at her housekeeper who was so much

more. She knew the woman was just as concerned as she was. She loved the family almost as much as Jo did, considering them a replacement for the family Bridget never got to have. She put her fears into words. "I don't know how to contact Sarah. I mean if Doc White says I should. What will I do?" Jo asked the tears not far from her eyes.

Bridget gave her a quick hug. "Nothing you can do Miss Johanna. But don't start thinking like that. Doc White will be able to help Mr. Rick and he will be home soon."

Jo saw Bridget's fingers were crossed. She didn't believe Rick was going to recover either. Jo's frustration needed an outlet.

"Oh Bridget, how could she do this to us? Why couldn't she have waited?"

Bridget's face darkened as she scowled. "Miss Sarah, I love the bones of her but she has a selfish streak a mile wide. You and Mr. Rick were the best parents you could be but she is just so stubborn." Bridget took a deep breath before continuing, "She will learn, Miss Johanna."

Johanna stared out onto the horizon wondering where Sarah was. Had she regretted her decision to elope? Was Edwin treating her kindly?

"Yes Bridget but not before she is badly hurt. I dread to think of how she is going to feel when she starts seeing Edwin Morgan for the man he really is."

"She is going to feel like a fool, just like I did." Bridget's voice shook. "Still there is no point in worryin' about her now. She made her bed. She is lucky though. You and Mr. Rick will take her in if she comes home."

"If..." Jo couldn't continue. She didn't want Sarah to be hurt by anyone yet if the girl stood in front of her, she would be hard pushed not to slap her.

"Come on inside Miss Johanna. Won't do Master Rick any good to be worrin' about you and all. Miss Della has everything running ship shape."

Jo looked at Bridget and giggled at the expression on her housekeeper's face. Once she started she couldn't stop. She knew her ma drove Bridget nuts, especially when she started cleaning Bridget's pristine kitchen. Bridget stared at her before she too dissolved into laughter. "Oh Miss Johanna, I swear I will have to do penance when the priest gets here. I love your ma but she needs to be banned from my kitchen or she may end up in the stove!"

Jo linked arms with Bridget thanking God once again for sending this lovely woman to live with them. She took one last look at the horizon.

"Don't fret Miss Johanna. Walking Tall and the others won't let anything happen to Almanzo. That boy be home soon, just you wait and see."

"How will he take the news about Sarah?"

"You mean because he loves her? I think he will want to thrash her backside and maybe punch Edwin and all. It may make him realize she is not the woman for him. She is his sister, maybe not through blood but sister still the same." Bridget sighed. "Miss Sarah ain't the right woman for Almanzo. She never was."

Jo stared at Bridget who once again proved she knew the family better than anyone. The Irish woman's accent and Irish way of saying things came out stronger when she was upset or angry.

"Maybe Almanzo will come back with an Indian bride. That would give the townsfolk something to talk about eh? Can you see Mrs. Morgan's face if she was to find out Miss Sarah had an Indian for a sister in law?"

Jo let her housekeeper lead her into the house praying Almanzo would return safely and soon. She didn't care who came back with him so long as her son was home.

CHAPTER 15

INDIAN CAMP

*A*lmanzo stared at his ma, fighting the urge to pinch himself to make sure this wasn't some nightmare. How could she have married his real pa's murderer?

"I thought your father had died in an accident. It was only years later, I found out the truth. Then it was too late. I was married to Price. As you know, there are few options for women who divorce their husbands. He kept telling me he would put me in a lunatic's asylum if I tried to do anything. He would keep you."

"So you stayed," he said bitterly even though he knew she was right. She hadn't much of a choice. He was torn between feeling pity for her, for the years of abuse she had suffered and anger at what her choices had meant for him.

She turned to him, taking one hand and using the other to turn his face to make him look at her.

"I had to," she said desperately. "Don't you see. I had to protect you. He used to beat you so badly."

She was begging him to understand. He didn't want to show her he did yet he was only hurting both of them. She had suffered enough. She didn't need his anger now.

"I remember you standing between us. You tried to protect me," he acknowledged.

"I didn't try hard enough. I will never forgive myself for what I allowed happen. When I saw you yesterday, I nearly died. I couldn't believe my eyes. But I should have left you believing I was dead," she murmured taking her hands away from him. As soon as she broke contact, he missed her touch.

"Why? I don't want you dead," he said automatically but realizing he meant what he was saying. "I don't. Truly."

She gazed at him again with sadness this time. "It would be easier for you if I were dead. You would not have to bear the shame of a mother who lived with Indians, who bore him a child."

"Ma, my best friend is Walking Tall, the Indian I rode in with."

"Did he rescue you? How were you found? Where have you been living all these years? With the Indians? Have you seen Price? I used to have nightmares he found you." Her questions tripped off her tongue one after the other as if she had been waiting years to know the answers.

"Steady Ma, I can't answer your questions if you keep asking the next one."

She smiled and his heart pounded. It was his ma. His

ma who had protected him, made him cakes, bought him candy whenever she could. His ma who had stayed up late, sponging him down and putting ointment on his cuts after a beating. This woman who had taken the blame for anything and everything he did as a child. The time he had gone fishing and forgotten to chop the wood. Or when he was held back in school and didn't get his chores finished. Suddenly his mind was flooded with images of how many times his ma had helped him, looked after him and done everything she could to take the beatings meant for him. He didn't think about the years he had spent hating her for abandoning him and the guilt at wanting to love the woman who had left him to die. He looked at her and broke down crying. She moved quickly and he found himself hugging her as if he would never let her go. She was doing the same to him. They stayed like that for what seemed like ages, her tears mixing with his. He realized she was saying she was sorry repeatedly. Whispering it into his hair.

"Ma, stop it. You didn't have a choice. You probably saved my life. Thank you. I am so glad I found you. Now you can come home with…" He stopped as her arms fell to her side and she broke contact. No, he wanted to shout. Don't stop holding me. I need you. Instead, he said, "I can't leave you here. You and Mia can come home with me. Rick and Jo will welcome you."

"We cannot leave. You know how they will treat your sister. I cannot do that to her. The Braves here accept her. She will marry one day, have a family of her own."

"Ma she might not get that chance." Quickly he told her the reason why he had come to the camp and the mood Harvey and his friends were stoking up in town. "They want the land to be free of Indians. All of them, no matter what their ages or sex."

His ma paled but then she looked stronger. "We will move to the reservation with the rest of the tribe."

"I don't think your Chief will allow that to happen. He said he was keeping the girls unless a promise was made to respect the treaty," Almanzo spoke quickly. He felt the time slipping away and he had to save his ma. He couldn't, he wouldn't lose her again.

"That's never going to happen. Nobody respects that treaty."

"I know that Ma and I suspect your Chief does too. But what's the alternative?" Almanzo forced himself to speak gently when all the while he wanted to grab her and run to safety. "The reservation is miles away. The land is poor, there are no buffalo to hunt, nothing grows. If he moves there he is condemning his people to starvation."

"If the tribe stays, they will be slaughtered." Her matter of fact acceptance of being murdered made him see how different their lives were now. She was a white woman. She could save herself and maybe her child too.

"Walking Tall and I are here to try to stop that happening. We want to convince the Chief to let us take the white women to town. There they can tell the sheriff what happened. Maybe it was Harvey and his friends who attacked the wagon train."

"Who is Harvey?" she asked.

"George Harvey." Almanzo almost spat the name out. "He is the son of a very wealthy man who has made a rather big name for himself in Portland. He owns a lot of land and businesses. A lot of people work for him, one way or another. He hates everyone but especially Indians and blacks. He is a fan of slavery and would move all Indians into the ocean never mind a reservation if he thought he could get away with it." Almanzo took a deep breath before adding, "unfortunately usually he can break the law as he has never been caught red handed."

"This Harvey sounds like Price, well aside from his money. He is full of hate. I wonder what happened to him to make him that way."

Almanzo was surprised to hear her reaction. He had never thought about Harvey being a victim of anything. He didn't want to either. As far as he was concerned, Harvey was a blight on society.

"He reminds me of Pa, I meant Mr. Price but he is worse. He is wealthy which means his words carry more weight. Also, he doesn't like to get his hands dirty, not unless he can't be tried for his crimes. If he wanted white folks killed, he would pay someone else. He likes to kill Indians though. He knows he won't have to face a jury." Almanzo didn't want to think of what Harvey would do if he found out about his ma and Mia. "Ma, Price is dead."

His ma paled, her hands shaking as she asked, "he came for you?"

"Not for me,"Almanzo said bitterly. He explained how

the gang had kidnapped Becky leading to Scott rescuing her. "All the would be kidnappers were killed, including Price."

"God forgive me but I am glad. He can't never hurt you again,"she said. "I will speak to the Chief. He sometimes listens to me."

"Why?"

"Brown Owl was his son."

CHAPTER 16

INDIAN CAMP

*T*illy and Fiona sat in the lodge whispering. Broken Wing had unbound Tilly's hands telling her she would have to put the binds back on when they went outside.

Then she had shown them how to do some beading. Fiona was better at it than Tilly but neither showed much talent. Tilly suspected Broken Wing was simply trying to occupy their time until they could leave. The hours passed by so slowly.

"Tilly, what will you do when we get out of here?"

Tilly looked up from her work at Fiona's question. She wasn't sure how to answer. What could she say?

"If your father survived, you will marry Richard. But, well, will you marry Richard if your father is dead?"

Tilly had told Fiona about seeing her father shot and falling off his horse.

"No." Tilly shuddered. "I am not going to marry that man regardless of whether Father is alive or not."

"But how will you break off the engagement? Can't he force you to get married?"

Tilly didn't know what her rights were under the law. She doubted she had many but hopefully she was allowed to marry a man of her own choosing. She was almost 18 years old.

"I may have to see a lawyer. But hopefully, Richard will have changed his mind."

"Why would he do that? Cook said he loves you."

Tilly stared at Fiona in shock. "Love? Cook must have been drinking again. Richard doesn't know the meaning of the word love. He wants to marry me for whatever money and property he thinks my father has. Nothing to do with me."

"Very important woman marry right man. Make everyone happier."

Tilly nearly fell over as Walking Tall stood in the lodge entrance. He didn't make any attempt to come inside. She guessed it was because they were not chaperoned by Broken Wing. Their minder had gone out earlier and yet to return.

"You shouldn't listen to private conversations. It's rude," Tilly responded crossly, wondering how much he had heard and understood.

"Then you shouldn't speak so loudly Fire Daughter. The whole camp can hear you."

Tilly wanted to stick her tongue out at the Indian. He

was always teasing her. She looked at Fiona but Fiona's whole attention was focused on Walking Tall. If she didn't know better, she would think Fiona fancied herself in love with this savage. Only he wasn't a savage was he? He had been nothing but kind since the first day they met.

"You marry Al. He would make fine husband. Give you strong babies."

Tilly flushed furiously torn between the desire to run away from the conversation and the need to know more. Did Almanzo not already have a girlfriend? Surely the women were queuing up to marry him. He was tall, broad shouldered, kind and made her laugh. He had a lovely face too, kind eyes and his lips. How would they feel if he kissed her?

A girl couldn't find much better. She felt Walking Tall accessing her. She looked into his eyes and saw he was smiling at her as if he could read her inner most thoughts. Her blush grew deeper.

"You need lessons in how to speak to ladies," she responded huffily.

"Walking Tall doesn't mean any disrespect. White men and women make it very difficult to have happy marriage. They should learn to live more freely." With those words, Walking Tall turned and left leaving Tilly wondering why he had sought them out in the first place. Had he come to tell them they were free to leave but been distracted by their conversation?

Fiona was still staring at the retreating figure. "He is so kind, isn't he? He has a lovely smile."

"Fiona Murphy, he is an Indian, not a potential suitor."

At Tilly's sharp tone, Fiona paled before turning on Tilly.

"No need to remind me. I am not simple. You can be Indian and be kind you know," Fiona said, her voice full of hurt.

"I'm sorry Fiona, I didn't mean to hurt your feelings. Being cooped up in here all day long is driving me insane." Tilly reached out to touch Fiona's hand. "Forgive me?"

Fiona nodded and smiled, giving Tilly's hand a quick squeeze. "What do you think of Almanzo? You were blushing when Walking Tall was teasing you. I like him a lot but he hasn't looked at me twice. He is mesmerized by you."

Was he really? Could Fiona be right? Tilly hoped she was but although Fiona was her best friend, she couldn't admit her feelings.

"Hush Fiona, he is not. He is only interested in his mother. Can you imagine finding out, after all these years, that your mother was living with Indians and raising a child?"

"He must be very hurt."

Fiona's statement confused Tilly. "Why? I should think he would be relieved to find her alive."

"Tilly! You sound like your father and Richard."

That was just about the biggest insult Fiona could throw at her. Tilly gulped for a couple of seconds trying to stop tears from filling her eyes.

"I didn't mean it nastily. But if you found your parents

wouldn't you be happy?" Tilly tried to explain her thought process.

"Yes, but not if they were living with a brother or sister. It would make me feel they really didn't want me."

Tilly didn't say anything. She hadn't thought of it from that point of view. Fiona was right.

"I mean, you don't leave a baby you want on a doorstep but I believe my ma wanted me but couldn't afford to keep me. Or she was in trouble and not allowed to have me or come back and find me," Fiona explained quietly. "It would be different if I found her years later and she was healthy and living with her own child."

Tilly took the beading work from her friend and put it to one side. She hugged Fiona close, both letting the tears fall freely for the first time since they had been taken to the Indian village.

"I never thought about what it was like not to know your parents, Fiona. I am so sorry. You must think I am very selfish."

"You aren't selfish, Tilly. To be honest, I think it is better not to have known my parents. I can pretend they were nice people. You don't have that luxury."

Tilly held Fiona at arm's length.

"Are you telling me you didn't appreciate my parents and all they did for you, Miss Murphy? After all who would have given you such a good position, working fourteen hours a day without pay?"

The girls giggled as Tilly imitated her mother's strident

tones. Then they fell quiet, each wondering what lay ahead of them.

"Tilly, if you marry Richard, what will happen to me? He won't let me stay with you. I might not be able to get a decent position. You know what they say about women who were rescued from Indians. They are never allowed to live a normal life."

"Fiona Murphy, where has your fighting spirit gone?" Tilly responded quickly. "I am not going to marry Richard and we will stick together. Nothing has happened to us. We still have our virtue. Any man who gets you as his wife will be lucky. You are so beautiful, inside and out, and you can cook and do stuff like that. Men like that."

Tilly hoped she sounded convincing. In her limited experience of men, she had no idea what they looked for in a girl who didn't have any money. She guessed they were both about to find out.

Yawning, she suggested they take a nap. It would help pass the time. Fiona fell asleep quickly leaving Tilly to think in private. Was Almanzo looking for a wife? She told herself she wasn't interested in the answer, yet she couldn't stop thinking about him.

Fiona would make a better match for him. She was pretty and she knew how to keep house, to cook, do laundry and grow vegetables. Tilly didn't know how to do any of those things. She barely knew how to make a bed.

She didn't like how she felt about Almanzo with Fiona. Closing her eyes she imagined them kissing and laughing together. Her stomach churned. She wanted Fiona to be happy, of course, she did. But she didn't want her to find happiness with Almanzo. She beat the ground in frustration. She was a horrible friend. Fiona deserved the best in life and if that meant Fiona had set her heart on Almanzo, Tilly should do everything to help her friend.

alking Tall found Almanzo by the river later that afternoon. He was concerned, Almanzo could see that from the expression in his eyes, but he didn't ask any questions. He simply sat and waited. He knew Almanzo would talk if he wanted to.

After a few minutes in silence, Almanzo asked what the Chief had decided to do.

"He is going to let the women return with us. Your mother spoke with him. For a long time."

"She said she would."

"Al, is she coming back with us?" Walking Tall asked, a worried expression on his face. "Did you tell her it was too dangerous for her to stay here?"

Almanzo stared into the river. He had told her but had he made it clear just how much danger she was in? He had said she and his sister were welcome to come with them but had he meant it? How would he feel when Harvey and his friends found out his ma was a squaw and his sister a half breed?

"You are finding it hard to understand her actions?" Walking Tall guessed, as always he was very good at reading Almanzo.

"Yes. I don't blame her anymore for leaving me behind. She gave me good reasons for that. But, why didn't she come looking for me? When she was better? The tribe would have..."

"What? Driven her, a white woman, into Portland? Can you really see that happening?" Walking Tall sounded sarcastic but the look he gave him was full of concern.

Almanzo shrugged but at the piercing look from his friend agreed it was a stupid thought.

"Your mother survived as best she could. From what has been said, she found happiness for a while. She has a child. Perhaps it is best to leave the past behind. Let her stay with the people she calls her own."

"But you know..." Almanzo started to speak but Walking Tall interrupted him.

"I know more than most her chances of living to old age are slim. Your sister's chances of living to adulthood are almost non-existent. But what would you have me say? Do you want me to force them to come with us?" Walking Tall asked before standing up. "We live in difficult times my friend. You cannot make this decision for your mother. She is grown woman who has had much sadness. She deserves to live out her life, however long it may be, in happiness."

Almanzo gazed at his friend. Although of similar age, Walking Tall was so wise. He understood more about human nature than Almanzo ever would.

"It is not true. In time, you will find understanding. Our paths have been different so our minds are too," Walking Tall said as if to underline the point.

"How do you do that? How do you know what I am thinking?" Almanzo asked in wonder.

"Most white people think with their heart and tell us with their eyes." Walking Tall smiled, his tone teasing. "Good white people." He put his arm around Almanzo's shoulders. "Come, my friend, we must go. We have spent too long here. People will be worried. I do not want to face Becky or Johanna if we stay too much longer."

"Are you admitting to fearing women?"

"Any man who says the Thompson women do not scare them is lying. Their husbands are brave and to be admired."

Almanzo burst out laughing. He knew Walking Tall adored the Thompson girls as he called Becky, Jo, and Eva despite them being married with different surnames. They were all strong-willed women but had hearts so big they would help the world if they could. He felt a strong need to be back with them. To tell them his story. Most of all to tell them he was no relation of Price. As they packed up their things, he wondered it was too late for Rick to formally adopt him. Almanzo Hughes had a much nicer sound than Almanzo Price.

"Fire Daughter and her friend are worried too. They feel your people will not accept them."

Almanzo frowned at his friend's words. He should have done more to put the women's minds at ease. He didn't like to think of Tilly being worried.

"Fire Daughter not wish to marry what you call fiancé?" Walking Tall stumbled over the unfamiliar word.

"She doesn't?" Almanzo wasn't questioning Walking Tall's knowledge but playing for time. He tried to sound casual, closing his eyes so Walking Tall couldn't do his usual thing and read his thoughts.

Walking Tall pushed Almanzo's shoulder playfully. "You cannot hide your feelings from me, my friend. This is first time a woman light big spark," he chuckled as Almanzo tried hard not to respond. "Fire Daughter feel the same way."

Almanzo's eyes widened. She did? How did Walking Tall know? Had she said something? No, she couldn't have. White women didn't talk about such stuff and certainly not with Indians.

"Fire Daughter make you a good wife. She is strong woman. I told her you make her good husband."

Almanzo groaned, feeling very sick. Although he knew Walking Tall was telling the truth, he begged "please say you didn't."

"Why? I did. I do not understand you white people. Men need women. Life is too hard without a good woman at your side. Why make it so difficult when you find the right one?"

Almanzo wasn't about to explain white courtship to his best friend. He was dying to know how Tilly had responded. He looked into his friend's face, surprised to see a concerned expression in Walking Tall's eyes. "Do not take long to make up mind. Things change quickly."

With that Walking Tall walked away leaving Almanzo alone with his thoughts. Things change quickly? That was an understatement. A week ago his life was normal, understandable if not enjoyable. Now, he had found his long lost ma, a sister he never knew he had, and a woman who lit up his body and mind like a piece of kindling.

CHAPTER 18

*H*e waited with his mother while Walking Tall and the Chief spoke about the women.

"I will come back soon to check on you both. Can you introduce me to Mia then?" Almanzo asked.

"Would you not like to meet her today? She is curious about you," Broken Wing said.

"She knows about me?"

"Yes Almanzo. I told her about you from the first day she was born. Of course, I believed you were dead then. Yesterday when you turned up here, she saw I was shocked. When she heard the other men calling your name, she asked were you my Almanzo?"

"Yes I would like to meet her," Almanzo pushed the words out past the lump in his throat. His mother hadn't forgotten about him or willingly abandoned him. He waited impatiently while Broken Wing, as she preferred to be called, came back with Mia. The young girl's eyes were wide open with curiosity. She was lighter skinned than Walking Tall but her hair was as dark as his. Her big brown eyes were so dark, they were almost black.

"Nice to meet you, Mia," he said rather formally.

"You make mama happy. I thank you for this," Mia said.

Her English although stilted was more fluent than he expected. "Are you happy here Mia?"

She looked at him, a confused expression on her face. "Yes, of course. This is my home."

He caught his mother's gaze over the young child's head. They exchanged a smile of understanding. Then Almanzo bent down to kiss Mia on the cheek.

"Next time I come I will bring you a gift. What would you like?" he asked her.

"Food. Sometimes we are hungry," Mia said emphasizing her point by rubbing her stomach.

"I will bring food but what about for you Mia? Would you like a doll?" Almanzo asked, keen to make a good impression on his sister.

"What is doll?" Mia asked in confusion.

"Bring her one with you when you return, Almanzo." His ma said smiling at him. "It will make a nice surprise."

Mia took her mother's hand as she asked. "Will you come back, big brother?"

He liked being called brother. He smiled warmly at the child before confirming "Yes Mia. Soon."

"Will you bring Fire Daughter back too? I like her a lot."

Looking up, Almanzo caught his ma's stare. She was waiting for his answer.

"Fire Daughter may not be able to come with me. She has other plans," he explained quickly and quietly.

"Oh, I thought you were going to share her blanket. Have you not asked her?"

Almanzo flushed bright red. He knew Indian children were far more open about romance than whites were but still this was a little too much for him to take in. He looked to his ma for help but she was smiling widely.

"I have only just met her, Mia. I can't ask her that."

"She likes you a lot. She is always looking at you. Like you look at her. Under your eyes like this."

Mia did a good impression of looking at Almanzo sheepishly. He had to change the conversation. If Tilly heard what his sister was saying...

He kissed her cheek again and swung her into the air making her laugh. Then he turned to his mother. "Thank you, Ma." It was only three little words but they spoke volumes. He pulled his mother into a hug. She nestled her head on his shoulder.

"I am so proud of the man you became Almanzo."

He gulped back the lump in his throat and resisted the urge to pick her up, put her on his horse and take her back to the Hughes where she would be safe.

CHAPTER 19

*D*ella looked up as Scott rode into the homestead.

White faced, Della faced her son in law, her back stiff. "What prognosis did the Doc give?"

Scott wished he hadn't met Jo in town and she hadn't asked him to do this task. He couldn't look Della in the face. It wasn't his place to tell her she would be burying Rick soon enough. Instead he played for time.

"Doc wouldn't comment. On a better note, I've heard Almanzo and the women are on their way home."

"Praise be," Bridget announced, revealing the fact she was listening to their conversation.

"Bridget, come out here and show yourself woman. You shouldn't be eavesdropping. You might not hear good things," Scott teased, thanking God Bridget was there.

Bridget came out smiling. "The news I just heard was

the best ever. I am going to go bake Mr. Almanzo's favorite dinner."

"Maybe just bake him a few pies, Bridget. He may want to stay in town for a night or two until we know more."

Bridget's face turned as pale as Della's. Scott wanted to shoot himself.

"Don't look at me like that. The sheriff wants to talk to Almanzo about the ladies and what happened. There are some details about the massacre that don't make sense. Almanzo will want to visit with Rick too. Now put that smile back on your face and make me a coffee please, Miss Bridget."

Scott's flirting made her smile. When she had gone back into the kitchen he suggested to Della the adults come back into town. "David and Eva, Becky and yourself. Do you want to get Paddy? There is bound to be trouble. Harvey is baying for blood and there is some new guy around, a suited up guy who presents himself as a gentleman. Name of Richard Weston. Heard of him?"

Della shook her head.

"Something funny about him. Wouldn't take my eyes off his right hand. He seems to be very friendly with Harvey for someone who just supposedly arrived in town."

"Scott Jones, your instincts have never let you down before. Trust them now. I will leave Paddy where he is. Someone in this family might as well have a little peace as there is bound to be more trouble down the line."

"Della, wouldn't you prefer him by your side?" Scott

couldn't help asking, wondering if his mother in law had misunderstood how seriously ill Rick was.

"I surely would Scott love but Paddy isn't as young as he was. He will want to be in the middle of the fight. We will need his strength later."

Scott looked in admiration at the woman by his side. The true strength behind the Thompson family, this frail looking woman had protected her family from the first day he'd known her. She would go on doing that for as long as she is able.

"You are some woman, Della Thompson," he said placing a kiss on her cheek.

She was so flustered she was unable to respond.

"I will go get Becky and the children. Bridget and Carrie can mind them here. I've sent a man to David's to tell him to meet us in town. Can you be ready in a couple of hours?"

Della nodded, her gaze focused on some point behind him. He squeezed her arm once more before moving to the kitchen. He needed his coffee before he went home. He wasn't looking forward to breaking the news about Rick to Becky. At least she would be relieved to hear Almanzo was coming home.

CHAPTER 20

*A*lmanzo rode in front leaving the white women with Walking Tall. He said he was scouting ahead but he needed some space to sort out his feelings. He hated leaving his ma with the tribe. It would be so much safer if she came with them. Would it really? White women who lived with the Indians, whether by choice or not, were never accepted back into white society, not fully anyway. The children of such liaisons were always outsiders too. Maybe his ma had made the correct choice.

When they camped for the night, Tilly sought him out.

"Are you feeling any better?" she asked.

He was grateful for her concern but wished she had left him alone. He nodded, hoping by staying silent she would take the hint but instead, she took it as an invitation to sit down. He couldn't ask her to leave as that would be very rude.

"Do you know who survived the attack?" she asked, her voice trembling.

"No, I'm sorry but I don't. Were you traveling with your family?"

"My father and my fiancé. I know my father was hurt as I saw him fall off his horse but I didn't see Richard after the Indians arrived. I was with Fiona at the river bank. We'd sneaked off for a talk." At Almanzo's confused expression Tilly explained, "My Father didn't approve of our friendship."

"Sneaking off may have saved your lives, Tilly."

"Do you really believe they meant to kill all of us?"

Almanzo didn't answer. He didn't know. He could guess but guessing wasn't going to help anyone. "Don't get upset. You will feel better when you get back to your friends and hopefully your family."

"Maybe," she sighed but didn't elaborate. "Thank you for coming for us and for bringing us back safe."

"I can't take the credit. It was Walking Tall who did most of the negotiating."

"He is a fine man." She opened her mouth to say something else but closed it again.

"For an Indian?" Almanzo prompted.

"I didn't mean it that way. Not everyone shares the same values, Mr. Price."

"Don't call me that," his aggressive tone made her eyes widen. He immediately corrected himself. She didn't know his history so couldn't understand why he never wanted to be called Price again. "My name is Almanzo. I thought you said they were savages."

"Any man who abducts a woman is a savage regardless of their color. I didn't mean they were savages because they had red skin but because they had me bound like a dog."

Almanzo laughed at the indignant expression on her face.

"What are you laughing at?" she challenged, fire spitting out of her eyes.

"I think your hands were bound for their safety. Don't you?" he looked at her and saw she was fighting a smile. "Go on, smile. It won't break your face in two."

"You are a horrid man."

"I think you like me."

"Are you flirting with me Mr. ... Almanzo."

"I guess I am but I shouldn't. You are an engaged woman. I apologize," Almanzo said but actually, he wasn't sorry. Not one little bit. There was something about this woman that intrigued him. As soon as he was near her, his senses swam. He wanted to touch her, make her laugh, kiss her...

"Don't. Please." Her words interrupted his train of thought, which given the direction of his thoughts was a good thing.

At the look on her face, he didn't think she meant don't flirt. She didn't want him to mention her fiancé. Why? Was she worried he had died? Was it too painful to think of him? It would be completely understandable but somehow he got the impression she had another reason for her reluctance to talk about her fiancé. What was she trying to say?

"I better get back to Fiona. She doesn't like to be left alone for long. Goodnight Mr. Almanzo."

"Goodnight Miss Tilly," he responded but the atmosphere between them had changed. It was no longer just teasing. Something else hung in the air but neither of them wanted to acknowledge it. His heart was bruised from finding his mother and sister but what was her story?

* * *

TILLY MASTERSON WALKED SLOWLY BACK to where Fiona was waiting, thanking God again her friend had survived. She couldn't bear to lose Fiona.

Fiona had no family either. She was a foundling. Nobody knew who her parents were. The orphanage had trained her for domestic service. Her mother had engaged her when Fiona turned fourteen. She had worked in the kitchen with Cook who was a hard taskmaster but a human being. She turned a blind eye to Tilly's visits with Fiona. The two girls had become firm friends being of a similar age and both lonely. Tilly's father decided to move to Portland thinking his political ambitions would be easier to achieve. Cook wanted to stay in San Francisco but Tilly had talked Fiona into coming with the family. She believed Fiona would have a chance of a better future out here. Look how well those plans had turned out.

"You were gone a long time," Fiona accused when Tilly

slipped into the bedroll beside her.

"I was talking to Almanzo. I thought you were asleep."

"I was but then I heard an owl or something. I woke up. You were gone. I thought you might be in trouble. Again."

Tilly tried to curb her impatience. Fiona had been through a lot.

"As you can see, I am safe. I just needed a walk to clear my head," Tilly replied trying her best to keep the impatience from her tone.

"Were you thinking of Master Richard?"

Tilly shuddered. Richard had insisted Fiona call him Master. He didn't like the serving girl for reasons Tilly couldn't understand. The Irish girl may be whining now but usually she was a ray of sunshine. She smiled at everyone and seemed to think every day she woke up was a blessing. Richard said she was a brainless fool.

"I was wondering who would be there to meet us," Tilly explained.

"You mean who survived? Do you think they would prefer we died?" Fiona whispered the question Tilly had been asking herself all day. What could she answer? She didn't want to lie but she wasn't going to upset Fiona further. She decided to pretend to be asleep. It was the coward's way out but easier than admitting Richard would prefer her dead. She had listened to him talking about other cases of women who were rescued from the Indians. His view was the rescuers should have left them with the Indians. No respectable woman would allow herself be held captive. She was darn sure he wouldn't consider her wife material now but instead of being upset, she felt rather liberated. Closing her eyes, it wasn't Richard's face she saw but that of a boy reunited with his mother.

* * *

THE NEXT MORNING when they woke, they found Walking Tall and Almanzo in deep conversation.

"I will take you ladies into Portland. Our white friends will meet us there," Almanzo said.

"Where are Walking Tall and the other Braves going?" Tilly asked.

"They are not safe in Portland. They will go to their Chief and tell him what has happened."

Tilly nodded to confirm she understood. Then she turned to Walking Tall. "Thank you and your friends for coming to our rescue. We are forever grateful to you. Aren't we Fiona?"

Fiona nodded shyly, her gaze on the floor. Walking Tall took a couple of steps toward Fiona before placing a finger under her chin making her stare at him.

"You have kind heart and pretty face. Do not look at the floor but at the sky. Thank your God for saving you," Walking Tall smiled as Fiona stared at him, her mouth hanging open. "He must have great plans for your future."

"For me?" Fiona stammered.

"For both of you. You and Fire Daughter," Walking Tall said before laughing at the murderous expression on Tilly's face.

"Don't call me that name."

"Why? If I do, you will burn me with your temper?" Walking Tall answered Tilly.

Tilly looked as if she would explode. Almanzo decided it was time to intervene.

"Miss Tilly, Walking Tall only teases those he considers friends," Almanzo said. "It's an honor."

"Hmph." Her expression told everyone what she thought of the honor. Almanzo grinned at Walking Tall knowing the Indian brave would now go out of his way to tease his new friend.

"It is time to leave. We will meet again soon." Walking Tall jumped onto his horse and headed off toward Scott's ranch.

Almanzo and the women watched the Indians as they rode off. They waited until they could no longer see them.

"Are we ready?" Almanzo asked noticing Fiona had caught hold of Tilly's hand.

"Yes. We are," Tilly confirmed in a voice slightly less confident than her words. He helped her mount his horse. He was riding a spare one Walking Tall had brought with them. Fiona traveled behind him, her arms holding tight around his waist. He knew she was scared but was impressed she didn't complain.

They rode into town in silence. Almanzo praying his family and friends would be waiting for them and not Harvey's gang. He wondered briefly whether Tilly was praying her fiancé would be waiting for them.

CHAPTER 21

*T*here was a large crowd waiting around the sheriff's office. A shout went up as they rode into town with a few people running toward them. Almanzo recognized Jo, Becky, and Eva. He looked around but couldn't see their husbands although he knew they wouldn't be far away. With Harvey and other undesirables in town, Scott, David, and Rick wouldn't leave their wives alone for long.

He dismounted and helped Fiona down from the horse. He helped Tilly down too, his arms holding her for a fraction of a second longer than necessary. One of the men took hold of the horses.

"Almanzo, thank God. We didn't know what to think when you didn't come home." Jo threw her arms around him.

"Jo, I am fine. But the women need some assistance," he peeled her arms off him. Seeing her tear-filled eyes made him choke. He knew how much she loved him. How would she react to the news he had?

Eva took Tilly's hand and Becky put her arm around Fiona's shoulders.

"Excuse me, ladies, only Almanzo is my eldest son. I couldn't sleep for worrying about him."

Almanzo caught the rise of Tilly's eyebrows at Jo's comment but he didn't say anything. Jo was still speaking. "I am so selfish. You both must be exhausted."

"We need a bath. I imagine we don't smell too good," Tilly said shyly.

He couldn't believe his eyes. Was this the same girl who had fought off the Indians she believed to be attacking her? She seemed so... demure.

"Matilda Masterson. What is the meaning of this? How dare you just ride back into town as if nothing had happened?" An older but distinguished looking man said. "And who is this? You shouldn't be riding alone without an escort."

Everyone including Almanzo stared at the stranger who was shouting at Tilly.

"Richard," Tilly answered coldly. "You survived."

This was her fiancé? He looked old enough to be her father, maybe even her grandfather.

"Survived? Barely. I had to walk to the nearest town. By the time I arrived I was half dead. Out of my mind with worry about your fate and sorrow over your father.

"Father? Is he...dead?" Tilly asked.

"You were there when it happened. Didn't you see for yourself?" Richard's tone was dismissive.

Almanzo flexed his hands trying to keep his temper from rising. How would her fiancé know she had seen her father die? But before he could question that, Becky had seen and heard enough. Despite her pregnancy, she obviously felt the man needed teaching a lesson.

"I don't know who you are or how you are related to these young women but you should be ashamed of yourself. They have been through a horrible ordeal and here you are berating Miss Masterson in the middle of the street," Becky's tone would have cut through iron. The man flushed but not with shame. He was clearly angry.

"I don't see it is any of your business Miss..." his sneering contempt was evident for everyone to see, calling her a miss when her pregnancy was obvious. Almanzo almost chuckled waiting for Becky to put him back in his place. Before she got a chance, Scott stepped forward.

"That Miss you are treating rudely is my wife. Mrs. Rebecca Jones." Richard's eyes widened as Scott stood to face him, his hand resting on the gun in his belt. Almanzo had never known Scott to draw on anyone, but Richard being a stranger, wasn't to know that.

"Please keep your missus under control," the man spat back although he took a step backward.

There was an audible gasp behind him. Almanzo watched Tilly's face as she squirmed in embarrassment. How could a woman like her be engaged to this ...?

"He doesn't control me you arrogant old fool. I don't

know who you are or where you come from but in this town married folk work together, side by side. Now excuse me but I have better things to do than to stand here talking to a brainless twit." Becky turned so fast her skirts twirled causing some dust to rise in Richard's face.

"Ladies please follow me. My friend, Mrs. Newland, is heating up some water as we speak. Some bags from the abandoned wagon train arrived in town. If they don't hold any of your clothes, we can buy new ones from the store. You need a bath, a good hot meal, and a nice rest before you should deal with any inquiries. From anyone regardless of who they believe themselves to be," Becky threw the last remark in Richard's direction before she led the ladies away.

Three or four other women from the town fell in behind Becky as they closed ranks protectively around the two women. They escorted them to the Newlands store leaving Richard and the other men staring in their wake.

Almanzo saw a couple of the other townswomen staring after Tilly and Fiona. Mrs. Nolan and Mrs. Roberts being two he recognized. He didn't like the expressions on their face. They seemed to be frowning. Were they upset at Richard's treatment of his fiancé or was it more they were annoyed about the women surviving? He couldn't help thinking of the stories in the papers, where female captives of Indians had been treated badly by their own communities after being rescued. His attention was diverted by Scott.

Richard took a step forward at which point Scott

drawled. "I wouldn't do that if I were you. You haven't seen my wife's full temper and she is mighty handy with a gun. Ain't she fellas?"

A couple of other local men who admired Becky for the upstanding person she was answered in the affirmative. Richard stared at Scott for a couple of minutes before dismissing him as you would something you trod on.

"Sheriff, are you not in charge in this town? I demand to speak to my fiancé."

"Listen, fella, I don't know how you do things where you come from. But here we treat our women folk with respect. Leave your fiancé alone. She will be well cared for by Mrs. Jones and her friends." Sheriff Rodgers glared at Richard before turning his attention to Almanzo. "I figure you got something to tell us, son."

"Yes, Sir. We got trouble brewing."

"Was thinking it was something like that. Never a dull moment with you folks is there?" The sheriff's eyes twinkled showing he was joking although concerned. "Why don't we go to my office and you can fill me in on what's happening," Sheriff Rodgers said. "Deputy Davitt, please escort this individual to the hotel and get him some strong coffee."

The deputy moved to Richard's side to escort him to the hotel.

"I want to hear what the boy has to say." Richard's contemptuous tone was accompanied by a sneer.

"I ain't no boy, Mister. After your behavior, I reckon I

am more of a man than you ever were," Almanzo replied shortly.

Scott clapped him on the back and pushed him toward the sheriff's office before Richard could respond.

"See you did some growing up in the last few days," Scott murmured as they walked up the street.

"Where's Rick?" Almanzo asked.

Scott's expression changed. "He's not good son. The doctor told him to rest. He came into town but he is resting up at the doctor's office. He can't wait to see you but he knows you got to tell the sheriff what is going on first."

"Yes, sir." Almanzo walked to the Sheriff's office followed by a crowd of townsfolk who, eager to hear the news, spilled into the office including the empty cells. Those who couldn't fit, waited outside for their friends to fill them in on what was happening.

CHAPTER 22

*A*lmanzo outlined the events of the previous three days making sure everyone listening knew it was white men who attacked Tilly's train not Indians. He didn't mention Tilly being bound but told them the Indians had rescued the women and treated them very well. He emphasized the fact that the women were kept with the Indian maidens so didn't come to any harm. He could see some expressions of disbelief but he hoped most believed him. For Tilly and Fiona's sake as much as his new Indian friends. He didn't mention his ma. That story was for his family and friends first. Then he would tell the sheriff but the whole town had no need to know.

"Where are Harvey and his friends?" Almanzo asked. "Miss Masterson and her friend believe they would be able to identify the men who attacked their train," Almanzo stated.

"Almanzo Price, you cannot accuse Mr. Harvey of

committing this crime without proof," Mr. Bradley commented loudly.

"Why not? He told everyone it was Indians. In fact, he suggested it was Paco's tribe and they have done nothing but help the people around here." Almanzo stared Mr. Bradley down until the older man looked away. He more than most knew how much Paco had done for their wagon train. Almanzo looked around before he continued, "He must have some reason for wanting to deflect the blame onto someone innocent." Almanzo knew he was treading on dangerous ground as Harvey's family had a lot of influence in Portland. The murmuring around the crowd buzzed but Almanzo couldn't tell if they were against Harvey or annoyed with him and the women. A few of the people he recognized were not fans of Harvey making him feel a little bit better. But Harvey missing something as big as this made him uneasy. Usually, where there was trouble, Harvey was in the middle of things stirring it up. The fact he was missing suggested he was otherwise engaged, something that usually meant bad news for the Indians and other vulnerable members of their town. He shifted from one foot to the other, impatient to leave.

* * *

THE CROWD GREW LOUDER, making Almanzo uneasy. Sheriff Rodgers must have felt the situation was becoming dangerous as he coughed loudly and when that didn't work, he rapped his knuckles on his desk and shouted at everyone to be quiet.

"I will go speak to Harvey. I think you should go check on your pa. Rick Hughes is at the doctor's clinic."

"Thank you, Sheriff. "

"Don't leave town without speaking to me first, son."

"Are you saying I am in trouble sheriff?" Almanzo asked.

"Not at all but you are another potential witness. I don't want to have to go searching for you. Your ma and her sisters will skin me alive."

Relieved, Almanzo grinned at the sheriff before Scott nudged him. They headed toward the doctors. "What did the doc say was wrong with Rick?" Almanzo asked.

"Something to do with his heart."

Almanzo's stomach roiled. Rick was only in his thirties. How could he be so sick?

"Don't go in looking like that. You will have Rick summoning the undertaker. Doc White knows what he is doing. He sent for some new medicines."

Almanzo didn't like the fact Scott wouldn't look him in the eyes despite his joke. He wanted to introduce Tilly to Rick to see what his pa, for that's how he saw Rick, thought of her. But if he was unwell, now was not the time.

"Al, before we go in there is something you need to know."

Almanzo's heart beat even louder. "What?"

"Sarah ran away. She's eloped with Edwin Morgan."

Almanzo kicked a stone on the road out of sheer frustration. "What did she have to do that for? Can't she see he is an idiot?"

"Son, I know you have feelings for her but…"

"Scott the only feeling I have now is the urge to grab her and spank her. How could she do that to Jo and Rick?"

"They are hurt and angry too, Al. So don't go in there all guns blazing. Rick could do with some good news. Do you have any?"

Almanzo shut his eyes briefly thinking of Tilly. She was good news, he could feel it but as yet there was nothing definite. He shook his head briefly before forcing a smile on his face. He was not going to add to Rick's worries. Not now.

CHAPTER 23

Tilly paced back and forth across the room. She felt confined especially after spending the last few days out in the open. The bath had been glorious. She was so thankful the ladies had suggested they stay in the private house, rather than the hotel. The ladies had felt Tilly and Fiona needed time to come to terms with their ordeal in private. Richard was staying at the hotel and after his performance when they first rode in, Tilly didn't want to see him.

Fiona came out of a bedroom dressed in one of Tilly's gowns. She looked wonderful despite her recent ordeal. The sunburn was fading thanks to Broken Wing's lotions. Tilly sent Fiona a reassuring glance and was rewarded with a big smile.

"You must come out to Jo's place and meet Bridget. She is Irish too. She never stops speaking though," Becky said smiling.

"Fiona is like that. Once she starts, she never stops." Tilly teased her friend thankful to see her eyes were once again shining with interest in what was going on around her.

"Miss Masterson, your fiancé sent a message. He is waiting at the hotel to speak to you," Mrs. Newland said.

"Let him wait." Tilly retorted. "Sorry, I don't mean to be rude but I would prefer not to speak to him."

"I can understand that. If he was my fiancé I would be riding back to the Indian camp," Becky said taking a seat and easing her feet out of her shoes. She examined her ankles pulling a face.

"Becky!" Eva reprimanded her younger sister. "Please excuse my sister's manners, Miss Masterson."

Since she agreed with Becky, Tilly didn't say anything to Eva. She turned to Becky, "You are Becky? Almanzo told me a little about you."

"I can imagine," Eva replied. "Becky's exploits on the wagon train to Oregon are fast becoming a legend around these parts."

"Stop it, Eva. You sound like an old grump," Becky replied before turning her attention back to Tilly. "I apologize if I spoke out of turn. But since I am in trouble anyway, what is a girl like you doing marrying a man like him?" Becky's eyes twinkled mischievously. Tilly knew she would like the other woman. She really admired the way the blonde woman had put Richard in his place. For all her dainty looks, she was made of strong stuff. Tilly closed her eyes, remembering how Becky's husband had looked at his wife, with admiration and love. Would anyone ever look at her like that? Would Almanzo?

She took a deep breath but before she could reply, Fiona answered.

"Her father made her accept the proposal. If what Master Richard said was true, and Tilly's father is dead, then she should tell him to go play with some buffalo."

The women laughed at the idea of the stuffy little man they had seen downstairs trying to combat the Buffalo.

"I assume he is nicer in person than the image he portrayed downstairs?" Eva asked.

"Not really. He is what he is." Tilly replied.

"He has a lot of money and expects everyone to jump when he shouts. He is not a kind man, not like Almanzo," Fiona said, the look on her face making the older women smile.

For some reason, the dreamy expression on Fiona's face irritated Tilly. She shouldn't be telling these strange women anything about Richard, her father or anything else of a personal nature. Tilly didn't want to admit Fiona's appreciation of Almanzo was making her jealous.

"I think it is time we changed the conversation." The older woman owned the store and was putting a roof over their heads. Tilly was appalled to realize she had forgotten her name.

"Thank you very much, Mrs." Tilly faltered, embarrassment flooding her face. "I am so sorry I have forgotten your name."

"Newland dear. You are most welcome. I had a run in

with some Indians on the way to Oregon. It wasn't as unpleasant experience as what happened to you although they were an unmannerly lot. Not like Paco and his tribe. Lovely bunch of people they are."

"Walking Tall was very helpful to us," Tilly confirmed eagerly to make a good impression.

"He calls Tilly Fire Daughter. It makes her ..." Fiona stopped speaking as Tilly glared at her. The other women smiled but Fiona didn't share anymore.

"Downstairs ladies and let's all have some food and coffee." Mrs. Newland ushered them out of the room.

* * *

AFTER THEY HAD EATEN and were sitting in Mrs. Newlands sitting room, the sheriff called to see Tilly and Fiona. Johanna Hughes excused herself as she wanted to check on her husband and Almanzo. Becky and Eva asked if the ladies wanted them to leave but Tilly asked them to stay. So, they together with Mrs. Newland listened as they told their story to the sheriff.

"You are fully certain it was white men who attacked the wagon train?"

"Yes sir, although there were some Indians riding with them. They were armed with guns, not bows and arrows," Tilly confirmed.

"And these men? Would you recognize them again?"

"I am not sure sir, we saw them from a distance and

they were wearing bandanas around their faces. I guess to hide their identity," Fiona guessed

"We heard them speaking though so that may help identify them," Tilly suggested although she wasn't sure if that was proof in a court case.

"Ladies, I know you have both been through an ordeal and I hate to ask but I need to know everything that happened to you in the camp."

Tilly guessed by the color of the sheriff's face, he was as embarrassed as they were. She exchanged a glance with Fiona, suddenly tempted to announce they were both ruined. Then maybe they would get rid of Richard once and for all. But as soon as the thought came, it went away again. She couldn't do that to the Indians who had done their best to look after them. They had shared their food although there seemed to be a shortage. Compared to the fate that awaited women caught by other tribes, they had been incredibly lucky.

"No sir, nothing happened. We were treated well." She noticed him glancing at the rope burns on her wrists. "I had my wrists bound."

"You were tied up like an animal?" his voice raised in anger.

"No not like that," Tilly hastened to correct the sheriff. "The Indians had to tie my hands as I kept hitting them."

"She kept kicking them too. They called her Fire Daughter. She was very brave. I didn't do anything," Fiona said softly, shame written all over her face.

The sheriff looked from one to another. "Are you sure that was the extent of the abuse?"

"It wasn't abuse. The Indians were very kind to us. Much kinder than I was to them. Given what happened to the other people on our wagon train, I suspect if it weren't for the Braves who found us, we would both be dead by now," Fiona said firmly, her mouth a mutinous line daring anyone to argue with her.

The sheriff looked uncomfortable.

"Sheriff who did survive?" Tilly asked hesitantly. She didn't really want to know the answer but knew she had to ask the question. If she closed her eyes, she could still see the child trying to outrun the men on horseback. She shivered.

"Your fiancé Richard and a couple of his men."

Her eyes opened wider as she stared in shock at the Sheriff. He looked at her keenly before glancing away, a flush on his neck.

CHAPTER 24

"What of the other women and the children?" Tilly whispered.

"No other women. A couple of small children survived," the sheriff said looking troubled. "But they haven't said a word to us."

"The poor things they must be terrified. No offense to you or your town, Sheriff but they don't know you," Tilly hastily apologized. She didn't want to offend anyone. "They will speak to Fiona. She has a real gift with children."

"Could you come and see them now Miss Murphy? I hate to ask you but we have been very concerned. We also believe the children may know something but they seem terrified of Richard and his friends."

"Can't imagine why?" Becky said, sarcasm dripping from every word. Tilly looked up and caught her speculative glance. Had Becky come to the same conclusion she had? Should she say something?

"Yes, Sheriff I will come with you. Tilly, do you want to come too?" Fiona asked.

"Yes although I would like to find the preacher. Has he said a service for my father and the other victims?"

"They have been buried. I can assure you the service was respectable. Our new preacher is a fine man. A bit young but..." the sheriff was cut off by Mrs. Newland.

"The Reverend and his wife are a lovely young couple," Mrs. Newland spoke firmly. "They have been doing an admirable job looking after the poor little mites who were left all alone. I am sure it would help you to speak with him, Miss Masterson."

"Call me Tilly, please. Thank you so much for everything Mrs. Newland."

"Sheriff, these ladies are staying with me for the next few days. I have the room and they need privacy." Mrs. Newland smiled over at Tilly and Fiona but her kind eyes were full of concern. "There are people in this town who have nothing to do but gossip. Such unkind speculation will do nobody any good at all."

"Quite right," the sheriff responded but it was obvious he was uncomfortable with the notion of female gossip. Tilly guessed he couldn't wait to be back outside in the company of men.

"Mrs. Newland is a very kind woman. She helped save our lives on the trip to Oregon. She will look after you very well," Eva said putting her hand on the older woman's arm.

There was clearly a warm friendship between these

women. Tilly wondered if the rest of the townsfolk would be so accepting of her and Fiona. Somehow she doubted it.

"Ah Eva, don't be flattering me. I just did what I had to. Now, Tilly and Fiona, you don't mind if I call you by your first names, do you? It's less formal here in the West."

The two women didn't get a chance to say anything as Mrs. Newland continued talking. "I will have your beds ready by the time you get back. Don't stay too long, you both look like you could do with a good night's sleep."

Tilly thanked the lady. She wasn't sure how she was ever going to sleep again. How was she going to survive? One thing was sure, she wasn't going to marry Richard. With her father dead, she didn't have to. She sighed with relief but her new friends misinterpreted her feelings.

"Tilly, dear, you are overwhelmed. It is a lot to take in. Are you sure you wouldn't like to go straight to bed? I can go to see the children with Fiona?" Eva said. "You can speak to the Reverend tomorrow." Over Eva's shoulder, Tilly saw Becky nod slightly. She guessed Eva's sister wanted to speak to her.

"Thank you, Eva, that would be lovely if Fiona doesn't mind?"

"Not at all Tilly. At least you may escape having to talk to Richard. He won't bother with me." Fiona smiled to show she wasn't upset by this but her remark was yet another reminder of how wrong Richard was for Tilly. She loved Fiona and didn't want to spend any time with someone who looked down on a person because they didn't have the same level of material wealth.

But if Richard was so rich, why would he be involved in a wagon train robbery? It didn't make any sense. Plus, he and Father were friends so why kill him? Why kill anyone? The risk of discovery was very big. But then he had made huge efforts to kill any potential witnesses. Surely he hadn't killed the older children but given the comments made by Mrs. Newland and the others, it appeared as if the children staying with the preacher were very young. She closed her eyes trying not to see the children playing as they had done the night before the attack.

Fiona coughed to gain her attention, her expression asking Tilly should she stay. Tilly shook her head and smiled back hoping to reassure Fiona she was all right.

Tilly said goodbye to Eva, the sheriff and gave Fiona a quick hug. She wasn't surprised when Becky offered to show her the way to where Fiona and herself would sleep. Mrs. Newland said she had dishes to do.

"You want to speak to me in private?" Tilly asked as soon as they got to the bedroom and Becky closed the door. "Should you not be resting?"

"I am pregnant, not ill," Becky tempered her remark with a smile. "I think you know who was behind the robbery on the Wagon Train." Becky looked at her, her eyes so piercing Tilly felt they could read her mind.

"I don't. At least not for certain." Tilly said looking everywhere but at Becky.

"But?"

Becky wasn't going to let this drop. Tilly looked at the woman and then asked in a low voice. "Does it not strike you as odd that the only survivors of the wagon train are Richard and his men and a couple of very young children?"

"Yes, it did. From the first moment I heard but we were given some story about Richard being out hunting at the time of the attack."

Tilly started to laugh but her laugh became hysterical very quickly. Becky slapped her across the face and when Tilly started to cry pulled her close into a hug.

"Your poor dear, losing your father and now hearing this about your fiancé. I shouldn't have said anything, I'm sorry," Becky apologized.

"I hate him," Tilly said softly but firmly.

"Your fiancé? Well, I have to say that doesn't surprise me," Becky confirmed.

"My father. This is all his fault," Tilly whispered.

Becky looked stunned. Tilly guessed the other girl thought her wicked for speaking so badly about her recently deceased father. But the truth was, he was the one to blame. He had insisted on coming here just as he had arranged her marriage. He didn't think to ask her what she thought. As far as her father was concerned, women didn't have opinions. They did what they were told, first by their fathers and then by their husbands. Tilly had tried to argue Richard was too old for her but her father had insisted she needed a firm hand. She could still hear him now. Praying for her to learn from her wicked ways. She couldn't remember anything she had ever done which was truly bad. She had continued a friendship with Fiona behind her parents back but that was the sum total of her rebellion.

She didn't read books she shouldn't or go out with men. She didn't sit beside anyone at church. The only men she was allowed meet were friends of her parents. When her mother was alive, she had complained constantly of the trial of having such a dimwitted ugly daughter.

Tilly poured all this out as she sobbed on Becky's shoulder. She rarely cried and never in front of someone she had just met. But there was something about the woman that made her trust her. Or maybe it was just the events of the last few days had finally caught up with her. Either way, she was sitting on a bed, sobbing as she told a stranger details of her life she had never shared with anyone. Even Fiona didn't know everything she had just told Becky.

* * *

AFTER A WHILE, she dried her eyes. "I'm sorry. I don't well I usually can control myself," she mumbled.

"Don't apologize. You have been through an ordeal. Thank goodness Al and Walking Tall found you."

Tilly wondered if she should mention who else Almanzo found but decided not to. It wasn't any of her business. "Did I hear your husband say there was something wrong with Almanzo's friend?"

"Yes, his pa. My sister Jo's husband, Rick is very ill. Poor Almanzo between Rick being sick and Sarah eloping, his heart will be broken."

Sarah? Who was she? Did Almanzo have a girlfriend but then why would Walking Tall have said anything. The

Indian didn't seem the type to joke about that type of thing. She itched to find out more, but she couldn't ask Becky no matter how nice she seemed. Almanzo was her family whereas Tilly was a stranger.

"I hope his pa gets better," Tilly said meaning every word but what she really wanted to ask was how long Almanzo had loved Sarah.

"I don't think that is going to happen but we will have to wait and see what Doc White says. Anyway, he is home safe and you and your friend are too. Things can only get better now, can't they?"

CHAPTER 25

*A*lmanzo stood at the doctors office not wanting to open the door. He knew he had to face up to the fact Rick was seriously ill but he didn't want to. For as long as he could remember, Rick had been his rock. A tower of strength who guided his decisions but didn't tell him what to do. He always let Almanzo make the final choice but under his guidance Almanzo rarely made a mistake. As he dithered, Scott gave him a gentle push through the door.

"About time you got back son, I thought Jo was going to ride all over the country looking for you," Rick said as Almanzo stared in horror at the old looking man in the bed. He looked so small, so frail. So unlike Rick. The silence continued. Almanzo gulped before speaking too quickly.

"I know you were worried Rick, and I am sorry but there was a reason why I was so delayed," Almanzo apologized hoping his face didn't give away his grief at the sight of his adoptive father. Rick looked awful, much worse than he had earlier in the week.

"This reason a pretty lady with a sorry excuse for a fiancé?" Scott teasingly asked.

Despite coloring, Almanzo dodged the question. "I have some news. It's good, I think but maybe I should wait for Jo to be here."

"Tell me now son. I could do with some good news."

Almanzo hesitated on hearing the exhaustion in Rick's voice. His adopted father was breathing hard too if the hollow at the base of his throat was anything to go by. Maybe he should let the man rest.

"I would love if you were to adopt me. Officially like. So, I can change my name to yours."

"Adopt you?" Rick asked as if he hadn't heard properly.

"Yes, sir. I know I said no all the other times you asked me but I changed my mind," Almanzo said.

"Son there is nothing more I would like but I think you might be too late now."

Almanzo paled as the implication of Rick's words hit him.

"Rick means you are probably too old, son." Scott clarified so gently that Almanzo thought the words were just for him alone. Almanzo released his breath as Scott squeezed his shoulder.

"Can I ask Judge Ryder when he comes back?" Almanzo asked.

"Yes, son you can. But despite what the piece of paper

says, you know you are and always will be part of my family."

"I know Rick." Almanzo looked at the man who had rescued him not just from the trail but also from repeating the same mistakes Price had made. This man, Scott Jones, and David Clarke had shown him how real men treat their women, their families, and other human beings. His eyes filled up but he wasn't going to cry. It would only embarrass them all.

"So what happened on your trip to make you change your mind?" Rick asked, curiosity making him sit up straighter.

"I found my ma."

The two men stared at him, horror and shock on their faces.

"Your ma? I thought she died." Rick's eyes were thoughtful as he examined Almanzo's face.

"We all did. Where has she been living? Why didn't she come to Portland?" Scott asked, his tone suggesting he had tried Almanzo's ma for neglect and found her guilty.

"Easy Scott let Almanzo answer."

"She's living with the same tribe of Indians who rescued Tilly and Fiona. She has been for years. I have a soon to be seven-year-old sister. Mia."

"How?" Scott asked, "Your ma believed Indians were savages."

"I don't think she did. Mr. Price certainly held that view. I don't think my ma had an opinion for the time she was married to Price. She hated him but was too scared to leave him."

"Because of you?" Scott asked raising his eyebrow.

"Yes but not in the way you think. Price wasn't my pa. She was pregnant when she married him but he told her he would have her locked up in an asylum and keep me if she ever told anyone. Or if she ever tried to leave."

"How did she explain leaving you alone?" Rick asked.

"She said she had to or he would have killed me outright," Almanzo paused. "Just like he did my real father."

"He was an evil son of a…."

"I hope you are not using foul language in front of my son, Mr. Jones," Jo said as she walked into the clinic closing the door behind her.

"No ma'am." Scott winked at Almanzo.

"How much did you hear?" Rick asked his wife.

"Enough. I am really pleased you found your ma, Almanzo."

Almanzo would have laughed under any other circumstances. The look on Jo's face showed she was anything but pleased.

"Jo, don't lie. Not now. You aren't pleased at all, are you?" Almanzo asked her.

"No, I'm not," Jo exclaimed.

"Jo!" Rick admonished.

"I'm sorry Rick but I have to tell the truth. The last time she left him, she nearly destroyed him. I don't want that to happen again. Not to my son." Jo's voice quivered with tears.

Almanzo had to restrain himself from going to Jo and giving her a hug. Instead, he said, "Jo, you are like a mother to me. I am very grateful to you and Rick for everything you did. To everyone who looked after me but this is my mother. She explained everything about what happened. If it weren't for her going with Price, I wouldn't have stood a chance. Believe what you will, but she told me the truth." Almanzo pushed his fingers so hard into the palms of his hands, he nearly drew blood. He hated the hurt look on Jo's face but he wasn't about to denounce his ma. Ma had made mistakes but leaving him behind wasn't one of them. She had tried her best to save his life.

"Where is she now? How come she didn't come back with you?" Jo asked quietly.

"Would you if you had been living with Indians for years and had a half-breed daughter?"

Jo flushed at his tone.

"Almanzo, keep a civil tone. Your ma, I mean Jo, deserves better," Rick corrected him.

"I apologize. I didn't mean to be rude. I just…. well, it has been a big shock."

Jo came closer to him and put her arm around his shoulders.

"I shouldn't have said those things about your ma without hearing her side. I am the one who should be sorry. I guess I am just a little bit jealous. She has the right to have such an amazing person call her ma."

Almanzo couldn't speak. He looked into Jo's eyes and saw her pain, weariness, and worry. He drew her into a hug before saying. "If my ma was dead, you would be the ma I want. I love you and I am grateful for everything you did."

Jo didn't respond verbally but hugged him tightly. He felt her tears on his neck and had to breathe deeply so he wouldn't end up crying too.

"Jo, how are the young ladies?" Scott asked. Almanzo suspected he was trying to change the subject.

"They are doing better than they were but Miss Masterson is somewhat upset with her fiancé," Jo said trying to smile.

"I'd say that was an understatement. She reminds me of Becky. The Indians had to bind Tilly's hands. For their safety."

Rick, Jo, and Scott laughed but Almanzo could see they were still concerned. If only he had a way to make everything better. For Rick to recover and for his ma and Mia to be welcome and happy in Portland. And Tilly?

CHAPTER 26

*A*lmanzo left Rick and Jo behind him at the doctor's clinic.

"Come on, let's get you some decent food," Scott said.

"Where is Harvey? He must have prayed for such an opportunity to kill as many Indians as he could." Almanzo didn't hide his bitterness. Scott understood better than most. His years of living with the Indians had given him a unique insight into their culture. It had also made him an outsider when it came to people like Harvey who had said often enough Scott was no better than a half breed despite being fully white.

"Scott, can I ask you something?" Almanzo asked, half hoping Scott would say no.

"Sure. Can you ask me while we eat? I'm starving'"

Almanzo nodded. He wasn't sure if he had the nerve to ask Scott what he wanted to know. Would he have taken his son to live in the white man's world if he had survived the attack that killed Scott's Indian wife?

They sat at the small restaurant, the hotel recently realized there were a lot of hungry cowboys who couldn't afford to eat in a regular hotel but would appreciate cheap well-cooked food. They made conversation until finally, Scott sat waiting for Almanzo to ask his question. Almanzo knew he would wait forever if he had too. Years of living with the Indians had taught him patience.

"I forgot what I wanted to ask."

"Almanzo, you might be a lot of things but a coward isn't one of them. Ask your question."

"I don't want to bring up bad memories," Almanzo played for time.

"You can't do that. Every day my family, the one I lost, are on my mind. I try to remember the good times but sometimes. Well as you know only too well, some days are easier than others."

"Having Becky and the children helps, though doesn't it?" Almanzo asked.

"Yes, but they are not replacements. Every life is valuable. Even those we do not like."

Almanzo colored as Scott had caught him thinking of Mr. Price, the man he had called Pa for so long.

"My ma had a baby girl with an Indian. He died. But Ma says she wants to stay living with the tribe. I told her we would make her welcome," Almanzo faltered. He had said that but he hadn't given any thought to where his ma would live. He lived with Rick and Jo and they might not welcome his ma and another child.

"She doesn't want to leave her child behind?"

"No, she wouldn't do that. But she won't bring the child to live in the white man's world."

"And you wanted to ask me what would I have done?" Scott asked.

Almanzo was glad Scott was so perceptive. It was easier than having to put his thoughts into words. "Do you agree with her?"

Scott examined the table for a while. Almanzo tried to sit still but despite Walking Tall's lessons in patience, he still hadn't mastered the art of sitting quietly. Not when he was desperate for answers.

"I think I can understand your ma's reasons. Whether I agree or not is not relevant. What matters is your ma. I do know it is unlikely she would be accepted back into our society. Not when she has evidence of living with the Indians in every sense of the word."

"Becky, Eva, and Jo would accept her. Mrs. Newland too." Almanzo didn't know why he was arguing. He knew Scott shared his beliefs.

"Our family would but most the town folks wouldn't. Your ma would be called vile names and worse. If the men of the town got it into their heads, they may... Almanzo, you have to respect your ma's decision."

"But I can't leave her now I have found her. I spent way too much time away from her as it is." Almanzo hated the desperation in his voice.

"That's the boy talking not the man you are now. You are grown up. You don't need your ma."

"No Scott, I don't need her. I want her." Almanzo clarified his thoughts out loud. "I want her to meet my wife, my children. I want to get to know her better. Now she is free of him."

"I can understand your reasons but you are not thinking of your ma," Scott said, his tone firm but kind. "Or your little sister."

"You think I'm being selfish."

"We are all selfish sometimes. You have been through a lot over the last few days. Finding out the man you hated wasn't your father, after all, will have been a relief. But it will also have raised other questions. Maybe you understand why your ma didn't stay with you or never came looking for you but it still opened that wound. Take some time to think about what you want and why you want it. You will make the right choice. You have matured into a fine young man," Scott smiled as he complimented Almanzo.

"Thanks to you, Rick, Jo, David and everyone else including your Indian family."

"Yes, I think the time you spent with Paco, Walking Tall and the rest of the tribe has paid off. You don't plan on taking an Indian bride, do you?" Scott asked, his expression difficult to read. "You could ask your ma and sister to join the tribe. I am sure Paco would welcome you."

"No, I like everyone at the camp but I haven't found

love. Not there anyway." Almanzo felt his ears grow red. He wished he knew how to stop them doing that.

"Ah, I wondered if your interest in Miss Masterson wasn't a little more personal than her friend Fiona. But what of Sarah?"

Almanzo spewed his coffee. Sarah? What did Scott know about his feelings for the girl most considered his sister?

"Everyone except Sarah knew you had feelings for her. Jo and Rick were worried for a while with you two being as close as brother and sister. Sarah falling in love with Edwin focused their worries elsewhere."

Almanzo grimaced. How could Sarah have eloped with Edwin? Sarah was impulsive and acted without thought for others. He had imagined himself in love with her but she had never made him feel like Tilly did. With Tilly, she only had to glance at him and his body erupted in flames. He wanted to be with her the whole time. He'd wanted to punch Richard before he had even met him solely because he was her fiancé. Now he'd met him, he wouldn't let Tilly marry that man if he was the last man standing.

"I take it you have realized your feelings for Sarah weren't the love a man has for a woman?" Scott asked, an amused expression on his face.

"I love Sarah but as a sister. I never reacted to her like I do, I mean like I would with a woman I was in love with. Oh, heck I'm not having this conversation."

"Why not? The love of a good woman is the best thing on earth. So, what about her? Does she feel the same as you do?" Scott asked, grinning now like a school boy. Almanzo knew he was enjoying himself.

"Heck Scott I don't know do I? Until three days ago I never felt like this. Tilly, I mean Miss Masterson is engaged. She's obviously a woman of culture. She... she fought like an injured wild cat when the Indians brought her out to meet us. She thought we meant to... you know." Almanzo couldn't say what Tilly had thought. Group rape wasn't a subject up for discussion.

"She reminds me of someone," Scott said dryly.

Almanzo didn't reply. What could he offer Tilly? He didn't have any land or any real skills. Anyway, what was he going to do about his ma and sister?

Almanzo decided to concentrate on the most important subject being his ma. "About my ma and my sister. I don't think they are safe where they are."

"I guess your ma knows that. You can't force her to leave. You saw a little of how your new friends were greeted. Not by our ladies but other townsfolk. In case you didn't notice there was quite a bit of whispering and hard cold stares."

"Yeah, I saw," Almanzo nodded. He had tried to convince himself it was in his imagination but that was impossible now Scott had confirmed he had seen the same thing. "I think they did too. They would have to be blind not to."

"That prejudice is everywhere. Your ma might not be strong enough to survive. From what you said, she has spent most of her life-fighting someone or other. It might be time to let her live in peace." Scott was repeating what Walking Tall had said.

"But she could die," Almanzo repeated as if Scott wasn't aware of the danger. He couldn't help it. The thought of losing his ma again so quickly after finding her was too hard to stomach.

"Anyone of us could die at any minute. Living in Portland isn't any guarantee of that." Scott stopped talking. Almanzo guessed he was thinking of Rick. What guarantees were there? None really. Any one of them could die tomorrow. They could be bitten by a snake, thrown by a horse, get a chill or any of a number of things that could kill them. Like heart disease.

Scott was right. His ma was old enough to make her own decisions. He had to find the guts to give her that freedom. He glanced at Scott wanting to thank him for making him see sense but he found his throat was too clogged up to speak.

"Give it a few days before you make any big decisions. About anything." Scott stood up. "I think it's time I found my wife and took her home. Della Thompson loves my children but I don't think she planned on being alone with them this long."

Almanzo grinned thinking of Della. She would be in her element. Family meant the world to her. What was family anyway? Was it your blood relations like his ma and Mia? Or was it the people who had loved him, raised them like their own and provided him with everything he needed and more from the age of ten? Jo, Rick, Sarah,

Carrie and the twins felt like his family, his real family, yet they weren't related at all. The Thompson clan had accepted him as one of their own, never treating him differently. Or was it his future family he should concentrate on? Could he move with Tilly somewhere assuming she agreed he was the man for her and she didn't want to live in Portland? He scratched his head in frustration. He hadn't even asked her to dinner yet here he was planning a life with her.

CHAPTER 27

*T*he next morning, Almanzo called to Mrs. Newland's to see if the ladies wanted to go for a walk. He figured they may be getting claustrophobic. Fiona declined but Tilly seemed pleased. Or was he reading things that weren't there? They walked through the town but thankfully didn't meet her fiancé. Tilly had said it was a bit early for him to be up and around town.

"I guess it was called Portland after the harbor?" Tilly asked.

"No. It was a wager. Two men founded this town, William Overton and Asa Lovejoy. Overton didn't have the money to file his claim so he sold half his claim to Lovejoy and the other half to Pettygrove. Lovejoy wanted to call it Boston and Pettygrove wanted to call it Portland. Legend has it they bet a penny. Pettygrove won."

"How fascinating. It doesn't look a bit like Portland

Maine," Tilly commented, her innocent remark reminding Almanzo, Miss Masterson had traveled extensively.

"I guess the men were homesick." He couldn't think of anything to say.

"What about you? Do you want to move back East or is this your home?" Tilly asked him.

Almanzo looked around the streets of his neighborhood. "I don't want to move back East but I am not sure this town is what I want either. It is growing so fast and I find my views can be very different to others who live here."

"You mean about the Indians?" Tilly probed. She seemed genuinely interested.

"Yes and the black people. Oregon is a free state but that doesn't mean there is no slavery here. A lot of settlers brought their slaves with them. People tend to ignore that fact rather than deal with it. Most people who voted against slavery also voted to make it illegal for persons of color to live here."

"But aren't Indians persons of color?" Tilly asked, looked perplexed.

"Yes, but they are allowed – at least to a certain extent. If an Indian man has a white father, he can file a claim. Not sure how many do though but they have that choice. But Blacks don't. They cannot file claims or anything. It is so unfair on them."

"Life is unfair. Especially when you are a woman. An Indian man who has a white father can file a claim but an

Indian woman with a white father couldn't. A woman is always a second class citizen regardless of her color."

He looked at her waiting for her to explain how she could be as badly off as an Indian woman.

"I know people see me and think I am well off. I couldn't possibly have any problems given my extensive wardrobe of nice clothes. My father was wealthy so I never starved. At least not for love." She stopped as if unsure she should be telling him.

"You weren't happy?" he prompted.

"That's an understatement. I wasn't allowed any friends. I couldn't go out, not alone. My mother had to accompany me everywhere. The only place I went was to church and even then my parents sat either side of me. I think they thought I would run off with the local saloon owner."

"I wouldn't recommend that. Mrs. Dell, his wife, may take exception," Almanzo said smiling.

She smiled back at him appreciating him making a joke. "Fiona was my first friend. Not that my parents agreed with us being friends. They believed I shouldn't mix with servants. Richard is worse, he insists she calls him master."

"Fiona seems like a nice girl. Where are her family?" Almanzo asked wanting to divert the conversation away from Richard. Her fiancé.

"Nobody knows. She grew up in the orphanage. She started working for my father a few years back. Now she will never have to be a servant again." Tilly's tone was firm. There would be no arguing with that decision.

"Why?" Almanzo was curious. How could Tilly guarantee Fiona's financial future? His stomach churned. Did it mean she was wealthy? If she had money, he wouldn't be able to court her. What did he have to offer an heiress?

"I will inherit money from my father. I intend to give some of it to Fiona. She can pursue her dream of working in an orphanage. She won't need to earn an income. She loves being near children."

"And you? What do you plan on doing?" He didn't want to hear her say she was leaving yet he had to know.

* * *

TILLY GAZED UP AT HIM. Could she admit to not knowing what she was going to do? To hoping he would suggest she stay in Portland so they could get to know each other better. But he stayed silent. She had to say something. Anything. "It's quite a pretty town isn't it?"

Almanzo burst out laughing. "That's one word for it. You are seeing it at its best, in the sunshine. Wait until the rains come. Then the streets become a mass of mud."

"But you have boardwalks at least. Some towns don't have them." Why was she talking about a boardwalk? He must think she was stupid.

"I guess we are lucky. You should stay away from the Port area. All sorts coming and going. It is not safe for decent women or children for that matter. There have been stories of children being kidnapped to work in the mines in Alaska."

"Children? Where were their parents? Surely people wouldn't do that?" Tilly was horrified.

Almanzo stood and observed her. She couldn't tell what he was thinking.

"What?" she asked.

"I am just wondering how you stay so innocent. You luckily survived a massacre, were taken captive by Indians even if it was for your own safety. Your father is dead and there is a possibility the man you were engaged to had a hand in all three events. Yet you wonder if people could be cruel enough to kidnap children."

She hung her head. Hearing him talk like that did make her feel stupid.

He leaned over and put his finger under her chin forcing her to look at him. "Please don't be ashamed. It's a lovely quality you have. You seem to see the good in every situation."

She raised her eyes to his, the look of admiration on his face taking her breath away. They stood staring at each other until flushing he turned away and pointed out some other places.

"To the southwest lies Goose Hollow."

"What a funny name," she said trying to follow his lead and ignore the undercurrent between them.

"They call it that as the women raise geese and let them run free through the Tanner Creek Gulch. Many of their husbands are away working in the gold mines."

They walked for a little bit in silence but it wasn't

uncomfortable. She was glad he wasn't one of those people who had to fill every silence with words.

"What do the people you are living with do?" She asked.

"Rick and Jo are both school teachers although Jo only works a few hours here and there now. She is too busy with her twins and running the farm. We grow wheat and raise cattle. Jo's sister Becky lives on the next ranch. Her husband Scott raises horses and he also has fields of wheat. He and Rick help each other out. Eva and David, she's the twins elder sister have a cattle ranch as do her parents, Paddy and Della Thompson. David writes for the newspaper. He will probably want to interview you and Fiona but only when you are ready."

Tilly felt the color drain from her face. She couldn't allow that. She would ruin whatever reputation she had left. "I am not sure I want to be the subject of gossip."

"Oh no David, isn't like that. The newspaper is one of the few that is fair to everyone including the Indians. You can trust him." Almanzo clearly looked up to this David person.

"It must be nice to be surrounded by family," Tilly said trying to move away from the topic of the interview.

"It is especially for the children as they have so many friends to play with. We kept in contact with most of the families who traveled with us to Oregon. Mrs. Newland, you met already. Mr. and Mrs. Bradley run the post office, well Mr. Bradley does. Mrs. Bradley runs a boarding house. She is ever so busy with all the miners and other people coming here. Milly and Stan have a ranch not too far away from Becky's.

"You have a lot of friends," Tilly said wistfully.

"It wasn't always like that. The man I called Pa wasn't a pleasant man and he didn't let me play with most children. He hated Indians with a passion rivaling that of your friend Richard."

"He isn't my friend," she protested hotly but Almanzo ignored her remark.

"Price made me believe Indians were savages. But thankfully spending time with Walking Tall and his family has shown me Price was wrong. Indians are just the same as white folk. Some good, some bad and a lot in between."

His expression made her laugh. She was enjoying her time with him. He was very interesting to speak to. She'd never have believed the history of a small town from the way it was named to the dates the first bank and hospital was opened would have held her attention. But then he could probably talk about anything and she would listen just to hear his voice.

"What are you going to do Miss Masterson?"

She was caught off guard by his direct question so she didn't answer. He took her silence as censure.

"I apologize I had no right to ask."

"Please don't. I wasn't angry. I just don't know what to say. I don't know what to do."

"I have to go back to the ranch. Jo is collecting Rick from the clinic today and I want to be with Carrie and Bridget when they get back," he said softly.

"You should have said so earlier not stayed with me. Jo needs you with her," Tilly said feeling guilty at keeping him from his loved ones.

"Jo wanted it to be just her and Rick and well... I didn't argue too much. I wanted to see you."

Tilly looked him in the eyes, seeing the truth there. She stared at him as he moved his face closer to hers. He moved so slowly, she knew he was giving her the chance to pull away but she didn't. When his lips touched hers, she almost gasped with pleasure. His kiss, although brief, seared through her.

"Tilly Masterson, you make me feel alive."

CHAPTER 28

*J*o twisted her hands as she reached the doors of the clinic, regretting her decision not to accept Almanzo's offer of company. Doc White had suggested she call in first thing this morning. Whatever the doc said, she and Rick would deal with it. Together. That's what the marriage vows said. In sickness and in health. She didn't expect sickness to strike so young though.

The doctor was waiting for her, a grave expression on his face. He followed her into the room where Rick was lying in bed.

"Mrs. Hughes thank you for coming in. I wanted to speak to you both. That way there can be no misunderstanding."

Rick and Jo exchanged a look before Jo focused back on the doctors face.

"Mr. Hughes, you have a heart condition commonly known as dropsy. You will have to stop working with immediate effect. In addition, you must take this powder medication."

"Doc, I'm grateful to you for your help but I can't give up work and I won't take medicines every day. I was perfectly fine until a couple of months ago. My father lived to be a good age, I expect I so shall I."

"You won't," the doc said harshly before making an obvious effort to modulate his tone, "unless you follow my instructions. If you keep working and don't take any medication you will be dead in a month or so."

Jo had to hold onto the arm of the seat although she was already sitting down. The room spun as the doctor's words sank in.

She stared at her husband who had focused his gaze on the doctor. His face showed disbelief but there was also fear. She didn't remember the last time she had seen Rick afraid of anything. He had been a bit wary about childbirth but that was usual for a lot of men. She had to help him. She would deal with her own fears later. Standing up, she walked over to her husband's side as he lay on the bed, and took his hand.

"Thank you, doctor, for being so frank with us. We will take your advice. Rick will resign as the school teacher," Jo said firmly.

"Jo, I can't. We can't live on thin air." Rick protested.

"Our family cannot live without you," she whispered,

bending down to brush her lips against his. It was a kiss not of passion but love. She wanted to show him just how much he meant to her never mind everyone else. "Where do we get this digitalis?"

"I will ask Mrs. Newland to stock it. We must make sure she carries enough stock at all times. You will need to keep some powders in your home. Keep them away from children. This is not something you want anyone else to take by accident."

Jo nodded. She was trying to keep calm and confident yet inside she wanted to scream. Rick was only in his thirties, how did he get so ill? Why him? Why not someone horrible? But she couldn't think like that. It wasn't up to her who lived to be an old man and who died young.

"Is there anything else we should know, Doctor?" she asked not taking her eyes off her husband.

The doctor sighed deeply. Jo got the impression he was trying to stay cheerful despite the news he was delivering.

"Mr. Hughes, Rick, you need to look after yourself. Get to know the signs when you have overdone things. You must be careful."

"What signs?" Jo asked.

"His feet and ankles will swell. You may notice his hands are swollen too Mrs. Hughes. He may find it hard to breathe. He will get tired easily. He should take regular rest but don't stay in bed all day. We want you to make the most of your life."

The rest of the doctor's sentence remained unspoken but Jo and Rick knew what he meant. This diagnosis had destroyed any hopes of them living together into their twilight years.

Jo kept rubbing Rick's hand.

"Thank you, Doc. I will make sure he does what you say. Medicine is improving all the time. I am sure in the coming years, you will have even more advice to give us." She smiled, determined to remain positive. Her husband was going to live to see his little girls grow up. He was going to give them away at their wedding. He was going to do all the things her own father had done for her. She wasn't going to let Rick leave them. Not without an enormous fight.

"Doc, what does this mean for my girls?" Rick asked.

Jo stilled as fear enveloped her. Trust Rick to think of their children. Her whole focus had been on him.

"Do you mean is there a chance you could pass this condition on to your children?" Doc White clarified.

"Yes. I don't mean like you would a cold. But is it something you are born with?"

"It might be but there is no way of knowing. You said your father lived to an old age. What did your mother die from?"

"We think childbirth but we aren't certain,'" Jo said quietly when Rick failed to answer.

"I am hopeful you just got unlucky. By all means, keep an eye on your girls. If they seem to tire easily or get more colds, coughs than children their age, let me know. To be honest, there is much to learn about this condition and the heart in general." Doc White looked at them frankly. "As your wife said, Mr. Hughes, we are making progress all the time. What matters most is getting you fitter so you can enjoy the time you have. Don't spend that worrying about the future. Anyone picking up a paper knows the future may be more precarious than any of us could have envisaged ten years ago."

Jo knew Doc White was referring to the political instability and threat of war but she couldn't find it comforting.

"Thank you, Doctor. We appreciate your frankness." Jo said, giving her husband's hand a squeeze. The news seemed to have hit Rick as he didn't respond. She tried to project her strength to him.

* * *

SHE HELPED Rick get dressed again before paying the doctor's bill and walking outside. As they walked down the street arm in arm, Rick said "Jo, I can't stop working. We have to eat."

"Yes you can and you will. I can get a job. Not at the school," she said quickly knowing how much Rick hated the new school regime.

"You can't ride into town every day. It's not safe for a start and it's too far, to then work for hours on your feet," he protested. She glanced at him lovingly. He was still thinking of her. Protecting her.

"Rick Hughes, we will find a way. We just have to. I am not giving up on you, on us or on our family. I just won't." She stared up into the face of the man she loved more than life itself. She couldn't believe he was now living under this death sentence. She wanted him to take her into his arms and tell her it had all been a bad dream. To wake her up out of this nightmare.

He pulled her to him, holding her very close. She felt a tear hit her face. It wasn't hers. She hugged him closer despite the fact they were on the main street in town. Who cared who saw them?

After a couple of minutes during which they both composed themselves, she asked him if he wanted to go and get something to eat.

"Darling, let's just go home. I've missed the children, Bridget and most of all lying next to my beautiful wife."

She smiled through her tears but couldn't say anything. She simply nodded and they headed to the blacksmith where their wagon was waiting. She'd asked the blacksmith to check the horses to see if new shoes were needed. Rick went straight to the wagon while Jo paid the bill. James or Blacky as everyone called him asked her how Rick was. She smiled and assured him he was fine.

"Do you think he will be back at school soon Mrs. Hughes? My girls sure miss him teaching them. He is a mighty fine teacher. The best."

Jo gulped not wanting to embarrass either of them. She turned toward the wagon. "I don't know yet Blacky. We will see how he is in a few days."

"You tell him to get well. We're all thinking of him and the family Mrs. Hughes."

Jo squeezed Blacky's arm having lost the ability to

speak. Then she forced a smile on her face as she walked back toward her husband and their wagon. What would they tell the children? It would be easy to fool the twins into thinking everything was fine but not Carrie. Almanzo already guessed the situation was serious but did he know just how deadly Rick's illness had become?

CHAPTER 29

They drove out to their house in silence, Rick having fallen asleep beside her despite the bumps and grooves on the track. Jo looked at his sleeping face. She loved him so much and couldn't contemplate living without him. He had to follow the doctor's advice. It was the only hope they had.

How would she manage the ranch? It was a lot of work and apart from Almanzo, they didn't have any more men to help her. They hired casual workers as and when they needed them. Could she keep the ranch going? Thankfully they had proved their claim and paid off the mortgage so she didn't have to worry about the bank repossessing. She wondered if it was worth working for a few hours every day. But that would mean leaving Rick alone. What happened if he had another turn and she wasn't there to help him?

The journey home seemed to pass in seconds. Rick

woke up as she drew up outside the house. Almanzo was waiting for them. She gave him a look telling him they would speak later. He didn't question them but offered to take care of the horses so they could go straight inside.

"Bridget cooked up a feast while you were gone," Almanzo said as he drove the wagon toward the barn.

Jo exchanged a glance with Rick. She didn't think she could eat but she would have to force down some food. It would be rude not to.

Rick put his arm around her shoulders, kissing her gently on the forehead.

"Try to smile darling. We don't want to worry the children."

She smiled up at him, doing her best not to run away and cry. She had to be strong. The time for tears would be later when everyone else was asleep. She could last until then.

* * *

WHEN THEY ENTERED THE KITCHEN, their twins were waiting at the table. Carrie was helping Bridget.

Rick sat down while Jo checked if there was anything she could do to help.

"No Miss Johanna, you just sit down and enjoy your food. The twins helped me cook dinner. Didn't you girls?"

"Yes Ma, we helped a lot. We ate already because you were gone so long," Lena whined.

"Thank you." Jo bent over each of the girls to give them

a kiss. Their innocent happy little faces made it even harder to keep the tears at bay. She caught Rick's gaze on her. She blew him a kiss before taking her seat.

"Almanzo is just putting the horses away. He will be in shortly," Jo said to Bridget as she took her seat.

"Almanzo has a girl Ma. Her name is Matilda but we have to call her Tilly," Nancy said before she was interrupted by her twin.

"She is coming on Sunday and bringing her friend to meet Bridget," Lena said. "Do you think Al will marry Tilly?"

"Al is going to marry Sarah. We all know that." Nancy was so firm in her belief she threw her eyes up to heaven at the idea Al would marry anyone else.

"He ain't. Sarah got married already. Remember," Lena said pointedly.

"We don't use the word ain't," Jo corrected her daughter.

"Sorry, Ma. I didn't mean to upset you. Bridget said we were to be good. That you had a long day." Lena stuck her thumb in her mouth. Jo would have smiled on any other day. It was Lena's sure fire method of getting out of trouble. Sucking her thumb and acting years younger than she was. But tonight she was too tired, scared and angry about Rick being ill, to deal with Lena. Before she could rebuke the little girl, Carrie swooped in. "Come on girls, you got to see Ma and Pa. Now, first one to the bedroom gets to choose the story."

The twins were gone before you could blink an eye. Jo

sent up a prayer for thanks. Her adopted daughter was worth her weight in gold and then some. She had such a kind heart and a real instinct for people.

"Bridget, why don't you sit with us? You haven't eaten yet have you?"

"No Miss Johanna. I was so nervous, I couldn't taste a morsel. But I don't want to intrude," Bridget said twisting her apron as she always did when nervous.

"Bridget, sit down and eat. You are part of this family whether you like it or not. Jo will need you in the coming months…" Rick flicked a gaze at his wife and corrected his words "years. She will need someone to rely on. Help her through."

"Mr. Rick you are scaring me. You sound like you are dying," Bridget's comment fell into silence. Nobody spoke. Almanzo came in just at that minute. He looked around.

"What's wrong. Why are you all so quiet? Normally I can't get a word in for all the chattering…."Almanzo's voice died away too.

"Al, sit down, please. We have some news," Rick spoke softly. Almanzo sat down straight away.

Jo reached for Rick's hand and held onto it tightly as he explained what the doctor had said. He left out the bit about him needing to quit his job. Jo waited for him to finish and then spoke.

"What Rick is trying to tell you is that he has been told to stop working. Effective immediately." Jo's tone was firm but nobody was arguing. They were all staring at Rick.

"I think the doc is being a bit dramatic, Jo." Rick protested but Jo ignored him.

"We will have to pull together and find a way to make the ranch more profitable. Rick will need a lot of rest. He is not to be worried about anything," Jo said, her gaze on her husband.

"Jo, I am still alive. You can't treat me as a helpless child," Rick protested.

Jo stopped. Was that what she was doing? She was trying to protect him but was she going too far? She looked at her husband, the look in his eyes telling her he understood.

"Sorry, I just want you to get better," she whispered.

"I won't get better. We have to face facts. But I am not at death's door just yet…" Rick was interrupted by the door opening.

"Who is at death's door?" Carrie asked her face white as she stepped into the room

"How long were you listening?" Rick snapped.

"I didn't listen on purpose," Carrie replied quickly, her eyes widening in her pale face. Rick rarely snapped. "The twins fell asleep almost as soon as their heads hit the pillow. I came back as I haven't eaten yet."

"Sorry, darling I didn't mean to snap at you. Come, sit down and eat," Rick apologized.

"I can't. What is wrong with you?" Carrie addressed Rick.

"I have a heart condition. The doctor has given me some powders and told me to stop working."

Carrie paled. "That sounds serious. Are you dying?" she asked in her usual direct way.

All heads turned to look at Rick but he was staring at Jo. She gazed back at him for a couple of seconds before squeezing his hand. Jo answered, "Carrie, darling, nobody knows what is going to happen. We have to pray and we need to make Rick rest more."

Jo let Rick's hand go so she could cuddle her adopted daughter. Carrie had lost her real parents and was now facing the prospect of losing her uncle, the man she called Pa all before she reached fifteen years of age. Life could be very cruel at times.

CHAPTER 30

*A*lmanzo gripped the sides of the chair he was sitting on. He couldn't believe what he was hearing. Rick had always been so healthy. He was young too. What would they do without him?

"Jo, Rick, I can take over the ranch. I know most of what's needed and if I have any questions, I can ask Rick," Almanzo said, proud his voice was not shaking. He actually sounded confident even though he wasn't sure exactly how you ran a ranch. But he would learn.

"Thank you, son. I appreciate that. Right now, let's not make any decisions other than to eat Bridget's dessert. I am sure she cooked my favorite pie today." Rick's tiredness shone through his voice.

"Mr. Rick, every pie is your favorite," Bridget teased back as she stood up to serve dessert. Almanzo looked at her closely. He saw her eyes shimmering but she wouldn't give in to tears either.

"I'll get the cream. Ma, would you like some?"

Jo had been miles away but Carrie's question brought her attention back to the table. "No thank you, darling, but I would love some more coffee."

Carrie jumped up to get the coffee leaving Almanzo sitting with Rick and Jo.

"We hear you are having visitors on Sunday," Jo said.

"I can cancel. They will understand, "Almanzo offered immediately.

"Absolutely not. I want to see the girls again. I liked them and it's time Fiona met Bridget. They may know each other from home," Jo said.

Rick and Almanzo made the mistake of looking at each other before they burst into laughter. Jo looked mystified. Bridget and Carrie came back, Bridget carried pie covered in cream, and Carrie carried the coffee.

"Are you going to share the joke?" Bridget asked.

"I have no idea what I said, Bridget but apparently it was very funny." Jo didn't feel a bit amused.

"Bridget, my wife forgets Ireland is not a small town. She was wondering if you would know Fiona, Almanzo's Irish friend."

"Sure whether I know her or not, she is probably a cousin. Us Irish are all related in some sense. I can't see why that's funny," Bridget said but the men had started laughing again. This time everyone joined in because it was impossible not to. But if anyone had asked them what they had to laugh about, they couldn't have answered.

* * *

LATER IN THE privacy of their bedroom, Jo's body shuddered as she sobbed against Rick's chest. He worked his warm palms over her neck muscles desperate to give her comfort. "Shh...shhh Jo," he murmured as he ran his fingers through her hair, caressing her scalp gently kneading the stress away.

As her sobs subsided, he cupped her face in his palm, gazing at her tenderly.

"I'm still alive," he whispered kissing her forehead, her temple, her cheek before moving to claim her lips.

Her weeping stilled as she gave herself up to his embrace. Her eyelids closed under his kisses, her heart stuttering as he brushed his lips against hers before suckling on her earlobe.

"I love you more now than ever," he murmured softly against her ear. "I will always love you, support you, protect you..." Each word was punctuated by a kiss. She couldn't think straight as she lost herself in his caresses, his mouth and hands exploring her body. His lips moved to the sensitive spot between her ear and neck making her body hum with need for him. His need for her grew more insistent, his shallow breaths warm against her neck before he captured her mouth once more with his own.

Torn between her body's needs and her worry for him, she tried to push him away. "Rick, you need to be careful, your heart..." he silenced her with a kiss and then another one.

"Jo, I am loving my wife," he insisted as he took her mouth with his once more. "I want to cherish you, protect you and love you forever," he whispered as he played with her lips. He rose above her, staring into her eyes before he deepened their kiss. She tasted the salt of her tears. All thoughts of the future fled. He was here now. She moaned as his hands moved over her body, returning his passion as her mouth opened between his. Their kisses were both hungry and tender, uniting them body and soul. He clutched her closer, his uneven breathing matching hers.

* * *

She lay spent in her husband's arms, envying his deep contented sleep just a little bit. She loved watching him sleep. He looked like he had before the horrid illness had made him weak. Rick was right. They had to make the most of the time they had left together. They were luckier than many people. Few ever found real love. Their love for one another was deeper and purer than ever and it would help them both deal with whatever the future held.

CHAPTER 31

*A*lmanzo arranged to meet the girls after church on Sunday. He would drive them out to Jo's homestead and then drive them back to town later that evening. He was nervous not because he didn't think the family would welcome his guests but because it would show Tilly his background. She would see he wasn't well off. None of the land was his, all he owned were his clothes, his horse and a couple of other bits and pieces.

Sunday came very quickly and he was relieved and anxious at the same time. Jo decided to stay home as Rick wasn't feeling too good but he wouldn't hear of dinner being canceled. Bridget had everything under control. She was going to church, unusual for her. She normally waited until the catholic priest was around but today she must have felt the need of spiritual guidance. Carrie and the twins were coming too.

As Rick and Jo weren't around to drive, everyone traveled in the one wagon. The children would sit in the back with Bridget and Carrie allowing Fiona and Tilly to sit up front with him. It would be a squish but they would manage. They neared the church, parking the rig under the trees where the horses could find shelter from the sun. It was already very hot despite it only being 11 am. He spotted Tilly and Fiona up ahead. They were surrounded by a number of men but he noticed some of the women giving them the cold shoulder. Angry, he quickly explained to Bridget and Carrie what was happening. Bridget's face turned bright red.

"Heathens that's what they are. And them on their way into church. I will be having words with the Reverend."

Almanzo was in no doubt she would. He helped her down from the wagon and then she was gone. Her short form strode across the grass quicker than he had ever seen her move. Bridget had been a fantastic addition to their household but in that moment he loved her more than he ever had. He saw Eva and Becky arrive and they too followed Bridget's example. Carrie hung back waiting for Almanzo.

"Al, do you think Sarah will ever come back? How could she do this to them? When Rick is so ill?"

"Don't think too harshly of your sister, Carrie. She fancies herself in love. She will come back and probably apologize."

"I hope you are right. I think she has lost her mind. I hate Edwin. The things he said about Walking Tall and his family don't bear repeating."

Almanzo could only imagine but it wouldn't do getting Carrie all worked up outside of the church. He turned in time to see Stephen Thompson walking toward them, his gaze focused on Carrie. He poked Carrie gently and gestured toward Stephen.

"Why don't you two walk ahead and I will take the twins?"

Carrie's smile lit up her face. She leaned in and gave him a kiss on the cheek. "I don't care who your parents were, as far as I am concerned you are the best brother a girl could ever have."

Struck dumb for once, Almanzo took Nancy and Lena by the hand and walked slowly after Carrie and Stephen. This was what made up a family. It wasn't about shared blood lines but feelings.

He saw Tilly lingering at the door. Could she be waiting for him? He smiled in her direction and saw her turn a pretty shade of pink. He walked faster, telling the twins they were late. They were almost running by the time they reached the steps.

"AlmanzoMaand pa never let us run into the church. Reverend Polk won't like it," Nancy complained. Then she stopped and looked up at Tilly. "You have a really pretty dress. Were you waiting for Almanzo?"

Tilly paled and then flushed all at once. Almanzo could have swung Nancy into the air and kissed her but instead, he pretended he hadn't heard. He offered Tilly his arm and escorted her into the church, Fiona taking Lena's hand behind him. They were settled in their seat before he realized he was sitting behind Harvey. He groaned. Harvey turned and smirked in his direction. He was sitting beside Julia Bradley who looked as uncomfortable as her ma. Mr. Bradley, on the other hand, looked as if he had found a hundred dollars on the street. Rumor had it, he favored a match between Harvey and Julia. Almanzo hoped Julia would hold out for someone way more suitable. She was a nice girl who'd lost her pa on the trail out here. Almanzo hadn't met Mr. Long but his family had told him about how nice the man was. Mrs. Long had married Mr. Bradley at the same time Jo had married Rick and Becky had married Scott.

CHAPTER 32

*B*ridget had excelled herself as usual and the dinner was a huge success.

"You are a wonderful cook, Bridget. I don't think I have ever tasted such a magnificent meal."

"The beef almost melted on my tongue. You will have to give me lessons," Fiona said excitedly.

"Me too although I don't think a roast meal should be the first dinner I learn to cook."

Everyone laughed at the expression on Tilly's face except Almanzo. He was staring at her in awe. He had never met anyone like her. She knew her own shortcomings but laughed at them. Once dinner was over, Jo suggested the children go outside to play leaving the adults to enjoy their coffee in peace.

"You have lovely children, Mrs. Hughes, I mean Jo," Tilly corrected herself quickly.

"Thank you, Tilly. The twins are a handful at times but we are very lucky to have Carrie's help. She was always great with children."

Tilly exchanged a smile with the young girl who was beaming at her ma's praise.

"You have a very nice home, Jo. I love the colors you used," Fiona said looking around her. "I would love to have a house like this one day."

"I am sure you will, Fiona. We are lucky to have so many gifted friends. Walking Tall's family did a lot of the paintings."

"Walking Tall is such a nice man," Fiona said with feeling.

"Fiona fell in love with our rescuer," Tilly teased her friend.

"I wasn't the one falling in love," Fiona retorted hotly. Both Tilly and Almanzo turned pink making everyone else laugh at their embarrassment. Tilly could have killed Fiona. If she was sitting nearer she would kick her under the cover of the table.

"Thank you, Miss Murphy," Almanzo said bowing to Fiona sarcastically.

"You're welcome," Fiona replied in kind, her big smile showing her dimples. Then she turned her attention to Rick. "So Mr. Hughes do you think it likely we are going to have a war?"

Fiona's question, unexpected as it was, made everyone look at her.

Tilly almost groaned as Fiona started on her favorite

topic, her idol Abraham Lincoln. She adored the man and had often said if Ireland had a leader like him the British would have left years ago. Tilly didn't pretend to know enough to comment but she thought it best for them not to discuss it in public. They didn't know enough about the Hughes politics and beliefs. As guests, Tilly didn't want to upset anyone.

"Fiona, I don't think now is the time to discuss this." Tilly tried to deflect Fiona. But it didn't work.

"Why? It's an important topic and I am sure Mr. Hughes agrees Abraham Lincoln is just perfect," Fiona said.

* * *

RICK COUGHED. Almanzo thought he did it to hide a laugh. He was surprised at Fiona. She was the last person he expected to be political but then he hadn't expected her to tease him and Tilly either. She was really coming out of her shell.

"I don't think any politician could be called perfect, Miss Murphy."

"Fiona, please. I think he is wonderful. He believes in equality for everyone." Fiona's facial expression was one of total adoration.

"Call me Rick. As for believing in equality, I do not believe that's true."

"You don't believe in blacks and whites being equal? I just assumed you know... with your friends. And everything…" Fiona's discomfort was apparent not least because she stumbled and stuttered.

"Fiona, I apologize. I believe in equality for everyone," Rick clarified. "What I meant was, I do not believe your Mr. Lincoln believes in it."

"But he does. He is prepared to go to war to save the slaves. I think that's wonderful," Fiona insisted.

"He is prepared to go to war to save the Union. While he may not believe in slavery he certainly doesn't believe in equality. Did you read anything of his debates with Stephen Douglass two years ago when he was running for Senate? He said then he didn't believe black men should vote, intermarry with whites, hold office or serve on juries. That is not equality," Rick said softly in his best teachers voice.

"Oh, but I thought he said he believed in a better life for black people," Fiona continued to argue but her comments lacked her earlier conviction.

Rick stood up. "Excuse me for a minute, I will go find his speech. I have it in my office somewhere. If I can't find it, David Clarke, Jo's brother in law, wrote a good piece on it for our newspaper. "

"Once you get my husband started on politics, I am afraid he will never stop talking, Fiona." Jo smiled at the young girl who had flushed red by this point.

"I feel a bit silly now. I really believed Lincoln was anti-slavery."

"He may yet change his mind. I don't know what to believe when politicians start talking. They all seem to say different things depending on what audience is listening. I know one thing though, most are against women getting the vote," Jo said.

"Jo is very much on the side of women voting," Almanzo said, sending a teasing glance at the woman who had raised him.

"Why wouldn't she be? Don't tell me you are one of these men who believe a woman hasn't got a capable mind to form an opinion?" Tilly asked sarcastically.

"Oh, now you've done it Almanzo. Tilly's lost her high opinion of you," Carrie teased him. He looked up and caught Tilly's eye, a lovely pink color spreading across her face.

"I believe in votes for women. I just don't think it will happen anytime soon," Almanzo replied quickly.

He was saved from further conversation by Rick's return. He was carrying a sheaf of papers.

"This is what Mr. Lincoln said. I can't quote the whole speech but the main points were: "I will say then that I am not, nor ever have been, in favor of bringing about in any way the social and political equality of the white and black races.""

"Oh, how did I get it so wrong?" Fiona almost wailed.

"Fiona it is confusing for a lot of people, not just you. He did end his speech with what has been taken as his dislike of slavery. He said and I quote "like all men, blacks had the right to improve their condition in society and to enjoy the fruits of their labor. In this way, they were equal to white men, and for this reason, slavery was inherently unjust."

"So what he means is he is against slavery but at the same time he doesn't believe in equality between blacks and whites," Tilly clarified.

"Yes, Tilly. That appears to be it in a nutshell."

CHAPTER 33

*A*lmanzo escorted Tilly and Fiona back to Mrs. Newland's where they continued to stay. The ladies had insisted on paying Mrs. Newland for board and lodging despite Mrs. Newland's protesting she didn't want their money. She loved having company in the house. Fiona made some excuse to go inside leaving Almanzo and Tilly standing on the porch. Mrs. Newland had grown some hanging ferns to give her a bit of privacy when she wanted to spend some time thinking, away from the hustle and bustle of the store.

Tilly and Almanzo stood in silence for a couple of minutes. Almanzo was desperate to say something but his words all dried up. Tilly seemed to be waiting too but when he remained silent, she said,

"Thank you so much Mr. Price for rescuing us, I am so sorry Fiona teased you so dreadfully in front of your lovely family."

He opened his mouth to tell her not to call him that name turning slightly just as she pressed a kiss to his cheek. Her lips were so close, he almost tasted the sweet smell of her minty breath.

They froze as their gazes locked, his pulse thundering as he waited for her to pull back. Only she didn't. Her gaze slipped to his mouth as her tongue grazed her upper lip.

"Tilly, I…" he whispered knowing he should move away but the roaring in his ears demanding he get closer. Her eyelids flickered closed as he brushed her lips.

She jolted at the feel of his touch, he stilled, breathing heavily as he waited for her to make the next move. She groaned softly. All his restraint fled as moving slightly behind the privacy offered by the greenery, he gathered her into his arms raining down kisses on her forehead, eyelids, nose before finally taking her mouth once more.

"God help me Tilly but I want you more than I've ever wanted any woman."

Blood pounding in his veins, he explored the base of her throat, her soft moan exciting him further. "Marry me."

Her eyelids opened revealing eyes blackened with desire. She looked at him but her unfocused gaze didn't reveal she had heard him. His mouth took hers as he deepened the kiss.

Her senses twirled, her breathing ragged as she clung to him. His hands roamed her back, urging her closer as his lips moved to the curve of her neck. A fire lit in her belly, her skin tingling at his touch, her mouth wanting his once more. She reached up for him.

A noise from the store somewhere behind her had the effect of an ice cold bucket of water. She sprang away from him, her heavy breathing matching his.

He tried to take her hand but she grabbed it back.

"I'm sorry. I shouldn't…. I couldn't…" he stammered.

"Mr. Price. I'm an engaged woman. I shouldn't have behaved so…so wantonly. It's me who should apologize." She bent her head, wishing the ground would open or she could disappear. He put a finger under her chin and forced her to look at him.

"Tilly Masterson, I don't regret kissing you. Not for a second. I want you for my wife. I warn you, I usually get what I want."

His words, while arrogant, filled her with hope. She smiled shyly then her mind flew to Richard.

"What of my…. Richard Weston."

"Do you want to marry Mr. Weston?"

She gazed into his eyes before she shook her head.

"I need to hear you say it," he prompted.

"No. Father wanted me to marry him. I don't even like him," she replied.

He pulled her into his arms, this time kissing the top of her head in a protective fashion. "Nobody is going to force you to do anything you don't want to do. I promise."

She wished she could believe him. She wanted to. Desperately. But from what she had seen of her father and then Richard, stopping those men from achieving what they wanted wouldn't be easy.

"So will you marry me?" he whispered. "I very much want to continue what we started."

She giggled at the flirtatious look in his eyes.

"You best ask me when I am a single lady. I don't think one is allowed two fiancés."

He burst out laughing as he swung her into the air before setting her back on her feet. "Life with you sure won't be boring, will it Miss Tilly?"

CHAPTER 34

*R*ichard showed no signs of returning back to San Francisco. He seemed to be watching her closely. Every time Tilly took a walk, they would meet on the street. He never mentioned their courtship or plans for the future. She felt like a mouse being taunted by a large cat.

"Fiona, can you come to the hotel with me today. I want to speak to Richard and need a chaperone."

"A chaperone? I didn't think you wanted to marry him anymore. I thought you liked Almanzo?" Fiona's confused expression would have made Tilly smile if she wasn't so concerned about Richard's motives.

"I am not going to seduce him. I want you there to make sure he doesn't try to put me in a delicate situation. I have to know what is going on. He is making me nervous, watching me all day with that silly smile playing on his lips."

"He makes me feel sick. I wish he had died in the raid."

Tilly opened her mouth to rebuke Fiona but she couldn't. Her friend had only put Tilly's own thoughts into words.

"I know it's evil of me Tilly, but how did such a horrible man escape when so many died. It doesn't make sense."

Tilly sat on the bed. "No, it doesn't. Lots of things don't make sense. Like how Richard knows that man Harvey. Richard told Pa he didn't know anyone in Portland yet he and Harvey behave like they are old friends.'

"Exactly. And how come your pa was killed and Richard was left unhurt? I think you should bring the sheriff with you Tilly."

"I can't. What do I say to a lawman? This man is my former fiancé and I think he murdered my father?" Tilly said mimicking her mother's voice once again. "They would laugh at me. We need to have some proof."

"Like what?"

"Did the children say anything to you?"

Fiona shook her head sadly. "Those poor little mites. They have nobody now. Almanzo said someone was trying to send them off to an orphanage. They don't stand a chance. I should know." Fiona hiccupped as tears flowed unchecked down her cheeks.

Tilly took Fiona's hands in hers. "Don't cry Fiona, we still have time to change things. They haven't left yet. Maybe they could stay in Portland?"

"How? There aren't enough well off families who can afford more children. In fairness to the sheriff, he said he didn't want the boys being adopted as unpaid workers. He is a kind man under all that gruffness."

Tilly wasn't really listening. She hadn't said anything to Fiona about what she had discussed with Almanzo. She hadn't wanted to raise Fiona's hopes until she knew more about her financial position. She had no idea how much her father's estate was worth but surely it would be enough to help the children and Fiona.

"Come on Fiona, dress up like a real lady. Both of us are going to see Richard Weston and find out once and for all what is going on." When Fiona didn't jump up, Tilly pulled her to her feet. "Remember you are his equal now. You are no longer anyone's servant. Now go put on my green dress, it suits your hair and coloring so much better."

With a smile on her face, Fiona did as she was bid.

* * *

THE TWO YOUNG women caused quite a stir on the board-walk as they walked toward the hotel. "Smile, pretend you are going to visit your favorite aunt," Tilly hissed at Fiona.

"I don't have an aunt," Fiona hissed back.

"Good morning ladies, what a lovely vision you make. Are you quite recovered from your ordeal?"

Tilly resisted the urge to slap the stranger's face as he sneered at them. She could see the contempt in his eyes. Once more her mimicking abilities saved her.

"Why thank you, Sir, we are truly recovered. We are just about to meet with a friend in the hotel. Enjoy your day," she shrilled in a tone her mother has used for her most important guests. Her charm worked too as the man looked uncomfortable. Tilly wasn't about to wait for him to recover. "Come along Fiona, it is getting rather warm and the air is less than cordial."

Fiona giggled at the expression on the man's face as he processed Tilly's insult. He didn't have time to say anything as they left him standing in their wake.

CHAPTER 35

*T*illy asked to speak to Richard Weston but declined the invitation to go to his room pretending she hadn't heard it. Instead, she told the hotel worker, they would wait at a table. "Please arrange for some coffee as we are quite thirsty."

The hotel worker looked bemused at being ordered around by a young girl. Despite the rumors around town about her being kidnapped and ravaged by savages, she looked and acted like a real lady. It was more than his job was worth to insult someone wealthy.

"Tilly, everyone is staring at us."

"They are admiring the view. We are quite presentable scrubbed up like this," Tilly replied trying her best not to let Fiona know she was also terrified. "Put a smile on your face and enjoy it. Richard will be furious with us."

"That's good enough for me." Fiona smiled and her true beauty shone out. Tilly berated herself for not doing more to help her friend when she had worked all hours for Tilly's parents.

She heard Richard before she saw him. His anger reached them in waves.

"Miss Masterson, what are you doing in a hotel lobby? Your parents would be horrified."

"Given they are dead, I don't think their opinion matters much. It was preferable to being shown to your room. Now we need to speak. Please sit down, I would prefer to talk in private," Tilly pressed her knees into the table in a hope to stop them shaking. She didn't look at his face knowing by his breathing, he was struggling to keep his temper under control. She waited for the fear to move down her back but nothing happened. He didn't have that effect on her anymore. Despite not being afraid, she decided a little bit of charm wouldn't hurt.

"Dear Richard, please do sit down. Everyone is staring at us. I need your help."

His grin reminded her again of a cat stalking a mouse. She shivered with revulsion.

"Excuse my manners Miss Masterson. The events of recent days have had an effect. Of course, I will do everything in my assistance to help you. We were to be married after all. That should count for something."

"Were?" Tilly knew she shouldn't ask but she had to know. Was he really setting her free? Could she plan a future with someone else? Was it really that easy?

Richard glanced at her to Fiona and back again. "Perhaps it would be best to speak in private?"

"Fiona is staying with me. I need a chaperone. There has been enough talk already." Tilly appealed to the needs of society rather than admit she didn't want to be alone with him.

Richard's eyes narrowed but after several seconds he sighed. "I guess you should try to protect what little reputation you currently hold."

Tilly heard Fiona's breath hiss but she pretended she hadn't. She didn't let Richard see any reaction to his insult but stayed quiet leaving him to continue talking.

"You know I hold you in very high regard my dear and looked forward to making you my wife but that is now impossible."

"Why?" Tilly couldn't resist baiting him despite Fiona's kick under the table.

"Miss Masterson, surely you are not that innocent. A man of my position cannot marry a woman with such a blemished character. It simply wouldn't do. The best solution would be for you to move East and perhaps join a convent. Devote yourself to a life of service. Take her with you, the nuns are always in need of more scrubbers."

The knuckles on Tilly's clasped hands tightened at the insult but she wasn't going to play his game. She refused to lose her temper. She saw Fiona was ready to tip her coffee over him. She hoped her friend would hold back.

"I see. Well, I guess there is nothing I can do to change your mind despite the fact that my honor and that of Fiona's are truly intact. The Indians were nothing but kind to us," she ignored his reaction but turned to smile at Fiona.

"The fact you can speak like that about the men who murdered your father shows me my decision is the correct one," Richard said pompously.

"How was my father killed? Did you see it happening?" Tilly asked, her heart beating quickly. Would he admit his involvement?

"Yes, but I was too busy fighting for my own life to save him. I still feel guilty, Charles being such a good friend," he said causing Tilly to look away. She might not have loved her father as a daughter should but he was still her family. The insincerity dripping from Richard's voice made her temper flare once more.

"Did he not have a chance?" Tilly prompted.

"No. They walked right up to him and shot him. He didn't get his gun out. It all happened so fast," Richard answered.

Tilly held onto the table. He was lying but why? She had seen her father make a desperate bid to escape.

"Are you sure? Father usually had his gun nearby."

"Miss Masterson, Matilda, I know what I saw."

"We were lucky to escape with our lives, Miss Tilly," Fiona whispered causing Richard to stare at her for a couple of seconds before turning his attention back to Tilly. "Where were you? I looked in your wagon..."

How did he have time to look in the wagon when he was so desperately fighting for his life? Tilly glanced at

Fiona who looked as if she was about to answer but at Tilly's look, she closed her mouth once more.

"It was God's will, I guess," Tilly said, making a sign of the cross with her hand. "We were so lucky. All those people killed. You must feel very lucky too, Richard, to have survived when the only other survivors were a few young children." Tilly stroked his arm in a gesture of affection. As she suspected it had the right effect.

"I feel so lucky I chose that morning to go hunting with some of the men. If I had stayed behind, I too would have been dead and buried."

"Hunting?" Tilly put her head on one side as if very confused. "But I thought you said you saw my father killed?"

Richards' eyes flared for a second as he probed hers. Had he guessed she knew something? She struggled to maintain a bemused expression.

"I heard the screams and shots and came back to help. As I rode into camp, I saw your father get shot. Now if you don't mind ladies, it is getting rather late and I have some business to take care of."

"Thank you so much, Richard, for speaking to us. We know you are a very busy man. Could you just help with one or two last details?" Tilly asked sweetly.

Richard, annoyed though he looked, couldn't really refuse given she had used all her charm. Thank God mother insisted I take those classes in becoming a real lady.

"Who would I approach in town? I mean I know you

and Father had contacts in Portland but I cannot remember their names?"

"Approach for what my dear? I don't know anyone in Portland, not well enough to discuss financial matters. You must have misunderstood. Now I do have somewhere to be. Please excuse me?"

"I hope you find the happiness you deserve Richard," Tilly continued sweetly watching him preen. "Before we go our separate ways, could you please let me know where my father's papers are being stored? They weren't with his personal effects when they were returned to me."

"Weren't they? They must have been lost. So much tragedy," Richard's glib response didn't fool Tilly. She knew he was hiding something.

"I am sure someone holds them. They, as you well know, are valuable and considering my future depends on them, I should like to know where they are," Tilly stated firmly.

"Your future? But my dear, didn't your father tell you? He made me his heir. You, as my wife, would have benefited of course but now the engagement has been broken.... Well, you understand."

Shock reverberated through Tilly. She stared at Richard, his mouth opening and closing as he spoke but she couldn't hear a word he was saying. Her mind had shut down as soon as he said he had inherited everything. That couldn't be true. Wasn't she penniless? Was she?

"Come on Miss Tilly, you need to come home now," Fiona gripped Tilly's elbow in a strong grip pulling her to her feet. "As for you Master Richard, there is no way you are telling the truth. Mr. Masterson wouldn't do that to his only child. He just wouldn't."

"Of course, the faithful servant. And who in the world wouldn't listen to a common foundling with a taste for a life she can't afford. I applaud your loyalty. Maybe you will be able to coach your mistress in the ways to please a man, then both of you will have a few pennies at least."

Fiona held her hand up, her face a mask of anger, but at the last minute let it drop to her side.

"Come on Miss Tilly, we are leaving." She dragged her mistress to the front of the hotel and out in the direction of Mrs. Newlands.

CHAPTER 36

*M*rs. Newland took one look at Tilly and ushered both girls into her front room away from the nosy eyes of the store's customers.

"Whatever happened? The poor girl looks like she saw a ghost?"

"A ghost would have been nicer. She's had a bad shock. Can I make her some tea with sugar?"

"You sit with her dear, I will make the tea," Mrs. Newland said, fussing around Tilly like a bee around honey. "If you girls have not been through enough. Lord almighty what are these times coming to?"

Fiona didn't answer. She was too busy thinking ahead. Richard Weston had planned all of this, she knew that. But knowing it and proving it was another thing altogether. She had to get help for Tilly but from who? They didn't know anyone very well and it wouldn't do for people to think they were penniless. Which apart from a couple of dollars in Tilly's purse, they were. Almanzo. He would help them.

"Tilly you stay right here with Mrs. Newland. She has just gone to make you tea. I will be back soon," Fiona said quickly not wanting to tell Tilly where she was going. Tilly's pride may stop her asking for help. She moved quickly, catching Mrs. Newland as she came back into the room.

"I will be back in a few minutes. I forgot something."

Mrs. Newland was looking at Tilly with concern. "You go dear, I will look after young Tilly. Poor girl, the shock of losing her father must have finally hit her."

Fiona let Mrs. Newland think that. It was easier than explaining how her father had fleeced Tilly and left her high and dry. If what Richard said was true. But despite her low opinion of Richard, Fiona couldn't help feeling Mr. Masterson had a part to play in all of this. He had been willing to marry Tilly off to the man so he must have trusted him or at least liked him a professional level.

SHE HURRIED DOWN THE STREET, ignoring the admiring glances she was getting. Where would Almanzo be? Maybe he wasn't even in town?

He'd told them to go to Blacky if they ever needed help. Today was that day. Fiona took a deep breath and tried to calm herself before approaching the blacksmith. She saw him glance at her and then look again as he realized she was making her way toward him. He wiped his hands on his apron drawing attention to the fact that apart from the leather piece, his chest and arms were naked. He was so tall and strong, the perfect man to shelter a damsel in distress. She gave herself a good talking to. Now was not a scene out of one of the penny dreadful books Cook had often lent to her. The Masterson's didn't hold with their servants reading but Cook's attitude was what she did in her own time was none of their business.

"Miss Murphy? Are you alright? You seem a little…."

Fiona rescued the poor man as he struggled for the polite word to cover her actions.

"Mr. Blacky. We need help. Almanzo told us to come to you if we need his assistance. Do you know where he is?"

"Aye, he's at Rick's ranch. Is there something I could help you with?" Blacky looked up shyly. "I would like to if I could."

"Thank you Blacky but much as I would love to ask you to punch someone I think it would get us both into trouble. Could you please send for Almanzo and ask him to come to Newland's store. As soon as he can."

Troubled looking, it was clear Blacky was torn between wanting to know more and wanting to respect her privacy.

"Consider it done Miss Murphy. Would you like me to walk you back to the store?

She would love him to do that. The thought of bumping into Richard Weston terrified her as she wasn't at all sure she could stop herself from hitting him. She would be arrested and of no help to Tilly.

"Thank you kindly but no. You can help best by finding Almanzo," Fiona smiled her thanks and turned to go back to Newland's store. She felt the blacksmith's eyes on her. He was probably wondering if the sun had gone to her head or her recent experiences with Indians had damaged her mind. How she wished she was back among the Indians. At least there they had been safe. She smiled at the thoughts of being safer among so called savages but realizing people were staring at her now, she put her head down and walked quickly back to Newland's store and its relative safety.

IT TOOK ABOUT two to three hours for Almanzo to arrive by which time Mrs. Newland had called the doctor and given Tilly a sedative. Fiona wanted to ask for one as well but she couldn't. Someone had to watch over Tilly and also tell Almanzo what was going on. She sat by the bed watching Tilly carefully while Doctor White and Mrs. Newland chatted. They had decided it was delayed shock that had affected Tilly and Fiona wasn't going to disabuse them. They might not believe her. After all, despite her current clothes, she was a foundling and Richard Weston was a rich honorable businessman. Well, he was rich. The rest was just perception but Fiona had been around long enough to know that sometimes it was how one looked and behaved that mattered. People jumped to conclusions despite evidence to the contrary. The town thinking they had been ravaged by Indians was proof of that despite the fact they had shown up clear headed and unmarked. If they had been subjected to gross indecencies they would hardly look like they did.

CHAPTER 37

*D*oc White had left and Mrs. Newland had gone to help in the store when Almanzo knocked at the door. She opened it and seeing his face, promptly burst into tears. He took her by the hand and led her into the private sitting room.

"Fiona, what is wrong? Mrs. Newland said Doc White had to give Tilly some medication. What happened to her?" Almanzo asked kindly.

Fiona looked at his white face, seeing the panic in his eyes. She sought to reassure him.

"Tilly will be fine. They think it was delayed shock over the death of her father. I let them think it and Doc White gave her something to make her sleep. She will be the better of it."

"What do you mean you let them think it?"

Almanzo looked as if he was struggling to keep up. She'd confused him.

He looked at her sternly. "What upset Tilly? Tell me the truth?"

Fiona wavered. It had been one thing sending for him thinking he would rescue them but it was another thing looking at him and realizing it wasn't her secret to share. Would Tilly want this man to know she was penniless?

"Fiona, please. I am going out of my mind now."

"We went to see Richard Weston." At the thundercloud expression on his face, Fiona faltered. Then she started talking quickly while looking at the floor. She explained what had transpired between them. As she spoke, Almanzo got to his feet, walking back and forth across the small room. He was like a caged wild animal. She finished the story and then watched him silently. The silence lingered for a few minutes.

"I would like to see him hung up."

She couldn't agree more but that wouldn't help Tilly. "Do you think he is right? Could her father do that to her?"

"I don't know about the legal stuff. I will have to ask Rick or maybe David. Would that be alright? They know more about that sort of stuff."

Fiona nodded. She didn't think Tilly would care who knew so long as Almanzo trusted their ability to help them.

"Fiona, what was Mr. Masterson like? Could he do something like this?"

Fiona picked at her gown. What was she supposed to say? He was dead, so didn't that mean he was a kind hearted man generous to everyone who crossed his path. That's what they would have said at the funeral. It was what they always said. But in reality, he had been a mean miserable man who believed anyone who found joy in anything was inherently evil. He had treated Tilly, his own daughter, like a possession. She couldn't remember Mr. Masterson ever saying anything pleasant to Tilly or anyone else.

"Your silence says it all."

"Sorry Almanzo, I had to think. He wasn't a very nice man. He wasn't kind or caring towards Tilly. He didn't beat her but he did force her to marry Richard..." Fiona glanced at Almanzo who had stopped pacing but was now standing with his hands bunched up together. "But I don't think he would have given all his money away. But then he didn't have any sons and if Tilly had married Richard, it would all be his anyway. Wouldn't it?"

Almanzo didn't react. He looked as if he had stopped listening as he stared out the window.

"What?"

"Did Weston talk about having any friends in town?"

"No. He said he knew nobody but we don't know if that was the truth. Tilly said her father spoke about having contacts here."

"They seem very friendly for two people who have just met didn't they?"

Almanzo beckoned Fiona to the window. She glanced out and stepped back quickly as if he could see her.

"Who is that he is speaking to?"

"That my dear Fiona is Mr. George Harvey. He has his sights set on being governor of Portland when it is to use his expression white, rich and trash free. He considers a range of people trash but has a particular hatred for Indians, blacks, and anyone suspected of being supporters."

"Your best friend then?" Fiona joked as she tried to reduce the tension in the room.

"We are as close as brothers," Almanzo replied in kind, his sarcasm making them both smile. Then he looked out the window again.

"I don't trust Harvey as far as I could throw him. Given what you have told me about this Weston guy, I trust their budding friendship even less. Is there anything else you need to tell me?"

Fiona wondered if she should mention Richard's convenient hunting trip.

"Go on Fiona, tell me. I won't tell anyone unless they need to know."

"It could be nothing but it was something, Master Richard..." Almanzo raised his eyebrows making her blush., "I mean Weston said. He told us he was spared as he had gone hunting."

"Lucky man."

"Well, that's just it. It must have been luck as I never knew Weston to go hunting. He usually paid a younger man to do it on his behalf. Why go hunting that day?"

"You think he knew the attack was likely to happen?"

Fiona didn't know what to think or believe anymore. Her whole world had turned upside down.

"Who knew the attack was likely to happen?" Tilly walked into the room, holding a hand to her head as if nursing a headache. "Almanzo, what are you doing here? Is Rick alright?"

"He is fine, thank you. I came here to visit with you both but Fiona said you were feeling a little tired."

Tilly eyed Fiona but when she didn't look back, Tilly paled.

"You told him? What did you tell him? How could you?"

"Tilly, we needed help."

"You had no right to do that. Telling my secrets. I trusted you."

"Stop it Fire Daughter," At Almanzo's use of the horrible name Tilly rounded on him but she didn't get a chance to say anything. He continued talking. "You can't blame Fiona. She was right to send for me. You are in trouble and you need help."

"I don't need anything of the sort." She said, wishing her voice wouldn't shake so much. She desperately wanted to tell him everything and let him take care of her but she couldn't do that. He had enough issues of his own with his mother and now his adoptive father being ill. "We can handle things. Thank you for coming."

Almanzo laughed. She stared at him haughtily but he continued to laugh.

"Excuse me. I don't see the joke."

"You are not in one of your society evenings now Miss Tilly. You are in trouble and you should be thanking your friend for trying to save your backside.

"Almanzo Price watch your language."

"No, I won't as you don't seem to listen unless I shock

you. Tilly, when are you going to wake up and see your life is in danger. You and Fiona both."

Fiona paled and sat on the couch. Tilly shook but she just put out a hand to steady herself.

"Listen to me, Tilly, please. You are the only adult survivors of the attack apart from Richard and his men. Whoever planned these attacks won't like leaving loose ends. I think you should arrange to leave Portland at once.'

"I, I mean we have nowhere to go. There is nobody left in San Francisco."

Almanzo paced again. "You are best staying here in town in full sight of everyone. Mrs. Newland doesn't need to know. You can pretend to be grieving deeply. I will speak to Sheriff Rodgers and also to David, Scott and … Rick."

His pause made her heart break especially when seeing the desperation flitting through his eyes. She took a step toward him but stopped. Nothing about his demeanor suggested he saw her as anything other than what was the term he used? A loose end.

CHAPTER 38

*J*o, Becky, Eva, and their ma sat in silence at Becky's table after Jo told them what Doc White had said. The forlorn expressions on their faces, testament to their love for Rick.

"We are family. Jo, you focus on Rick and getting him better. Your pa and I have some savings."

The girls focused on their ma. Savings? That was a word for rich people.

"Your pa lent some fellas some money to start mining. They promised to pay him back along with ten percent of what they earned. Some earned quite a bit. We put the money in the bank. We should be able to buy whatever you need." Ma smiled self-consciously. "So long as you don't have huge debts."

"Thanks, Ma. But we will be all right. We only had a small mortgage as Rick had the money he got from his pa.

We paid it off years ago. We don't owe anyone any money. We are luckier than most."

"What about Rick going back east for a second opinion?" Eva suggested. "I know Doc White is a good man but he isn't as qualified as some of the doctors in Boston or New York."

"I don't think that's an option. At least not at the moment as the journey is so difficult. Maybe when he gets a bit better," Jo said, trying to stay positive. Would her husband's condition improve?

Becky didn't say anything. She sat there, a pensive look on her face. Jo wished she could have avoided telling her twin. She knew this pregnancy was more difficult than her previous ones.

"How does Rick feel about his enforced rest?" Eva asked.

"He's not happy but what can he do? He knows what the doctor said and he knows how much we need him."

"Just be careful Jo, don't turn him into an invalid before his time. Rick is a proud man," her ma said hesitating for a couple of seconds. "Just like all our men. He needs to be head of his household. Don't steal that away from him."

Jo swallowed hard. Her ma didn't understand. Paddy, her pa hadn't been sick a day in his life, well apart from the brief time on the trail. It had been ma they nearly lost.

"I am sure Jo knows what's best. She's the one living this. We can do everything to help, but we have to respect their wishes too," Eva said softly winking at her sister behind their ma's back. Their ma's heart was in the right place but sometimes she could take over without meaning to. Della Thompson was a strong woman, she couldn't have had the daughters she did otherwise. They could clash at times, being so similar.

"Have you heard anything from Sarah?" Becky asked.

Jo shook her head but couldn't answer as her ma exclaimed. "What is it with that young lady? She never thinks through the consequences of her actions?"

"Be fair ma, she's only 18. She's young," Jo automatically defended her adopted daughter although secretly she agreed. She was annoyed Sarah had upset Rick but then in fairness she hadn't known how ill he was.

"We were 17 when we met Scott and Rick. Were we as wild as she is?" Becky asked before realizing they were all looking at her. "What?"

"Are you serious? Do we need to remind you that you rode into a fort full of soldiers almost naked?" Della asked Becky as Eva and Jo grinned.

"Ma, I was not naked. My dress was a little torn and anyway I was in the middle of a rescue attempt," Becky clarified rather indignantly.

"What about that time Scott nearly shot you when you rode off on your own?" Eva asked her.

"I needed to speak to him," Becky said huffily. "I am not a bit like Sarah."

Her mother and sisters giggled making Becky stick her tongue out at them.

"Very mature Rebecca Jones," Della chastised her

daughter. "I guess, in comparison to you, Sarah isn't too bad."

"Sarah has been struggling for a while. Since she found out the truth about her pa," Jo defended Sarah again. She could still see her face when Rick explained her father had run out on her ma a couple of years prior to them leaving their home. Rick didn't know if his brother in law was dead or alive but he'd told Sarah about the other women whom her pa had made pregnant and deserted. Sarah had run outside to vomit. She was so upset, Jo had wondered if they did the right thing telling her the truth. But Rick was adamant she needed to know her nightmares weren't some bad man coming to get her but details she was remembering about her own Pa.

"But Rick told her the full story years ago," Eva said her expression telling them exactly what she thought of that excuse.

"Yes and only because she kept having nightmares but I think it left Sarah looking for love," Jo speculated. "I think we failed her somehow. Edwin isn't the right man for Sarah, regardless of his opinions, which are detestable. He isn't firm enough. She needs someone like Scott, who will let her be herself but keep her in line at the same time. Just like he did with Becky."

"Jo, you take that back. I don't answer to Scott. We are equals," Becky protested.

"I know that sister dear but he does curb your more impulsive actions," Jo replied, smiling at her sister.

"He should have curbed her a bit more. I thought that

Richard person was going to hit her," Eva said but she wasn't smiling.

"What did you do in town Becky? Why am I only hearing of this now?" Della asked, her face wearing the expression they all knew well. Their ma was furious.

"Relax ma. I just told one of the men who survived the wagon train massacre how he should speak to his fiancé. You would have hit him with your rolling pin." Becky echoed her ma's threat. "He was so rude. You should have heard the way he spoke to Tilly. He more or less told her she should have stayed with the Indians. No self-respecting woman would have returned alive."

"Nonsense. If he loved her, he wouldn't care about anything other than she returned safe." Ma had very firm views on how men should behave. "Maybe I should bring my rolling pin to town after all."

Ma was all riled up making Jo wish she had never mentioned anything. Ma was easily upset these days, she was so wound up over the threat of war. At least Rick was safe from that threat. She should thank the Lord for small blessings. There was no way the Army would let him enlist. How many men would go if a war was declared? More importantly, who would survive. She shuddered as the image of Stephen or Almanzo marching off to battle flashed into her head.

"Jo, are you all right? You are very pale," Becky held Jo's hand, studying her carefully.

"It has been a rather stressful few days. A good night

sleep will do me the world of good. On that point, I am going to go home."

"I will drive you back and then David can drive me home. He and Scott were at your house earlier. Ma are you staying with Becky or coming with us?" Eva asked.

"I will stay here. I plan on letting your sister have a sleep in tomorrow. She's not going to get much chance with four children underfoot."

"Don't remind me Ma. Why did I think having lots of children was a good idea?" Becky said ruefully rubbing her small bump.

"You love being a ma. If anyone from Virgil had told me you would have the largest family out of all my daughters, I would have thought they hit their head," Ma said.

Jo looked at her sisters. She was lucky to have such a supportive family. They would help her get through the weeks and years ahead. But now she needed some privacy. She took her leave and headed back to her own home with Eva. Thankful her sister didn't chatter but remained quiet, she let her thoughts linger on her husband. Ma was right, she shouldn't make him feel like an invalid. He would hate that.

CHAPTER 39

*E*va had remained silent on the trip, but not because she was upset over Rick. She was. Her brother in law was a lovely man and a wonderful husband and father. But it wasn't what had upset Eva. She felt selfish even thinking about herself but her ma's words had hit home. Her mother or sisters didn't know but she would have loved to have more children. But it just didn't happen. It wasn't for want of trying but every month they were disappointed. She wondered if she should go speak to Doctor White. He was a nice man but she would be so embarrassed having to ask him questions like that. But who else could she ask?

Mrs. Newland maybe? She acted as midwife sometimes. She was good at it too but did she know anything about trying to get pregnant? David thought they should just accept things the way they were. They were lucky to have their two boys, but she would love a little girl. She idolized

251

Jo's twins, Nancy and Lena. They made her laugh particularly, Nancy, who was an old soul. Paco said her spirit had roamed the earth before. Eva didn't know if she believed that, but Nancy was wise beyond her years.

Impatiently, she focused on getting back to Jo's house. Indulging in self-pity wasn't good for anyone. She had a healthy husband, two fine boys, a lovely extended family and a working profitable farm. She should be happy with her lot. Jo needed her support now.

* * *

WHEN THEY GOT BACK to Jo's the lights were all on. Something was wrong. Eva pulled up but Jo had already jumped down, running into the house. Eva said a quick prayer Rick was okay before tying up the horses and following her sister indoors. Everyone was awake including the twins.

"Is it Rick?" Eva asked her husband as he came forward to greet her.

"No, he's fine. There is trouble in town. I brought the boys over here with Jessie and his family. I want you to stay with them. Almanzo is coming with me."

"David, be careful. You know there are some people very mad with your latest articles."

"Being a newspaper man means I have to tell the truth, Eva. Most people respect that. Someone has to stand up to Harvey and his friends," he said before giving her a kiss on the cheek. "I will be back as soon as I can."

She linked arms with Jo as David and Almanzo rode off.

Jessie was out checking everything was fine around the ranch. Bridget was in the kitchen making cookies and bread. Bridget always started baking when she was worried.

The children were all tired and acting up. Eva guessed that although the adults were trying to appear cheerful, the children had picked up on their anxiety.

"I hope Becky and Ma will be all right."

"Scott will make sure someone is with them. He won't leave them alone. Why don't you start a story with the children? I want to check on Rick."

Eva gave her sister's hand a squeeze and then went to get the children settled. It was going to be a long night.

CHAPTER 40

"Almanzo, what do you think is going on?"

"I have no idea, David. Walking Tall sent a message with a younger brave, a boy of 13 or so to say to meet him at the crossing. He said to bring guns and men. I hope it's not a ploy to get us out in the open," Almanzo looked around him as he spoke. "Harvey has been itching to get a piece of us for a while now. You got him riled up with that piece you wrote about his slaves. He thought he had got away with it."

"He should have been jailed. Treating people like pieces of property is wrong. Slavery is banned in Oregon for good reason," David said heatedly. Almanzo knew David was furious the law hadn't punished Harvey by putting him in prison. He had paid a small fine and that was that.

"It's not because people love the blacks though is it? I don't think there were many who felt sorry for the Smith family. They just wanted them out of Portland."

"You are very perceptive, Almanzo. Unfortunately, you are also right. The men of Oregon voted against slavery but they also voted on the no blacks law in the State. So far Oregon is the only state to join the USA with a racial clause in their constitution. They don't have that in Alabama or other well-known slave states," David's voice was full of disgust.

"You aiming to become another John Brown?"

"No son. Eva would kill me," David joked then grew serious. "I don't believe in killing people over my views. I think Brown was wrong in wanting to arm slaves and others. Fighting is not the answer. I believe all people should be treated equally. Murders and mobs will not do the Black cause any favors."

They both fell silent as they drew closer to the crossing. Walking Tall was waiting for them.

"I am glad we are your friends. You are so noisy, if we were your enemy you would both be dead by now."

"Nice to see you too Walking Tall." David greeted the younger man. "Is your father here?"

"No, he has gone ahead. He told me to wait for you. He Who Runs is with him."

"Scott is here already?" David looked around him. "What is going on?"

"We kept scouts near the area where the Indian tribe who had the girls is camped. They noticed some white men acting suspiciously. They think they were spying on the Indians."

"You mean preparing to attack? Soldiers?"

"No, not soldiers but men from town. Militia." Walking Tall spat the hated word. The militia was often more ruthless than the soldiers.

"What are Paco and Scott going to do?" David asked.

"They will fight. If they have to." Walking Tall's tone suggested the fighting was inevitable.

"Guess your promise to Eva will be hard to keep," Almanzo said to David. David didn't get a chance to reply as a cry went up.

"The attack has begun. Come. Quickly." Walking Tall shouted as he rushed toward the noise.

They rode out as fast as the horses could carry them. Up ahead they spotted smoke and heard gunshots. That couldn't be the tribe who had offered the women shelter as they didn't have any guns.

Were Paco's Indians armed? Almanzo didn't think many of them had guns although both Paco and Walking Tall did. Scott had insisted on them learning how to use them although both had resisted at first. But as with most things, Scott being so persuasive had convinced them. Arrows didn't work too well against guns.

* * *

THEY CAME to the top of the ridge. The scene below was one of devastation. Many of the lodges were in flames. As they watched, a group of men chased down some children, killing them as if hunting animals.

His ma and Mia were down there. Without another thought, Almanzo raced down into the fray. He jumped from his horse to check on the women and children. He saw things that would haunt him forever. But still, he kept looking. David, Walking Tall and their men had come in from the right with Paco and Scott already fighting on the left. The attackers finally saw they were outnumbered and made a run for it. Almanzo looked up to see Walking Tall and his men chasing after them. There was no sign of Paco or Scott. David had dismounted and was looking around him in horror.

Almanzo kept moving, kept looking. There were so many bodies, most of them dead. There were some who were still living. He asked them if they had seen Broken Wing and Mia but they couldn't understand him. They didn't speak English. Frantic, he moved faster and faster. Some Indians from Paco's group were helping the survivors.

Almanzo almost fell over the Chief. The old man was still alive although badly wounded. With tears in his eyes, Almanzo stopped to help the man who had been so welcoming to him. He gently lifted the man to bring him to where the other survivors were being helped.

"Broken Wing. You found her?" The Chief asked.

Almanzo shook his head, having lost the ability to speak.

"She ran, with Mia. Over there," despite the pain, the Chief pointed in the direction of a hill. "Go. Help."

"I will help you first," Almanzo insisted.

"Too late for me. Go. Please. Mia. Look after her," the Chief was gasping, desperate to get the words out.

"I will. Hold on. We can help."

The Chief gave him a sad smile and that was it. He was gone. Almanzo stared at the bundle in his arms. NO!

He didn't realize he had shouted until the other Indians stared at him. He placed the body on the ground respectfully. David moved quickly to his side to check the Chief. He closed the man's eyes.

"Friend of yours?"

"He was kind. He is my sister's grandfather. I have to go find her."

"Al, the men… they may have taken captives."

"For their sake, they better not have touched them." With a last look at the Chief, Almanzo turned and mounted a horse. It wasn't his but it didn't matter. Thanks to Walking Tall, there wasn't a horse he couldn't ride. He pushed it in the direction of the hill.

"Al, wait. Let me come with you." David's voice came from behind him but he didn't have time to wait. His ma needed him. He pushed the horse faster and faster, his rage mounting. Whoever had done this was going to pay. He would make sure of that. No matter the cost. He kept going until he spotted something or someone on the ground up ahead. Jumping from the horse, he ran screaming no as he reached her. His ma was breathing but barely.

"They have Mia," his ma said breathing heavily. "Get her back. Please."

"Ma, I will get Mia but let me get you to help."

"No time. Go, find my daughter, please. I let you down. I cannot do that to her. Please, Almanzo. Please."

His ma beseeched him even as the blood mark spread. He stared at it in horror, torn between dragging her onto the horse and taking her back and doing what she wanted and going for his sister.

They both heard the horses at the same time. Almanzo turned around drawing his gun. David jumped off closely followed by Scott.

"Ma is hurt. Bad. They have Mia." Almanzo spoke quickly fighting back his horror and tears. "Can you take Ma to help? I have to get Mia."

"David, take Almanzo's ma back to the camp. Al, I am going with you."

"Thank you."

"I can come too," David suggested.

"No David, you are needed back there. They have so many wounded. Plus you will keep Paco in line," Scott's concern for his friend made his tone sharp.

"Paco's wounded?" Almanzo's heart jumped. Walking Tall should be with his father.

"Yes, but he'll live. If he's sensible!" Scott's facial expression was impossible to read. Almanzo hugged his ma. "I'm going to find Mia. Please hold on. We will be back."

His ma put her hand to his face. "I never stopped loving you. So proud..."

"Ma!"

"Al, she hasn't died. She's passed out. Go. I will look

after her, I promise," David said, lifting his ma gently from the ground.

Almanzo jumped back on his horse. Scott had already raced ahead so he pushed his horse to follow. He didn't want to think of how scared his little sister would be. He'd been terrified when he has abandoned alone but he had been a ten-year-old boy. She was a little girl. He kept riding hard hearing Scott speak to the two Indians with them. He spoke their language too fast for Almanzo to understand. He guessed he had told them to spread out and look for Mia as both Indians took off in different directions. They kept pushing the horses wondering just how far ahead of them the riders had got.

CHAPTER 41

*D*arkness fell and still no sign of the men or his sister. Almanzo wanted to keep going but Scott insisted on stopping. They had to rest the horses. It was too dangerous for the animals to continue pushing them at the pace they had taken.

"Do you think we missed them? We couldn't have been that far behind them," Almanzo asked breathing heavily.

"We haven't missed them but they got at least an hour start on what I imagine were fresh horses. We will find them," Scott said.

"You can't know that." Almanzo didn't know why he argued, maybe it was frustration at not catching Harvey and his friends.

"No, but I can promise you we won't go back until we find them," Scott snapped.

Almanzo knew his friend wasn't angry with him but with the situation, they were in. Ma was injured and Paco hurt. Maybe some other people Scott loved were also hurt. Walking Tall whistled before he walked into the camp leading his horse. The two Indians who had separated from them earlier soon answered him.

"We make camp here. My men will be back shortly. One has found something," Walking Tall said in greeting.

Almanzo stared at him in awe. Even after all these years, it amazed him how much the Indians could communicate in a series of what sounded like bird calls.

Without thinking, Almanzo started to prepare a fire. Walking Tall stopped him, a grin on his face. "This is why we can always track white men. You do not think beyond your stomach."

"I need coffee," Almanzo said churlishly.

"You need to keep out of sight. Smoke travels long distance."

Almanzo couldn't believe he hadn't thought of that.

"Don't blame yourself. You have more important things on your mind," Scott said as he came back from hobbling his horse.

"I swear I will scalp them myself if they touch a hair on her head," Almanzo meant every word.

"This is your Indian sister, the one you weren't at all sure you wanted."

Almanzo hung his head, shame coursing through his body. Scott had known despite Almanzo's words to the contrary. He had wished his ma would leave the Indian camp and Mia behind and come back to live in Portland with him. If Mia wasn't there, their neighbors would have less to speak about. How could he have been so selfish?

His ma would never have left her daughter. He wouldn't help the twinge of jealousy that ran through his blood but then his brain kicked in. His ma hadn't meant to leave him, she had done what she thought best to save his life. Now she was doing exactly the same for Mia. When he thought of the smiling little girl in the hands of strange men who didn't see her as a person, the rage boiled within him.

"Do not let anger cloud your vision. You have to focus. Find Mia first. Revenge comes later," Walking Tall counseled him as Scott fetched some water for the horses.

THEY SAT on the ground chewing some food. Walking Tall stopped chewing, listening intently his hand on the knife at his waist. The bird call came and he visibly relaxed. The two Indian scouts joined them. They spoke too fast for Almanzo to follow but he caught words here and there.

"What did they say?" Almanzo finally asked, losing patience.

"They have found the camp and your sister. It is up ahead, about an hour from here."

"So let's go," Almanzo jumped to his feet.

"There are twenty of them and only five of us. We need to plan this carefully. They know we are coming so we have lost the element of surprise.

"What then?" Almanzo was impatient to get going.

"Patience son, we can't risk your sister being killed," Scott said quietly

"She is still alive?" Relief made the tears spring into his eyes but he blinked them away.

"Yes," Scott said, "for the moment."

Almanzo tried to be patient as the Indians and Scott talked out their plan. Eventually, they decided on the best course of action. He waited as they outlined it.

"It's risky but it's the best chance we have," Scott said.

"They will kill her, won't they?" Almanzo asked even though he knew these men had no way of knowing how the kidnapper's minds worked.

"We won't give them time to do that," Walking Tall said, his hand gripping Almanzo's in a gesture of support.

The Indians were so convinced this was the best way Almanzo couldn't argue. Anyway, he didn't have a better plan. He agreed albeit reluctantly. They waited until it was nearly dawn and then they moved out but they took off in a different direction from where the men holding Mia were camped. As the Indians had said, they were expecting to be hit from behind. Scott had suggested getting in front of the kidnappers and coming at them from that direction. Hopefully, it would buy a little time. Almanzo had to grab Mia leaving five men to each of the other four. He thought the odds were dreadful but they seemed confident.

They pushed the horses hard as they made a wide arc. They didn't want to alert their target of their presence.

When they reached the spot Walking Tall had recommended, the brave let out a long bird call. Then they waited. Soon it was answered.

"Mia is a good girl. Very brave. Very quick." Walking Tall said approvingly making Almanzo feel proud of his sister. "She knows we are here. She will be waiting," Walking Tall confirmed.

The group hid the horses and then split up. Almanzo guessed his friends planned on getting the men alone, hopefully killing a couple to reduce the odds against them. He took the knife out of his waist. He had never killed anything before, well apart from when he went hunting but even then he used a gun. It was far less personal than a knife. But if he had too, he would. He had promised his ma, he would bring Mia home.

His heart thudding, he made his way carefully to where the men were camped. Keeping an eye out for sentries, he saw Scott take care of one of them. He had never seen Scott kill a man before. He didn't have any choice. There were too many of them and they didn't have time for backup. Almanzo moved on closer. He spotted his sister. She was looking around her but without moving her head. She was clever. She spotted him quickly and blinked rapidly. She didn't smile or otherwise show any sign she had seen him.

There was a man standing beside her but her gaze was focused on a group of trees to one side of the clearing. She wanted him to come from that side. What was she trying to tell him?

He moved closer but her look of alarm in her eyes told

him he had made a mistake. He retreated slightly and she relaxed a little but still kept looking in the direction the tree. Then he saw what she was trying to tell him. Harvey was hidden behind a bush, his gun aimed at Mia. Ready to hit anyone who tried to rescue her. Almanzo doubled back. He didn't know if any of the others would see Harvey. He couldn't take the chance. He had to deal with him. He had his knife. He made his way very slowly until he was standing behind Harvey. The man hadn't moved, his concentration focused on Mia, his finger hovering over the trigger. Almanzo didn't want to do anything to make that finger move. He hadn't come this far for Mia to die from a stray bullet. He had to disarm Harvey without giving him a chance to fire.

He took a step forward, snapping a twig in the process. Harvey swung around, shooting. Blackness descended, his last thought being one of Tilly….

CHAPTER 42

"Thank you, Mrs. Newland, I feel much better today. Fiona has been a great comfort to me," Tilly said to the pleasant lady whose house they were staying in.

"You girls are wise to stick together. A problem shared and all that. Goodness look at the time. Mr. Newland will think I have been kidnapped." Mrs. Newland was still talking as she left the room closing the door behind her.

Tilly jumped out of the bed and strode over to the window, all semblance of a girl grieving deeply had gone.

"Fiona, there is something wrong. I can feel it. Nobody has seen or mentioned Richard in the last two days."

"I thought you hated Richard. Why are you thinking about him?"

"I would prefer to know where he is. I saw him talking to Mr. Harvey the day before yesterday. They stopped talking when I walked by. I think they were planning something."

"Like what?"

"I don't know but Almanzo doesn't like Harvey. Says he can't be trusted."

Fiona grinned at Tilly. "Almanzo isn't fond of Richard either but I can understand his reasons."

Tilly flushed at Fiona's good-natured teasing. Almanzo hadn't come back after they had told him about their meeting with Richard. He'd left saying he had to speak to his friends and they heard nothing since. Maybe he was staying away on purpose? Was he shocked? No, it must be something else. Maybe his sister had returned. What was her name? Sarah. Or Rick was worse. She couldn't bear staying in town another day.

"Maybe we could take a ride out to see Bridget again?"

"Bridget? Is that what you are calling him these days?"

"Fiona, stop it. I am worried. I think Richard is planning something. Something horrible."

"You should go to see the sheriff. Tell him your misgivings about the rescue and what Richard has told you since."

Fiona was right. She should speak to the Sheriff. Richard had changed his story about the raid more than once. She didn't have anything concrete but maybe the Sheriff could investigate what Richard had said about her father's businesses. There had to be some paperwork proving Richard was not her father's sole heir despite what he said.

"We have to do something. I can't sit here all day."

The two women made their way to the sheriff's office. He was out but Deputy Davitt was there. He made the girls feel welcome. Fiona explained what Richard had said about the massacre.

"I know it's not much but how did he know those details? We never told him. He doesn't like me being friends with Tilly, I mean Miss Masterson."

"There is more. Richard Weston has told me my father made him his sole heir prior to us making this trip. Is it possible to check whether that is the truth? I know my father had some old fashioned views but making a man who wasn't family his heir, seems rather odd to me."

"Rather suspicious he died soon afterward too. Isn't it?" Fiona asked. If Tilly hadn't been distracted by her worries, she would have smiled at Fiona playing detective while batting her eyelashes at the single deputy.

"Thank you for coming in ladies. I will discuss this matter with the Sheriff and we will send a telegram to the sheriff's office in San Francisco. Perhaps they will be able to enlighten us. In the meantime, perhaps you ladies should continue to stay with Mrs. Newland. It might be safer than wandering around the countryside right now."

"But we hoped…"

"Thank you, Deputy. I promise Miss Masterson and I will not leave town without telling you first."

Fiona half dragged a protesting Tilly out the door. "Tilly, we need to get some horses."

"But I thought…"

Fiona nudged her friend before turning and smiling back at the deputy.

"You like him a lot don't you?"

"I wouldn't spit on him if he was on fire. Can't you see he is in on whatever is going on here? Up to his sweaty old armpits.'

Tilly looked at Fiona in confusion.

"Tilly Masterson, I didn't survive 14 years in the orphanage system without learning a trick or two. We need to get out of town. Now. Before it's too late. Do you have money in your purse?

Tilly nodded, not trusting herself to speak. She had thought Fiona had set her heart on the Deputy. Her friend had her totally fooled.

"Right let's go hire a buggy or some horses or something to get us to the Hughes place. We will be safe there."

Tilly followed this new Fiona toward the blacksmith. He agreed to rent them a buggy when they explained they were calling to see Jo Hughes.

"Ask Mr. Rick when he is coming back to school. My children miss his teaching."

"We will, thank you kindly Mr. Black."

The blacksmith laughed loudly startling Tilly. "Sorry Miss but my name ain't black. The men call me Blacky due to my job. You have a good day now." He turned his attention back to Fiona. "You look lovely today Miss Murphy. You take care now too, you hear?"

"Yes Blacky, I will. Say hi to the boys for me."

"Will do Miss Murphy."

Tilly looked at Fiona with new eyes. Blacky or whatever his name was, seemed smitten by Fiona and judging by the pink tinge to her friend's face, his interest was returned.

Fiona ignored her as she took the reins. "Can you drive?" Tilly asked her.

"No, but neither can you so between the both of us we will have to learn and fast."

They had only been to the Hughes place once, but it wasn't difficult to find. As they came down the track, they were met by Jo, Bridget, and Rick all fully armed.

"It's Tilly and Fiona. Why are you here? Who's chasing ye?" Bridget said, relief making her voice louder than usual.

"It's a long story but the short version is Fiona thought we would be safer here."

"Come inside and get something to drink. Carrie, can you take their rig to the barn please," Jo asked. " Give those poor horses a drink. You have run them hard on such a hot day."

Tilly apologized. "Sorry Jo, we wouldn't have pushed them but it was imperative we get out of town. Fiona thinks Deputy Davitt may be working with Richard."

"Your fiancé and Davitt? I find that hard to believe. Richard has only just arrived in town. Davitt has lived here years.

"Richard is working with a man called Harvey. We didn't make the connection until the other day when Almanzo called. Fiona remembered my father and Richard speaking about some connection in Portland. We think it was Harvey."

"Did you tell Almanzo?"

"Yes, why didn't he tell you? He said he was going to consult with you over some other issues..." Tilly trailed off not wanting to admit to these people everything Richard had said.

"We haven't had a chance to speak to Almanzo, he had to ride out in a hurry," Rick explained. "Davitt and Harvey are friendly, always have been from what I've heard. What did the sheriff say?"

"Before you answer my husband, come into the house. Otherwise, the both of you will melt."

Tilly pushed her hair back out of her eyes. Jo was right, the sweat was rolling down her back not that she would admit to it. Ladies didn't sweat.

They followed Jo into the kitchen and after several glasses of cool water, they told Rick, Jo, and Bridget the story of how Richard was now Tilly's father's heir. Bridget laughed when Tilly mimicked Fiona's attempts to flirt with the Deputy.

"Poor Davitt, I almost feel sorry for him. He hasn't had much luck in the female department."

"Given how bad he smells, and those teeth, I cannot say I am surprised."

"But how did Richard become your father's heir? Do you not have any other relatives?" Rick asked.

"Apart from me, you mean?" Tilly responded more sharply than she meant to be.

"Sorry Miss Masterson I wasn't trying to be rude but it would be normal for a guardian to be appointed as you are still underage. I would have thought your father would appoint a family member though."

"Well, Richard was my fiancé. My father's decision, my opinion didn't matter." Tilly knew she sounded bitter. She was.

"Even so, it seems rather convenient your father makes him his heir and then your father dies in a suspicious attack. What did Deputy Davitt suggest you do?"

"He said to stay with Mrs. Newland. He would tell the sheriff and send a telegram to San Francisco."

"That sounds sensible advice."

"Do you think we should have stayed in town?" Tilly asked, suddenly feeling bad at intruding on these people she barely knew.

"Not at all my dear. I believe you should always trust your instinct. My wife would welcome a distraction. Bridget loves to entertain so please feel welcome to stay as long as you wish."

"My husband is going to lie down ladies. I will be back in a few minutes. In the meantime, Bridget and Carrie will be happy to look after you."

"Thank you, Jo."

"Where is Almanzo?" Fiona asked Bridget as soon as Jo and Rick had gone. The Irish woman turned pale.

"He hasn't come back yet. He took off a few days ago. Miss Johanna and Mr. Rick are worried about him but they won't admit to that."

"Who is he with? Where did he go?" Tilly asked, her heart hammering against her chest.

"He rode out with Paco, Walking Tall and Scott Jones a couple of nights ago. "

"Where did they go?"

"We don't rightly know, Tilly. But don't you start worrying your pretty head about it now. Those Indians will keep Mr. Almanzo safe. They treat him as one of their own." Bridget sounded confident but she couldn't keep the worry from her eyes.

Tilly said a quick prayer to help Almanzo come home soon. She couldn't bear to lose him.

Bridget gave them small tasks to do, more to keep their minds and hands occupied rather than to make them work. They sat peeling beans and corn but there was no conversation. Each of the women was caught up in their own thoughts.

Jo came back about a half an hour later. "I believe you are right about Deputy Davitt. My husband likes to see the good in everyone but I haven't trusted that man in a long time. Is there anyone in San Francisco you know you can trust? Someone who would know your father's wishes?"

"Yes, his solicitor. He was my godfather. Used to visit us all the time until Mother died and Father and Richard became friendlier. I could send him a telegram." Tilly wondered how far the nearest telegraph office was. In San Francisco, you didn't have to walk that far to find one. Out here in the middle of nowhere, you probably had to travel miles.

"I think it would be best if you didn't go back into town for a while. Who knows you came here?" Jo said, her expression thoughtful.

"The man at the blacksmiths. He said to tell your husband his children were missing him."

"Blacky. He isn't a gossip. I will go into town and see what I can find out." Jo stood, taking her bonnet from the peg.

"Miss Johanna, I do not think that is wise. Let me go. People don't really take much notice of me."

"No Bridget, you stay here and look after everyone. I won't be long."

Bridget looked like she was going to argue but Jo's mouth was set in a determined line. Tilly stood up.

"I will go with you. You can't go alone."

"No thank you, Tilly. I think it's safer if you stay here." Jo said, her tone telling Tilly not to argue. "Give me your godfather's details. I know the man in the telegraph office, he is discrete."

Tilly wrote out the information for Jo while she went to tell her husband she was heading to town. Bridget kneaded some bread furiously. The women stood at the door waving Jo off. It would take her the best part of the day to drive the wagon into town and back. She had promised to call at Newlands store and if it was safe, she would bring back some of Tilly's and Fiona's personal belongings.

* * *

Tilly, Fiona, and Bridget spent the day doing chores and entertaining the children. Bridget laughed a lot at Tilly's expense.

"It is going to take you a while to settle down as a homesteader Miss Tilly. Didn't you ever do any chores at home?" Bridget asked as she showed Tilly how to peel a potato without losing half the vegetable.

Tilly colored as Fiona giggled.

"Miss Tilly dusted a bit sometimes but otherwise she left everything to us servants." Tilly made a sound but Fiona ignored her. "In fairness to Tilly, the mistress of the house would have needed sleeping salts if she saw her precious daughter working."

Tilly smiled at the reference to her mother. Fiona was being kind to her employer who would have taken to her bed for days rather than allow her child do anything menial.

"I am eager to learn. Fiona has shown me some things but I don't know anything about farming," Tilly said.

"You can come and milk the cow with me. I will show you how to do it," Nancy piped up, her little face lit up with excitement at the thought of showing an adult how to do something. "I won't let you near Daisy. She has a nasty temper and it hurts if she kicks."

"I don't think Miss Tilly is ready for milking just yet, Nancy darling."

The disappointment on the child's face caused by Bridget's remark was too much for Tilly.

"Of course I am. Why don't you take me to meet the

cows now and later we can milk them together?" Tilly bent down so she was the same height as Nancy.

Nancy beamed putting her tiny hand into Tilly's larger one.

"But Miss Tilly you are going to ruin your clothes," Bridget argued.

"Dresses can be washed," Tilly said, still holding Nancy's hand.

"That will be something I will be showing you how to do, next. Then you might be less willing to get covered in cow muck." Fiona grumbled making Bridget and Tilly laugh.

CHAPTER 43

"*H*e's coming round, careful now. Watch his arm,"
Scott shouted a warning.

Almanzo tried to lift his head but stopped at the pain.
His stomach roiled as the pain hit him in waves.

"Drink some of this my brother. It will help with pain,"
the child gave him a drink. He screwed up his mouth at the
taste but she insisted he drink more. He wanted to talk to
her. Ask her something but what? His mind strived for
information but instead found blackness. He gave in to it
again.

He came to sometime later. The men were speaking
very loudly, their noise hurting his ears.

"Why are you talking so loud?"

Walking Tall looked from David to Scott, his concern
obvious.

"Al, we are whispering. You were shot and you hit your

head hard when you fell. You will be fine but we want to try to get you back to town."

"Shot? Why?"

"Don't you remember son?" Scott asked leaving Almanzo to stare back at him. No, he didn't remember did he? He closed his eyes, screwing them up against the pain. He probed his mind but couldn't remember anything.

"Stop forcing your thoughts, it will come back. Mia, give him some more water please."

Mia was here. Of course she was, she had given him the horrible drink earlier. So where was ma? She wouldn't let Mia far from her sight? He tried to look around but any movement hurt.

"Al, you need to keep your neck straight just until Doc White has a good look at you. Can you do that?"

He would have nodded but couldn't. He opened his mouth but nothing came out. He blinked before he fell back asleep.

* * *

"Almanzo, oh my goodness what happened. Is he okay?"

"He's fine Jo. Don't touch him. We want Doc White to have a look at him. I couldn't get the bullet out."

"Bullet?" Jo swayed until Scott grabbed her arm, supporting her down the street as the other men carried Almanzo.

"Harvey shot him. He was lucky he wasn't killed."

Jo looked into Scott's face seeing it ravaged with pain.

She looked at the other men. David looked unhurt although he was filthy and exhausted.

"Who? What?"

"There was a raid on the village. By the time we got there, lots of people had been killed. Walking Tall took Mia back to his wife. She will look after her."

"Almanzo's ma?"

"Dead, like the Chief and many others. Paco...."Scott couldn't continue but stared over Jo's shoulder.

"Paco is dead?"

Scott shook his head but his eyes filled with tears.

"Oh Scott, I am so sorry. What can I do?"

"Stay with Almanzo. Where's Becky? Still at home?"

"Yes with ma. Rick didn't want any of us to leave but when Tilly and Fiona came, I had to come into town. Thank God I did."

Jo ran to the doc's office to check on Almanzo. Doc White prepared to operate straight away, worried about the length of time infection setting in but the wound looked clean. Jo sat waiting and praying. It was bad enough Rick was seriously ill but now Almanzo. She couldn't lose both of them.

David sat with her, having sent a man back to the homestead to tell Eva and Rick where they were. Scott had gone to his own home to make sure Becky and his children were alright.

CHAPTER 44

The minutes passed slowly as Doc did everything he could to save Almanzo's arm. He came out to tell them the operation had gone well and the bullet was out.

"Can I see him please?"

"Yes Mrs. Hughes but he may not make sense,' Doc White replied. "He is better than he looks though."

David held Jo's elbow and she was glad of her brother in law's support. They stepped into the small room, Jo's breath catching in her throat. Almanzo looked so young and fragile, not at all like the strapping 18 year old who had rode into town only a few days before.

"He's strong Jo and Walking Tall looked after him as best he could. You know those two are as close as brothers."

"Poor Walking Tall. Scott told me Paco was hurt bad."

RACHEL WESSON

"I don't think he will recover," David said sadly. "Harvey and his men attacked before we got there. Paco didn't stand a chance but he tried to save some of the women and children. You know what he's like."

Jo did know. Paco would do anything to help anyone else particularly a child. She leaned over and kissed Almanzo on the forehead. "You get better fast, you hear me. Your family needs you. A certain young woman is waiting for you at home. Tilly loves you," she whispered into her son's ear. He didn't even blink.

Jo let David escort her back to the waiting room. "Go home David, Eva has been going out of her mind worrying about you. You need a bath and some decent food. I will stay here."

"I can't leave you alone..." David said, but she saw he was desperate to see his wife and children.

"Yes, you can. I am not alone anyway. I will call to Mrs. Newland later. Rick might be well enough to come back into town tomorrow with you. Just don't let him overdo it. Please."

"You are a tough lady Mrs. Hughes and we all love you for it."

Jo blinked back the tears at the unexpected compliment. David was a lovely man but he wasn't very talkative. She squeezed his arm and then he was gone. She sat in the office praying as the time passed. Soon the door opened and Mrs. Newland appeared followed by Mrs. Bradley and Julia

"What are you doing here?" Jo asked.

"Mrs. Bradley and Julia are going to sit with your son and you are coming home with me for a hot meal, Doc White had the sense to come earlier. So come on now," Mrs. Newland said. "No arguments."

Jo closed her mouth again. There was no point in protesting and she was very hungry. "Thank you so much ladies, and you too Julia."

"It's the least we can do. What did Doc White say? Is Almanzo going to be alright?"

Jo tried to smile but she failed. "I don't know yet honey. Doc White is doing all he can but Almanzo still hasn't woken up. All we can do is pray."

"We can do that while you get something to eat and have a rest. Jo, your family needs you. You can't fall sick on them. Not now."

Jo recognized her friend's guidance for the good advice it was. She thanked them again before she followed Mrs. Newland outside. The older woman offered Jo her arm and so linked they walked down the street toward the store.

"I wish I could do something to ease your troubles, Jo."

"You do already Mrs. Newland. You are so kind not only to me but to Tilly and Fiona. Those girls really need a mother figure and you are perfect."

Mrs. Newland smiled although her eyes were still sad. "Rick Hughes is a real favorite of mine. I know I shouldn't admit that but from the day I met him on the trail, I knew he was a good one. Almanzo is another good soul. I can't understand that man above sometimes. Why not hurt the wicked and leave nice people alone?"

Jo didn't answer. What could she say? She glanced in the direction of home. How was Rick? He would be worried sick about Almanzo. She half expected him to come into town. What was that light on the horizon?"

CHAPTER 45

"Jo? Jo? What is it?" Mrs Newland's cry caught her attention.

Jo blinked her eyes again to clear them but it was still there. There was only one thing that would light up so bright from this distance. A fire. "Mrs. Newland, rouse the town. My home is on fire," she screamed at the startled woman as she picked up her skirts and ran toward Blacky's. Her screams emptied the saloon and some other buildings.

"Fire, fire," she roared as loud as she could. She banged on the door to Blacky's, who finally came running. "Mrs. Hughes, what's wrong?"

"Blacky, my home's on fire. Look!"

Blacky and some men followed the direction of her gaze.

"Seems that might be just a small grass fire Mrs. Hughes. You stay here in town and I will go check it out."

"Blacky, my husband and the girls are out there. I am going with you. Mrs. Newland, please look after Almanzo."

Mrs. Newland had arrived at Blacky's some minutes after Jo, her face smeared with dirt and tears. She nodded so breathless she was unable to speak.

"Come on Blacky, we got to go now," Jo insisted.

Blacky had saddled up two horses. Jo didn't care about who would see her riding astride wearing a dress. She got into the saddle arranging her skirts quickly around her knees and took off. Her family was in danger. She had to get to them.

As they raced, she wondered if David had reached them in time. His wife and children were in the building too. Along with Bridget, Tilly, and Fiona. She pushed the horse harder as they saw the flames in the distance. There was no mistaking it for a small grass fire now. It looked like the whole house had gone up. She prayed harder than she ever had before. Please let them have gotten out.

* * *

DAVID RAN toward her as she dismounted.

"Where is everyone?" she asked, the smoke and ash hitting the back of her throat.

"Don't know Jo. You got to stay back, we are trying to stop it spreading over the back roof."

"Stay back? Not on your life. My children are in there." Jo pushed up her sleeves and joined the row of people transferring water with buckets and goodness knows what else from the well to the flames. Loads more people had followed her from town and soon there were other teams of people passing buckets from the stream at the back of the house to fight the fire.

She saw Scott arrive followed later by her ma driving a wagon, Becky and the children in the back. They were kept away from the flames. Scott arguing with Becky who eventually agreed to pass out drinks of water to thirsty men. Jo kept praying and just when all hope had been lost, the rain came. It fell down heavily beating out the rest of the flames. She stood in the pouring rain watching her home. How on earth could anyone have survived that? She fell to her knees, the sight of her precious home a blackened ruin proving too much for her.

"Come on Jo love, come away. This isn't helping..."

"Ma, I can't. Everyone I loved was in there. Where are they?"

Della didn't answer, she didn't have to. It was written all over her face. She believed Eva, Rick, the children, and Bridget were dead.

"Tilly and Fiona were there too. They came to us for safety."

"Why? Why did they need protection?" David shouted at her

"Stop shouting David, can't you see the state of her."

"Sorry didn't mean to shout. I've been shouting at people all night. Jo, tell me, please. I am worried sick about Eva. Maybe she and the children went home?"

"Paddy checked your home. There is nobody there," Della said softly.

David sat on the ground beside Jo, his devastation painful to watch.

"Tilly and Fiona believed Richard Weston, the man from the massacre was working with Harvey and Deputy Davitt. They were frightened. They thought they were planning something."

"Harvey was too busy killing Indians and shooting Almanzo to worry about Tilly and Fiona," Jo spat.

"Almanzo was shot? Is he …."

"No Ma. he's with Doc White."

"Pa, pa …..

The three of them turned in disbelief at the sound of Eva's son calling David. Soon the little lad burst through the trees.

"I told them you would be here. They didn't want me to sneak out but I had to. That cellar smells real bad.'

"Cellar? Oh my God you got into the cellar. All of you?"

Her grandson didn't answer Della as David had him in a vice grip. Jo had already gone running in the direction the child had come from.

"Come on Della. We got a second chance.'

David half pulled, half dragged Della with him as he carried his son back the way the child had come. He had forgotten Rick had gone further with his cellar telling David he wanted a second means of escape from the house. They pushed through the vegetation until they came to what looked like a barn. Only the family knew the cellar ended here.

"Eva, come out darling. It's safe," David added his voice to Jo's who was shouting at her family to come out. Eva appeared, picking up her skirts and flying into David's arms. She was followed by Bridget carrying Lena and Carrie carrying Nancy. Tilly and Fiona came out holding hands, tears flowing down their cheeks. Jo hugged each one and then stood waiting. Rick would always be the last to leave, having made sure they were all safely accounted for. She smiled as she watched Della greet her daughter and grandchildren before glancing back at the building. Rick was taking his time. Was he ill? She pushed the door open but there was nobody inside.

CHAPTER 46

"*E*va, where's Rick?" Jo asked, a horrible suspicion making her stomach roil.

Eva paled, even more, right before her eyes.

"Isn't he with you? He said he was going for help. He told us to hide in the cellar. He wouldn't come with us. I thought when you were here he had come got you...." her sister's voice trailed off but Jo had stopped listening. She screamed Rick's name over and over and over again. He didn't come. Scott did. He slapped Jo hard holding her tight as the hysteria played out.

"Jo, Rick is a brave resourceful man. He loves you so much. We might still find him."

Jo looked into Scott's eyes knowing he didn't believe what he said.

"He's gone." she said.

* * *

IT TOOK some time to find Rick. He was lying near the front door, his gun by his side. To his left, lay Richard. The men carried Rick over to where his wife was waiting. She sat holding his body, crooning over him as if he was a new born babe. Her ma and sisters kept the children away. They knew their pa was gone. They didn't need to see this too.

Della moved to sit beside Jo, not touching her daughter but wanting Jo to know she was close. She waited as her child cried her eyes out for the man she loved. Della wiped away her own tears. She'd loved Rick like a son and would mourn his passing for the rest of her days. But she had to look after the living now. He would have wanted that.

"Jo, darling, let's go into town and see how Almanzo is doing."

"I can't leave Rick he needs me, Ma."

"Sweetheart, Rick will always be with you. Forever. His son needs you now. The girls want their ma. Come on darling. Let Rick go. We will ask Reverend Polk to do the service. Then you can say goodbye to him properly."

Jo looked at her husband's face. He almost looked like he was sleeping. He'd been shot in the back. She wished for a moment she'd been with him. There was no way she would have left his side, not for an instant.

"He died a hero protecting his family. Tilly and Fiona said he insisted they all get into the cellar. Eva was going to wait upstairs with him but he tricked her into going. He bought them time to get away. If he hadn't, the men would have found the cellar and then well... we don't want to think about what could have happened."

"Ma, I can't live without him."

"You can, and you will. You knew he was dying."

"Yes, but I thought we had some time together. Now, he's gone and I didn't get to say all those things I wanted to say. To tell him how I feel about him. How much I loved him. I love him so much ma."

"He knew that darling, everyone knows. You and Rick were a match made in Heaven. Nobody can take that from you. Try to take comfort from the fact he died a man. He protected his family. Family meant everything to Rick, you taught him that."

Jo closed her eyes remembering her first argument with Rick when she had believed he intended to abandon his nieces Carrie and Sarah. Sarah. How was she going to tell her? Where would she find her?

"Sarah….she doesn't know."

"Someone will tell her." Della knew she sounded dismissive but if she was honest Sarah was the last person on her mind. She was concerned about Jo and Almanzo. She didn't like the sound of what Scott had told her. Almanzo seemed to be badly injured and she wanted to be sure he wouldn't die. She didn't think Jo could cope with that on top of everything else.

"Come on darling, let's go. Al needs us. You need him."

Jo gave Rick one last hug before she placed him gently on the sheet beside her. She glanced up at Bridget who was crying softly beside her.

"Look after him for me please Bridget. I will be back later."

"Yes, Miss Johanna. I'll take right good care of him. I promise ye." Bridget's tears still flowed.

Jo gave her a weak smile in acknowledgment and then she stood up and taking her ma's arm walked toward the waiting wagon. She couldn't ride a horse back to town. Not in her state. As she walked, the people who were still gathered around parted allowing her passage. She spotted Tilly and Fiona, standing a little apart from everyone else. Fiona was crying on Tilly's shoulder but the older girl was staring into space, her white face frozen in an expression of terror. Jo shook off her ma's arm and went toward the younger women.

"Tilly, Fiona, come with me. We are going into town." Jo surprised herself by how normal her voice seemed.

Tilly stared at her, blinking rapidly but she didn't say anything. Fiona kept crying.

"Come on, into the wagon. We have to hurry," Jo repeated.

"Mrs. Hughes, this is all my fault." Tilly said, stopping Jo in her tracks. "I killed your husband just as surely as if I had pulled the trigger."

"Nonsense Tilly, you didn't do anything," Della said firmly.

"Richard was after me. He didn't even know your husband. If I hadn't been here, Rick would still be...."

"Dead," Jo replied, her voice cold. "Rick would have died soon from his illness. This way, he died saving people he loved. He may not have known you very long Tilly but he knew how important you were to our son. Please, get on the wagon now. I have to go see Almanzo."

Jo didn't wait to see if the girl followed her. She climbed into the wagon. They soon saw she was serious as they climbed in as well and then Della drove into town in silence. When they pulled up outside the clinic, Jo got down and walked in.

Tilly and Fiona weren't sure what to do.

"Mrs. Thompson, I tried to apologize to Jo but …. Well I don't know if she understood. She seems so…"

Della knew what the girl was trying to say. Jo seemed unemotionally involved but that was her daughter's way of coping. She would fall apart later in private. "Jo is dealing with things the best way she can. She always did put others first. She is very worried about Almanzo but she is concerned about you two as well. We all are."

"But it's our fault. If we hadn't gone to the homestead, Rick would still be alive. I told Tilly we had to go out to your family. I shouldn't have said anything," Fiona wailed as Tilly held her hand tightly.

"The only person responsible for what happened to my son in law is the man who pulled the trigger. You girls are not to blame. Rick would have insisted on protecting you. That was the man he was. Never believe you were to blame. Nobody in our family thinks that. Why don't you go with Mrs. Newland to her house, have a bath, get some rest and then come back? I am sure Almanzo would love to see you when he wakes up." Della smiled kindly but Tilly's reaction astounded her. The girl picked up her skirts and practically ran away. She looked at Fiona who stared after Tilly before turning to Della.

"I'm very sorry Mrs. Thompson, she is so upset. I will look after her." Fiona left too leaving Della with Mrs. Newland.

"I heard the news, Della. I can scarcely believe Rick Hughes is dead. He was a wonderful man, a good friend, neighbor and an amazing teacher. He did so much for this town. We shall miss him." Mrs. Newland wiped a tear from her face. "My home is yours for as long as you need it. Please tell Jo the same."

"Thank you, Dorothy. I must go in and see how my grandson is doing."

Della took the hug Mrs. Newland offered and then turned, taking a deep breath and headed into the doctor's clinic. She hoped and prayed good news awaited her.

CHAPTER 47

Tilly didn't care who saw her running through the street and into the store. She wanted to pack her bag and leave this town. It was one thing her life being in ruins but she had destroyed a whole family. Almanzo would never forgive her but even if he did, she couldn't forgive herself.

"Tilly, wait. Nobody blames you. None of this was your fault," Fiona cried but Tilly didn't look up.

Tilly took the small trunk Mrs. Newland had lent them and started throwing her things into it.

"Tilly, where are you going?"

"I don't know but we're leaving. We should never have gone there. Rick Hughes would still be alive." Tilly's heart beat faster. She closed her eyes but opened them again just as quickly. She could smell the smoke, the fear, hear Rick ordering them into the cellar. Eva arguing with him but he insisting they take the children to safety. He'd

296

promised to follow but at the last minute closed the trap door and put something on top. Eva had tried to open it but despite Tilly, Fiona and Bridget helping, it wouldn't move.

"Tilly, Rick knew what he was doing. He sacrificed himself so we could live. You can't repay that by running away. You need to stay here. Almanzo needs you by his side."

Tilly raised her tear stained face to Fiona. "Would you want me if I killed your father? He must hate me."

"Yes I would and no he doesn't. Now stop feeling sorry for yourself and help me get the bath ready. We both need to clean up and get back to help. Jo is at the hospital but the Hughes homestead needs cleaning. We have to salvage what we can. Standing around here crying isn't going to help anyone," Fiona spoke sternly as Tilly stared at her. Then she hugged Tilly close. "Tilly, you have wanted a loving family as long as I have known you. Someone to love you for the person you are rather than the person your parents felt you should be. You've found that with Almanzo. Don't throw it away. Don't let Master Richard take that from you too."

Tilly tried to smile at Fiona's intentional use of the word Master but she was too upset. She wanted to believe her friend but...the fire, the devastation, Almanzo being shot, it was all too much.

"Tilly you've fought back from the minute I met you. You can't stop fighting now."

Tilly hiccuped. "I don't think I can face those people."

"You have to. This isn't about you, Matilda Masterson, and the sooner you learn that the better."

Fiona slammed the door behind her leaving Tilly staring after her. She sat on the bed as shame overwhelmed her. Fiona was right. She was being selfish, running away instead of staying here facing up to what happened and helping the innocent victims rebuild their lives. Nancy and Lena had lost their father, Carrie too would need support and Jo. Almanzo was hurt, she didn't even know how badly.

She didn't need a bath. She needed a quick wash and then she'd go to the clinic. She had to see him. If only for a couple of seconds to see he was alright.

* * *

WHEN FIONA RETURNED, she looked a little sheepish. "I have the water boiling on the stove. I'm sorry for shouting at you."

"Don't be. I deserved it. But I don't have time for a bath. I have to check on Almanzo," Tilly said.

"I'm coming too. We need a quick wash and can have a bath later."

The girls washed up and changed before heading back to the clinic. As they approached they saw Scott up ahead.

"How is Almanzo?" Tilly asked.

"He hasn't regained consciousness yet. The doc is worried about him and Jo."

"Jo?"

"She just sits and stares at him, hasn't made a sound. Della tried to get her to go back with her but she refused."

Tilly hugged herself. Poor Jo was probably trying to make sense of what had happened. "Can I go in?"

"Yes, try to get Jo to rest if you can. I have to go to speak to the Sheriff."

Tilly was about to push the door when she remembered Broken Wing. "Mr. Jones, what happened to Almanzo's ma?"

Scott stared at the ground before looking up, a bleak expression on his face. "We were too late. She died along with most of the Indians who sheltered you."

Tilly blinked back the tears. "Does he know?"

"He knew she was injured. She sent him to rescue Mia."

Tilly's heart nearly stopped. The sweet little girl with the lovely smile who'd helped Broken Wing to look after them. "Oh no, please tell me Mia survived."

He nodded. "Walking Tall has her. She is safer with Paco and his friends at least for the moment."

Tilly noticed the strain when he mentioned Paco but she didn't want to inquire any further. He seemed in a hurry to get going.

She took a deep breath and pushed open the door of the clinic. Doc White looked up and showed her into Almanzo's room.

She stared at his white face. He looked so young lying on the bed, so vulnerable. His arm was in a sling but otherwise, he looked unmarked.

"Can I speak to him?" She asked the doctor.

"Please do. I don't know if he can hear you though." The doctor put his arm on Jo's shoulder. "Mrs. Hughes I am ordering you to bed. You need to rest."

Jo didn't reply but sat holding Almanzo's hand in hers, staring at him.

"Jo, please try to rest. I will look after Almanzo for you," Tilly said softly.

Jo looked up into her face. "I can't lose him as well."

"You won't. But you have to do what the doctor says. The twins need their ma."

Jo didn't blink but stood up and followed the doctor out of the room.

"She is going to make herself ill," Fiona commented.

"It's her way. I can't imagine what she is going through. They were so much in love."

Fiona let out a sob but tried to turn it into a cough. Tilly gave her a quick hug and then turned her attention to Almanzo. Drawing the chair closer to the bed, she sat and held his hand.

"Tilly, I am going to go ask Blacky to take me out to the homestead. I need to work."

Tilly nodded in response to Fiona, not taking her eyes off Almanzo. She heard the door close behind her.

"Almanzo, I know you can hear me. You need to wake up. Jo needs you. The girls want their big brother back. You can't sleep anymore," Tilly said softly watching his face for a reaction but none came. She continued talking about this and that, all the time stroking his hand.

CHAPTER 48

Almanzo saw gray instead of black. Flickers of light. He heard her speaking to him. Tilly. She was here. But where were they? He tried to open his eyes wider but they wouldn't move. He had to let her know he could hear her. Forcing his fingers to move, he tried to squeeze her hand.

"Almanzo, you moved. I know you did. Do it again."

He tried but this time his body wouldn't co-operate.

"Darling, please try. I need you to tell me you can hear me. Can you open your eyes?"

He heard her desperation. Straining hard, he focused on his eyes. He had to open them, he just had too.

"You did it, you're going to get better."

He winced as she kissed him, her body hitting against his wound.

"Oh I hurt you, I'm so sorry. Doc White, Doc White, come in here quick…"

She was making so much noise his head hurt. He wanted to tell her to be quiet but his mouth wouldn't work. The wave of blackness started falling, he was ready to sleep once more.

"Don't you dare go back to sleep. You have to show the Doc and Jo you're awake. Listen to me."

How could he do anything but listen? She was screaming at him. He opened his eyes again – making out not figures but murky images. Then he closed them as the brightness hurt. This time he was going to sleep.

"He's passed out again hasn't he?"

"Yes Miss but that is okay. His body and mind need to recover. The fact he regained consciousness means he should be okay now. Mrs. Hughes, it may take a while but your son is coming back to us."

Jo stared at Almanzo and then the doctor before her eyes came to rest on Tilly. "Thank you," she murmured.

Tilly moved off the bed quickly and drew Jo into a hug. "Mrs. Hughes, Jo, please go and rest now. Let your family look after you. The twins are worried and scared. They need their ma. Bridget wants to look after you too."

Jo's body shuddered as Tilly held her. The racking sobs brought tears to Tilly's eyes. She continued to hold Jo carefully as one would a child. She knew crying would help. Doc White disappeared and soon afterward, his assistant came in with a cup of tea for both of them.

"Doc White put extra sugar in it too. He's gone with Mrs. Newland. Seems a baby is in a hurry to be born."

Tilly smiled at the lady, thanking her for the tea. She

helped Jo sit down and then held the tea cup out to her, encouraging her to drink. As she drank, Jo started to talk about Rick. How they'd met, their wedding and their plans for the future. Tilly listened, sucking in her breath more than once as she tried to stop the tears falling.

"I was lucky Tilly. The love Rick and I shared, well it's rare. I know there are plenty of married people in Oregon but how many of them are as happy as we were?"

"He was a lovely man. He saved my life. I feel guilty for causing him to lose his."

Jo put the cup to one side and took Tilly's hands in hers. "Please don't feel that way. Rick died doing what he needed to do. Protecting his family and those they love. If you love Almanzo, Rick's son, as much as he did, that's payment enough."

"I do love him, Jo…"

"But?"

"What about the people of Portland? They don't care much for my having returned from the Indian camp. I don't want my reputation to adversely affect Almanzo. He is respected around these parts."

"Tilly Masterson, if I was feeling a little stronger, I would shake you. The local gossips will be talking about something new next week. You and Fiona were victims of a scheming madman just the same as Rick was. Nobody worth anything could hold that against such wonderful women. Now don't let me hear you talk that way again."

Tilly didn't reply, she couldn't.

They both sat in silence watching Almanzo's chest rise and fall with each breath. He looked like he was smiling.

"Did you know his ma died?" Tilly spoke without thinking. "Sorry, I meant Broken Wing."

"Yes, Scott told me. Almanzo will be devastated, he was so happy about finding her."

"Well, at least they got to find each other and make up before she died. Too many times people die without getting that chance."

"Are you talking about your father?" Jo asked gently.

"Not really. My father and I were never close. I was thinking of Fiona really, something she said a while ago about her parents. She doesn't know who they were or anything about them."

"That must be difficult. But she has a good friend in you."

"I think she may have found something more in Portland." Tilly thought of the way Blacky and Fiona acted around each other. Blacky was a widower with young children. Fiona could have the family she craved and a good man too. If only there was some money left over from her father's estate to give to Fiona as a wedding gift. She smiled at herself thinking of weddings when Fiona hadn't even admitted to liking Blacky in that way.

"Jo, did anyone say why Richard was trying to kill everyone?"

"No. I haven't spoken to anyone. Scott went to see the sheriff. Do you want to go and find out what is going on?"

Tilly shook her head firmly. "I want to be here when Almanzo wakes up. Everything else can wait."

Jo picked up her shawl and with a last kiss to Almanzo's forehead, she said, "I am going to find my girls. I will be back soon but I know he is in good hands."

"Thank you." Tilly stood and kissed Jo on the cheek then took her seat once more holding Almanzo's hand. As the time passed, her eyes grew heavy and she fell fast asleep still holding his hand.

$\mathcal{A}$lmanzo watched her sleep, content to lie there holding her hand. She snored softly making him laugh. Wait until she woke up and he would tease her about that. Girls hated knowing they snored.

Watching her, he thought of the events of the last few days. He knew his ma was dead. Her injuries had been too bad to recover from. He wondered if they had buried her yet. He hoped she had been given a traditional Indian burial as she seemed to have found peace with the tribe. He should check on Mia although he knew Walking Tall would look after her. His thoughts turned to Rick. He'd heard Jo and Tilly talking, not that they knew he was listening.

Rick was dead. It was hard to get that into his head yet he knew the man he considered his true father had died in the way he wanted. He had protected his family and Almanzo's girl. Almanzo held Tilly's hand tighter. Somehow, he would live through the hurt of losing those closest to him so long as this woman was by his side. They had a future thanks to the actions of Ma and Rick.

She stirred as he stroked her hand, her eyes opening slowly. She flushed a pretty pink catching him watching her.

"You're awake," she whispered.

"Couldn't sleep, someone kept snoring."

The tinge of pink grew darker. "I don't...." she stopped realizing he was teasing her. She kissed his hand. "How do you feel?"

"Like a bear played with me for an hour or so," he responded.

"Almanzo, you had us so worried. When you didn't wake up, we thought..."

"Don't Tilly. I'm alive and I will be fine. I need you to call Doc White to help me out of the bed. It wouldn't do for you to see me undressed. Not until we are married."

Tilly flushed such a deep color, she lit up the room. Springing back from the bed, she got flustered. "Heavens, I'll get the doc. Oh, he isn't here. He's gone to a birth. What, who..."

Almanzo was laughing now. She was in such a tizzy. She glared at him.

"Sorry, Tilly but you are not exactly helping. Just go outside and I will sort myself out."

"I can't let you try to get out of bed alone. I'll stay here but close my eyes. If you feel dizzy you can call me."

They were rescued by Doc Whites assistant who came in on hearing the laughter.

"Come on Miss, out you go and let the patient get dressed. Almanzo Price, you ain't got anything I never saw before. Now get dressed lad I don't have all day."

Tilly ran leaving him to the tender mercies of Doc White's assistant who was old enough to be his grandmother, not that it reduced his embarrassment any.

Thankfully, he was only slightly dizzy as he managed to get dressed. But the effort tired him out. He had to lie down again but this time fully clothed. Tilly came back in fussing over him, telling him he should have stayed in bed for a while to get better.

"Tilly Masterson if you keep nagging me, I am never going to marry you."

She stopped talking long enough to stick her tongue out at him. Surprising her, he grabbed her arm with his good hand and pulled her down to the bed for a kiss.

"Almanzo, the assistant may come back in."

"You heard her. Nothing she ain't seen before," he said before claiming her lips again. "I love you Miss Masterson and I don't care who knows it."

"I love you too Mr. Almanzo."

CHAPTER 50

"Tilly, Sheriff Rodgers is coming. You best tell the rest of them."

Tilly nodded in response before going into the house to tell Della, Jo and everyone else. They walked outside waiting for the Sheriff to dismount.

"Want some coffee, sheriff?" Della asked.

"In a minute please Mrs. Thompson," he replied before turning to Tilly. "I knew I recognized your Mr. Weston."

"He was not my Mr. Weston," she protested but the man didn't listen. He was too caught up in his story.

"His real name was, I believe, Henry Furlong and in 1840 he married the 14-year-old only child of a wealthy businessman by the name of Menton. He had been married before, a few times actually. Two years after the marriage, Menton was dead leaving all his riches to his daughter and her husband."

Tilly paled. Richard had done this before. "How did Mr. Menton die?" she asked.

"We are not sure my dear. Some said it was natural causes, others believe he was poisoned."

"What happened to his daughter, Richard's wife?" Tilly asked

"She died, in childbirth."

"The poor lady. At least Richard didn't murder his wife."

"Well, I guess not although by abandoning her, he left her in poverty. He ran off with another woman but she too was abandoned in San Francisco." The sheriff's tone left nobody in doubt who he held responsible for the woman's death.

Tilly shuddered. "How did my father meet him? He was always so careful with his business and his money."

"I believe your father was introduced to Weston by a mutual acquaintance, a US senator. Your father…" the man coughed as his cheeks turned pink.

"My father…" Tilly prompted. "Please speak freely. You cannot possibly diminish his reputation any further in my eyes."

The man coughed before continuing. "It would appear your father had made several investments in what one would call unsavory businesses. The risk versus the potential return was enough to ensure your father and men like him closed their eyes to the actual business practices. The results made people rich so they didn't ask any questions."

"What type of business was my father involved in, Sheriff?" Tilly's voice shook prompting Almanzo to step closer to her.

"Among other things, your father owned part of a slave plantation in the south. There are also a number of houses of ill repute."

Tilly sank into a seat as she swayed. Her father owned slaves and invested in brothels.

"Sheriff, does Miss Masterson really need to hear the rest of these details?" Almanzo asked, his tone slightly belligerent due to his worry for Tilly.

"Please continue Sheriff Rodgers. I want to know the truth. For once," Tilly said firmly.

The sheriff bowed his head slightly before continuing. "Mr. Weston wanted to run for office and believed he had a better chance in Oregon. He had a number of friends including your father, willing to vouch for him. His intent, we believe, was to marry you and become more respectable. Once he became a senator, then who knows what he was planning to do. He had a lot of supporters. People including our own…"

"George Harvey. I knew they were connected," Almanzo said.

"But why, if they were friends, did Richard kill my father?" Tilly asked Sheriff Rodgers.

"That my dear is not clear. We suspect from what Harvey has told us, your father may have changed his mind. It appears he may have had second thoughts about your relationship with Mr. Weston."

"I doubt that. They must have fallen out over money,"

Tilly said so quickly, the other people in the room smiled. She flushed not realizing she had spoken aloud.

"If your father treated money more highly than you darling, he deserved everything he got and more," Almanzo said with conviction.

"Almanzo, nobody deserves to be murdered," Jo remonstrated with her son.

"That's a matter of opinion Mrs. Hughes," Sheriff Rodgers said dryly.

"But why did Richard come after Tilly?" Almanzo asked.

"We don't believe he did. I know it looks that way but I think he may have been after David or more precisely Mrs. Clarke and the children.

"Eva? He wanted my sister and her babies" Jo said, her voice trembling with horror.

"Harvey told us Richard seemed to believe David Clarke knew all about his scheme and would publish information in the paper. He planned to take Mrs. Clarke hostage to blackmail David," Sheriff Rodgers explained to the startled group. "I think Mr. Weston may be completely mad."

"That's an understatement. I didn't know anything about Mr. Weston or his business dealings. I spoke to H…."

"Harvey. I knew he had to be involved in this," Almanzo interrupted. "Sheriff I know you can't lock him up for killing Indians but can you not press charges against him now? He killed my ma and she was white."

The sheriff looked so embarrassed Tilly felt sorry for

him. "I know son but from what I heard your ma looked and dressed like an Indian. Harvey couldn't have known she was white."

"He knew," Almanzo's tone suggested he could kill Harvey himself. Tilly gripped his hand tighter.

"Can't you try Harvey for shooting Almanzo?" Jo asked.

"No Mrs. Hughes, we don't have any witnesses. Almanzo doesn't remember who shot him and nobody else saw."

"What Sheriff Rodgers means is nobody white saw. I was busy but my Indian brothers saw him lift the gun and shoot Almanzo. Mia, Almanzo's sister also witnessed the attack." Scott's opinion about the law was clear from his expression.

Clearly uncomfortable, Sheriff Rodgers fingered his hat, the sweat beading on his forehead. "Now you good folks know I don't hold with Indians not being allowed to give evidence but the fact is my hands are tied. I can't try Harvey on the word of an Indian or a half breed."

"Don't call her that," Almanzo spat.

"Sorry son didn't mean no disrespect."

"It just isn't good enough. Nothing is going to stick to Harvey. He will get away with it." Almanzo put into words what the rest of them were thinking.

"Not necessarily," Fiona said, her eyes twinkling.

Everyone turned to look at the young Irish girl. "What are you up to now?" Tilly asked.

"We know Harvey knew Master Richard. Harvey

doesn't know how much we know so let's see if we can bluff him into telling us."

Everyone stared at Fiona. "You are all looking at me as if I have a bush growing out of my head. As I told Tilly, you don't survive in the orphanage system to the age of fourteen without learning a thing or two. Tilly can pretend she knows everything."

"But I don't. I only know what Sheriff Rodgers told us," Tilly said.

"Yes but Harvey doesn't know that," Fiona replied. "From what the others have said, he is a greedy little varmint and he thinks you are really well off."

"He hates me. He isn't going to believe Tilly would be on his side," Almanzo said, looking skeptical.

"He will if you and Tilly have a very public argument," Fiona insisted. "Perhaps about her owning a slave plantation. He knows your views on the subject. Tilly can pretend she feels the same as Harvey."

"I am not sure I am that good an actress," Tilly said doubtfully.

"You never let on to your parents we were friends, did you? You lived in their house. He'll believe you. He's a man and won't be able to resist a pretty face.'

"Nice to hear you have such a high opinion of us men, Miss Murphy! Come on folks, let Tilly talk this over with Almanzo. I need some coffee and some of Bridget's pies."

"Trust you to think of your stomach Scott Jones," Della called as the crowd dispersed into Della's house. Jo and her children had moved in until their home could be repaired.

"I don't know if this is a good idea Tilly, you could get hurt."

"I won't. You won't be far away. We have to try. He and his friends killed too many people, your ma, Rick, and my father plus those men and women traveling in our wagon train."

"Are you sure?" Almanzo asked, his eyes telling her she didn't have to do this.

Tilly wasn't at all sure she wanted to have anything to do with Harvey but she needed to do something. It would help ease the guilt she still felt over Rick being killed.

"None of this was your fault, Tilly."

She smiled at Almanzo as he put his arms around her gathering her close to him. "I know but I can't help how I feel. This may help."

"I hope Fiona knows what's she doing."

Tilly didn't reply but reached up to touch her lips against his.

"When this is over, will you marry me?"

"I thought you would never ask."

"I did but you were otherwise engaged if I remember correctly," he teased, the expression of love in his eyes making her breathless.

"Oh you, don't bring him into it again."

Almanzo captured her lips once more. There was no more talk or thoughts of anyone else.

CHAPTER 51

PORTLAND

Tilly quelled the nerves in her stomach. She was doing this for Almanzo and his family. She owed Rick and wanted Harvey and his friends to be convicted for their part in the tragedy. They stood in the center of the boardwalk near to the hotel.

"He's coming. Look unhappy," Almanzo prompted. Tilly tried to slap Almanzo's hand away but he grabbed her wrist holding it in a vice like grip.

"Nice to see your true colors, Miss Tilly. Just wanted a little fun until you buried your rich fiancé?"

She tore her hand free and slapped his face. "I didn't start anything as well you know. You kissed me first you varmint!"

"Excuse me Miss Masterson but is this man bothering you? Could I walk you to Mrs. Newlands?"

"Why thank you Mr...."Tilly flashed her eyelashes hoping she wasn't overdoing it. The man in front of her pushed his chest out as he swept his hat from his head. She stared at the buttons on his waistcoat straining across his belly.

"George Harvey, Miss at your assistance. Get lost farm boy," Harvey snarled at Almanzo as he held out his arm to Tilly. She took it giving Almanzo a dirty look in the process. At the look in his eyes, she wondered if she had been too convincing.

Mr. Harvey walked on a little bit, his grip on Tilly's arm forcing her to accompany him.

"Miss Masterson, I meant to pass on my condolences for the loss of your fiancé. Such a terrible tragedy. I hope it hasn't made you make plans to leave our little town."

Tilly forced a smile. How did anyone bear being near this idiot? She wished Fiona had been the one to make eyes at him. She wasn't nearly as good an actress as her friend believed her to be.

"Actually Mr. Harvey, may I call you George? I am a little bewildered. Between losing my father and Richard, I find myself all alone. I am rather worried I am vulnerable."

"My dear young lady, we can't have you feeling like that," he said, insincerity dripping from his words. "Why don't we go for a cup of coffee? We can sit in the hotel lounge and talk for a while."

"Thank you kindly. I would like that. I need a business-man's advice."

Tilly almost laughed as George Harvey puffed out his chest even further. Did he really believe he was that irre-sistible to women? She noticed a few people staring at her, walking down the street her hand on his arm. For a second she worried about her reputation and then decided to let them talk. They had little enough to worry about.

She sat at the table and waited for George to find a waiter to bring coffee. Fiona came in a few minutes later in the company of Blacky and Mrs. Newland. They sat at a nearby table, not too close to cause comment but close enough to come to her rescue. She relaxed a little bit.

George came back and took a seat, his knee uncomfortably close to hers. She wondered what Richard had told him about her. She decided to follow the script she had prepared with Almanzo, Scott and the Sheriff.

"What were you and young Price arguing about? It looked very serious. I thought you were friends." Harvey took a sip of his drink, his eyes assessing her. She swallowed hard, not wanting to mess this up.

"Friends? With a man like that?" Tilly held a hand to her chest, using a shocked voice. "I had to appear to be grateful for him rescuing Fiona and I."

"Richard didn't approve of him."

"Yes, I know and I quite agreed with my poor fiancé. Did you know his mother lived with the Indians? She was killed in that last raid."

"She shouldn't have been living with them. No decent woman would do that. She got what she deserved. Pity her kid got away."

Tilly's heart beat faster. How would he know Mia was unhurt if he hadn't been there. She gripped the table. What a vile man he was. She wanted to tip his coffee over him but instead, she smiled despite it hurting her face. She had to keep up the pretense to help Almanzo.

"I didn't hear about her child. Where is she now? In town?"

Harvey's eyes darkened as he looked at her, a suspicious frown on his face. She had to change the topic and quickly.

"Look, Mr. Harvey, forgive me for being blunt but I really don't care about the Indians. I have a problem and I need help." Tilly looked around her as if worried she would be overheard. Then she leaned closer to Harvey. "My father left some investments. I found out they include some land and other property down South. Mr. Price and his family believe I should hand them back to their rightful owners."

"Why? Your father didn't steal these investments did he?" Harvey asked.

"No of course not but..."Tilly lowered her voice and moved closer t him, "some people would not approve. He owned some slaves."

Harvey laughed a grotesque sound which made Tilly want to pick up her skirts and run. "Oh my dear, what nonsense. Your father was obviously an astute business-man. There is lots of money to be made in those and similar investments. If I told you how much I earned from recent sales of Indian lands you would marry me today."

"Marry you, sir?" Tilly hid an amused look as an air of panic crossed his face. "I'm afraid I am not in the market for a husband. I must mourn my fiancé."

"Of course, my dear. Quite right too. I didn't mean to be

uncouth. Now about these investments, what do you think you will do with them?"

"I was considering selling them but I believe it can be difficult. I also have some other items which, well, that is to say, I am not sure how my father came to own them."

"Can you tell me more?" Harvey asked.

Tilly hesitated as if she was afraid to trust him.

"Come Miss Masterson. You of all people must have known how close myself and Richard were. We owned a number of similar investments, in fact, he owns a share of my business on the docks."

Tilly smiled graciously. "Forgive me, Mr. Harvey. You can't be too careful especially a woman alone. Richard told me some of his business dealings but he didn't think I needed to know the details. I was going to ask Deputy Davitt for help, he seems so knowledgeable. But then I was worried. I mean, I don't think what my father did was legal." She whispered the last word so Harvey had to lean closer to hear her.

"Davitt does as he is told. Don't worry about him. How many investments are we talking about?"

"About twenty thousand dollars, I believe. My father seems to have owned a number of properties. I found several bills of sale only the money he had hidden in the wagon appears to have gone missing. I meant to ask Richard if he knew where it was but now. Oh Richard, how could he die and leave me?" Tilly started sobbing, blowing her nose loudly. She toned it down at bit at the dirty look

Fiona sent in her direction but Mr. Harvey appeared to be falling for her act.

"Please don't distress yourself my dear Miss Masterson. Such matters are not for a young lady to concern herself with. As it happens, Mr. Weston had confided in me some of the details you mention. I may be able to help you liquidate some of your father's holdings."

"But I don't remember my father owning so many properties. He never mentioned anything to mother."

"I expect he didn't. Women don't have the brains for this type of investment. You leave it all to me. I will take care of things."

"Can you really sell everything and give me the cash? I know it's vulgar to speak of money but I wish to return home. I don't want to stay in this town any longer than I must."

"Of course I can do that. There will be a small fee for my services you understand."

"But of course Mr. Harvey, George." Tilly patted him on the arm but when he moved closer she drew away hastily.

"Where are the papers Miss Masterson?"

"I hid them in Richard's room. I guessed that would be the last place people would look but the hotel has asked me to clear the room out by tomorrow."

"I can take his things for you. In fact, why don't we go to the room now and pack up his trunks."

Tilly adopted a horrified expression. "I can't go into a hotel room alone with you, Mr. Harvey. What would people say?"

He looked aggrieved for a moment.

"My maid, Miss Murphy, is having tea with a couple of her friends. Would you like her to accompany us? She is discrete – it helps she can't read or write."

"Well if you insist. I would prefer it was the two of us but I expect people will talk and I do have a reputation to consider." Tilly coughed. "And of course you do too Miss Masterson," he said patting her knee. She wanted to kick him.

Tilly called him every bad word she could think of as she walked across the room to speak to Fiona who came immediately acting the part of a dutiful maid. She even curtsied to Harvey. "My mistress said you require my help with packing."

"Miss Masterson will instruct you. We don't have all day so put your back into it," Harvey replied dismissively.

Fiona scowled at him, she didn't need any acting skills to show him what she thought. Tilly had to hide a smile. They walked up the hotel stairs toward the room. Harvey producing the key making Tilly curious as to how often he had searched the room before.

"Oh, I am so silly I forgot my shawl. Could you be a dear and retrieve it for me please Mr. Harvey?"

CHAPTER 52

George looked nothing like a gentlemen as he rushed back down the stairs leaving Tilly and Fiona alone for a few minutes. Fiona pulled the package out from under her skirt and shoved it under the mattress. Then she stood waiting, looking so innocent butter wouldn't melt in her mouth. George returned.

Tilly looked in a couple of places before turning to the mattress. "I believe he said it was kept in the best place so that must be it," she said pointing at the mattress.

"Under his bed?" Came the dubious sounding reply

"Well, the mattress. Under the bed would be easily uncovered."

Tilly couldn't look at Fiona as George pulled out the documents. Just as he laid them out on the bed, Fiona opened the door.

"Rather warm in here don't mind me opening the door do ye, Sir?"

"Shut that door, you stupid girl," He barked back

Fiona shut the door reluctantly.

Tilly grabbed one of the papers, "it says here something about …."

She didn't get to finish as the door burst open admitting the sheriff and some other men, Almanzo among them.

"What's the meaning of this? What are you doing here?" Harvey protested loudly as he pushed the papers to the floor.

"Protecting my fiancé from your evil games. What are you doing here?" Almanzo answered, drawing Tilly close.

"Fiancé? Who? You and her? Don't make me laugh. Even you are not low enough to marry an Indians leavings!"

Almanzo raised his fist but Tilly got in first as she whacked Harvey across the face. Her palm stung but it was worth it.

"Don't even think about it," Almanzo replied as Harvey took a step in Tilly's direction

"What's going on in here, Harvey," Sheriff Rodgers drawled.

"Mr. Harvey admitted everything to me, Sheriff. He told me about killing the Indians and selling their land. He offered to sell all my father's land claims even though I told him there were no such properties."

"She's lying. You can't believe her." Harvey looked as desperate as he sounded.

"He said he knew various people who had done this

before and had even invested himself. He was only going to take a small fee for his hard work, not every penny though."

"That was very honorable of you, Harvey." The Sheriff's sarcasm brought a flush to Harvey's face.

"Sheriff, he told me Mia was still alive. She is Almanzo's sister. He couldn't have known that unless he was present, as the little girl was smuggled out to another location. Also, he said your deputy would keep quiet and do as he was told."

"That right young lady?" Sheriff Rodgers gave Harvey a dirty look. "You'll be singing like a canary once you see what Judge is lined up to come visiting. He's got quite a reputation for landing people like you in prison. Come on, let's get you behind bars where you belong."

The sheriff dragged a protesting Harvey out of the room and down the stairs. David and Scott picked up the paperwork with Fiona's help. Blacky stood to watch over Fiona as if she was in a danger.

ALMANZO TOOK Tilly's arm and pulled her out of the room, dragging her into a kiss as soon as they were in relative privacy.

"Let me know never to make you angry. That's some right hand you got Miss Tilly."

"Do you think it will be enough to put him away. He is such a horrible man. You should have seen his face when he was talking about people." Tilly shivered. "He made me feel dirty just sitting with him. Oh Almanzo, how can people like that live with themselves."

"I don't know darling but let's get you back to Mrs. Newland's. You can have a bath and get some sleep. Then we can go see Reverend Polk and talk about our wedding."

"Our wedding?" she murmured.

"Yes, Miss Tilly. I don't think I can wait much longer to make you my wife. Not with the way you kiss me."

Tilly blushed at the way he looked at her, her insides bubbling with happiness. He loved her as much as she loved him. Even with the sadness of Rick's passing and the other deaths, she knew their friends and family would understand their hurry to get married. If they had learned anything over the last few weeks, it was life was short. When you had a chance of happiness, you had to grab it with both hands and not let go.

"Why don't we skip Mrs. Newland and go straight to see the Reverend?"

He swung her into the air. "Well Miss Tilly, you just got the best ideas."

Arm in arm, smiling widely they left their friends and the hotel behind them and headed in the direction of the church.

*A*lmanzo and Tilly stood outside their newly built home, surrounded by a mass of horses.

"They are a gift."

"You have given us so much already, Walking Tall," Tilly said warmly.

"Not from me, Fire Daughter." Walking Tall winked at Tilly as he used her old name. "They belonged to the Chief, so they should go to Mia now, but she wants you and your husband to have them."

Almanzo looked down at his sister, the tears in his eyes making it difficult to see her face clearly. She put her hand in his, a solemn expression on her face.

"I will see you soon, brother."

"Mia, would you not reconsider? You can stay here with Tilly and me." Almanzo wrapped his spare arm around his wife's waist. "Tilly would love some company while I am out working."

"Thank you brother and you too, Tilly, but it is not my place. I belong with my people."

"She will visit you often, we will bring her." Walking Tall put his arm protectively around the young child. She gazed up at him in adoration. "I have asked Mia to join my lodge. Be my daughter. She can teach my sons manners."

Almanzo held out his hand to the Indian brave who took it and then, dropping Mia's arm, grabbed the white man into a bear hug.

"Now you will smell like me again," Walking Tall said laughing as he released Almanzo.

"We will have to try to find you a new fragrance," Tilly joked as she sniffed the air making them all laugh despite their sorrow at the parting. Mia would take to the mountains with Walking Tall and what was left of his tribe. It would be safer up there. Plus Paco wanted to be buried in their original homelands. Despite everyone's best efforts, the Chief was not responding to treatment. He had stayed for the wedding but was keen to go home now.

Almanzo seemed to be lost for words, he stood silently watching those he loved make ready to leave. Tilly squeezed Almanzo's hand tightly dragging his attention back to the scene in front of him. She let go of his hand and ran back into the house returning quickly with a parcel under her arm.

"Mia, this is for you. From both of us."

Mia unwrapped the present and squealed in delight at the ragdoll the ladies had made for her. Tilly showed her the extra outfit they had fashioned. Mia hugged her first and then Almanzo.

"I promised you a doll. Ma said to bring it back with me..." he couldn't keep talking.

"She is beautiful. I am going to call her Lucy."

Almanzo nodded, too overcome to comment. He hadn't even known Mia knew her mother's English name. Then Walking Tall made the sign to move out. He pulled Mia up in front of him, his horse nickering softly.

"Stay safe my friend. We will be back next year and will expect to see a fine son."

Tilly blushed at Walking Tall's words as Almanzo started coughing. Walking Tall winked and then he was gone, Mia waving back at them until she was no more than a speck on the horizon.

Almanzo and Tilly stood arms entwined watching, long after their friends had disappeared into the horizon. Then Tilly took Almanzo's hand and led him down to the creek running behind their house.

TILLY LAY her head against her husband's bare chest, their feet in the babbling creek.

"We are so lucky aren't we darling?"

Almanzo dropped a kiss on his wife's head. Rick had left Almanzo land in his will. Unknown to his son, he had purchased the land some years ago. Johanna had given him the deed the day after Rick's funeral. Then everyone had got together to help build a small house for Tilly and him to live in. Tilly was overjoyed with her castle as she called it. Some castle. It had three rooms with a privy and barn outside but it was theirs. Best of all it had a small stream running at the back of the property where they loved to sit and watch the sun going down.

"I am so happy I could burst," Tilly said, her smile evident in her voice.

He drew her even closer. She was everything he'd ever wanted and more. He hoped they would have years together. She looked up at him, wariness written all over her face.

"Stop it. You promised not to think about it," she said, her voice pleading with him.

"I know Tilly but it's impossible to ignore the situation. Walking Tall believes war is coming and he doesn't read the newspapers. He's been listening to various reports from other tribes as well as the travelers he meets. Word from the forts..."

"Please don't talk about the chance of war tonight," she begged. "I want to sit here with you and be thankful for all the good things that have happened to us. Trouble will always find us, we don't have to go looking for it."

He wiped away a tear from her face, kissing her gently at first and then with more passion. All thoughts of the war disappeared as they melded together, the love for each other being the only thing that mattered.

* * *

THANK you so much for reading the fourth book of the Trails of Heart series. I hope you enjoy the continuing stories of the Thompson girls and the people who come in and out of their lives.

PREGNANT AND ALONE, Sarah Hughes finds herself in a village at the mercy of strangers. Along comes Bear who is determined to bring her home. She doesn't want to leave but having killed a man she is left with little choice.

On the run with an Indian who calls her a spoiled brat isn't the best of starts to romance. Over time, she comes to see the person behind the stony face.

Bear is intent on staying single due to his mixed heritage.

Can Sarah prove to herself and Bear, not to mention their respective friends that they belong together?

Oregon Disaster

HISTORICAL NOTE

The character Richard Weston is a fictional although his existence was sparked by reading the true story of an Oregon senator, Mr. John H. Mitchell. This senator's life story reads like a bad work of fiction. Not only was he eventually convicted of land fraud, aged 70, there are also rumors that he made a habit of marrying the daughters of wealthy businessmen. Later, when they had outgrown their usefulness, he would abandon them and move onto his next victim.

The Pig and Potato war

This incident really happened. In June 1859, a man who had claimed land under the Land Donation Act shot and killed a pig who was eating his potatoes. The pig was owned by an Irishman who worked for the Hudson Bay Company. The shooter offered the Irish man ten dollars for his pig, the Irishman wanted one hundred. When they couldn't settle, the British threatened to arrest the man who'd shot the pig. The Americans asked for military protection. The situation escalated and the President, Mr James Buchanan had to get involved. In the end it was resolved but there was a time when both sides appeared to be willing to go to war over the incident. Both sides agreed to joint military occupation of the Island with a token force of 100 men from each side. They lived in relative harmony for the next twelve years until the situation was finally resolved.

12 Days of Christmas - co -authored series.

The Maid - book 8

Clover Springs Mail Order Brides

Katie (Book 1)

Mary (Book 2)

Sorcha (Book 3)

Emer (Book 4)

Laura (Book 5)

Ellen (Book 6)

Thanksgiving in Clover Springs (book 7)

Christmas in Clover Springs (book8)

Erin (Book 9)

Eleanor (book 10)

Cathy (book 11)

Mrs. Grey

Clover Springs East

New York Bound (book 1)

New York Storm (book 2)

New York Hope (book 3)

ACKNOWLEDGMENTS

This book wouldn't have been possible without the help of so many people. Thanks to Erin Dameron-Hill for my fantastic covers. Erin is a gifted artist who makes my characters come to life.

I have an amazing editors, Julia and MacKenzie, and also use a wonderful proofreader. But sometimes errors slip through. I am very grateful to the ladies from my readers group who volunteered to proofread my book. Special thanks go to Marlene, Cindy, Meisje , Judith, Janet, Tamara, Cindi, Nethanja and Denise who all spotted errors (mine) that had slipped through.

Please join my Facebook group for readers of Historical fiction. Come join us for games, prizes, exclusive content, and first looks at my latest releases. Rachel's readers group

Last, but by no means least, huge thanks and love to my husband and my three children.